ChangelingPress.com

Saint/Rocket Duet

Harley Wylde

Saint/Rocket Duet

Harley Wylde

All rights reserved.
Copyright ©2020 Harley Wylde

ISBN: 9798664036114

Publisher:
Changeling Press LLC
315 N. Centre St.
Martinsburg, WV 25404
ChangelingPress.com

Printed in the U.S.A.

Editor: Crystal Esau
Cover Artist: Bryan Keller

The individual stories in this anthology have been previously released in E-Book format.

No part of this publication may be reproduced or shared by any electronic or mechanical means, including but not limited to reprinting, photocopying, or digital reproduction, without prior written permission from Changeling Press LLC.

This book contains sexually explicit scenes and adult language which some may find offensive and which is not appropriate for a young audience. Changeling Press books are for sale to adults, only, as defined by the laws of the country in which you made your purchase.

Table of Contents

Saint (Dixie Reapers 12)..4
   Prologue 5
   Chapter One..10
   Chapter Two 27
   Chapter Three...42
   Chapter Four...55
   Chapter Five 76
   Chapter Six..93
   Chapter Seven 104
   Chapter Eight..122
   Chapter Nine 133
   Epilogue 144
Rocket (Hades Abyss MC 2) 147
   Prologue 148
   Chapter One..153
   Chapter Two 167
   Chapter Three...184
   Chapter Four...195
   Chapter Five 215
   Chapter Six..225
   Chapter Seven 238
   Chapter Eight..250
   Chapter Nine 262
   Chapter Ten 274
   Epilogue 290
   From Harley..295
   Harley Wylde 296
   Changeling Press E-Books 297

Saint (Dixie Reapers 12)

Harley Wylde

Sofia -- I didn't know what to expect when a man loaded me and my sisters on his jet and brought us to the United States. I'm going somewhere different from my sisters, alone in a new country with strange men. The man called Saint has been ordered to take me, and I admit I'm terrified. Though he's as beautiful as an angel, there's a hardness in his eyes that scares me -- until I see him with his daughter. How can a man so gentle and kind with a child be bad? If only he'd turn some of that kindness my way... But I know he's right to keep his distance. I'm no good for either of them. It doesn't stop me from craving his touch, from needing his kisses like I need air. I can't regret our one night together, no matter the consequences.

Saint -- I've always followed orders without question, but this time I'm not so eager to help the club. Keeping Sofia under my roof, down the hall from my daughter, is the last thing I want. If the monsters from her past hurt Sofia or my sweet Delia, there will be hell to pay. No matter how much I need to harden my heart against the sexiest woman I've ever met, I can't. I want her, more than I've ever wanted anyone. I'm far from celibate, but Sofia's the kind of woman you keep. I allow myself one night, one taste, one chance to hear her scream my name. After, I put the walls back up and lock her out of my heart. It was a mistake, the biggest I've ever made. I need her, want her, can't live without her. But I did such a good job pushing her away, how will I ever win her back?

Prologue

Sofia

I was scared. More than that. I was downright terrified. My sister, Luciana, was trying to be brave, but I saw the tremor in her hands when she thought no one was watching. Our little sister, Violeta, had been crying off and on since we'd left Colombia. I couldn't blame her. I'd wanted to cry too. Living with our father had been a nightmare, but going off into the unknown? Even worse. I didn't know anything about the bikers who were going to claim us. I might have held it together a little better if I'd thought my sisters would be close by, but I'd heard we were being split up.

Mr. VanHorne had helped our father negotiate with some biker clubs in the States. A way to ensure the safety of his drugs, and whatever else he was into, and we were the consolation prize. His perfect little whores who had learned the hard way to do as we're told or face the consequences. I glanced at Violeta and Luciana, wondering what would happen to them when it was discovered they were both pregnant. If our father had known, he never would have let them go. He either would have wanted their boys to turn into monsters like him, or he'd have passed the girls around to his men. Neither fate was one I'd wish on anyone. Was it wrong I secretly hoped they would both miscarry? I didn't blame the babies for what had happened, but I worried about the kind of lives they would have. If I could spare them any pain or suffering, then I would.

I'd always adored children, and they'd seemed to like me. My father had used it against me several times. The first time, I'd been so scared I'd wet my pants. That was the day I'd learned that my father wasn't a man to be trifled with, or a man at all. I was certain he'd been possessed by *El Diablo* himself. No one could be that evil, not if they had a soul.

The jet touched down and my stomach flipped. This was it. I knew I would be the first to go, and I tried not to beg and plead to remain with my sisters. It wouldn't do me any good. The deals for us had already been made, and now we were expected to suffer in silence. Mr. VanHorne motioned for me to stand as we came to a stop and the steps were lowered. I walked toward him and fought back the bile rising in my throat. He placed a hand on my shoulder and helped me down the steps to the ground below. A group of men in black leather vests covered in patches waited for us.

"Torch, this is Sofia," Mr. VanHorne said, pushing me toward the silver-haired man.

Torch turned and motioned to a younger guy to step forward. He was tall, broad-shouldered, and had golden hair that gleamed in the sunlight -- and he looked utterly pissed off. I whimpered and urged my feet to move forward and not run in the opposite direction. When the man reached us, he practically sneered down at me and I knew that whatever I'd endured so far, the worst had probably yet to come.

"Sofia, this is Saint. You belong to him now," Mr. VanHorne said. "Be a good girl and do as he says."

"Yes, sir," I said softly, my gaze meeting Saint's before I flinched and looked away. He had the face of an angel, but the anger burning in his eyes made me wish I could just die right here and now.

"You'll ride with Saint on the back of his bike, Sofia," Torch said. "Do you have any luggage?"

Mr. VanHorne handed over a small bag I'd packed with just two changes of clothes. It was all my father had permitted me to bring. Torch eyed the bag, hefted it, then frowned.

"What the fuck, Casper? Is there even anything in here?" he asked.

"I'll provide a clothing allowance for her. Their father wanted them to pack light."

Torch shook his head and handed the bag to Saint. The blond man walked off and I followed, not knowing what else to do. He stuffed my duffle into a black leather bag on the side of his bike, then swung his leg over the seat. He stared at me expectantly and I realized I was supposed to get on too. I awkwardly climbed onto the bike, then didn't know what do. He sighed and reached back, grabbing my hands and put them on his waist.

"Hold on or you'll fall off," he said.

I fisted the leather of his vest and hung on as the bike started forward. I tried to keep some space between us, but by the time we'd left the airstrip, I was plastered to his back for fear of tumbling off the motorcycle. I hid my face against his back, and tried not to notice that he smelled really good. It felt like we were riding forever, but it was probably less than twenty minutes. When we came to a stop, I looked around and saw rows of homes and a larger building in the distance. I also saw a fenced area that looked like it had a playground, which I found odd for a group of bikers. Unless they were like my father, then... I shivered, no, I wouldn't think that.

"We're here. You can let go and get the fuck off," Saint said.

I scrambled to do as he said and landed on my ass for my trouble. He grunted and stared down at me before shutting off the motorcycle and getting off. The door to the house opened and a little girl flew down the steps.

"Daddy!" she screeched and threw herself at Saint, who caught her and smiled broadly.

He had a daughter? A daughter who seemed to adore him? I got up and brushed myself off, watching to see the darkness enter his eyes, but it never did. He looked younger, and more approachable with his daughter in his arms.

"Is that the girl who's going to live with us?" the little girl asked.

"Yes, Delia. This is Sofia, and she's going to stay with us for a bit."

For a bit. Right. Because he didn't plan to keep me. Just use me, then pass me along to someone else. I tried to swallow the knot in my throat and followed them into the house. Saint pointed to an open door down the hall.

"That's your room while you're here. Don't touch anything that isn't yours," he said, then walked off with his daughter still clinging to him.

I stared at that open door and wondered what I'd find inside. When I got the courage to go look, it was a rather nondescript room. Tan walls, brown bedding, and even the rug covering the wood floor was a combination of browns and creams. It wasn't a bad room, and at least it didn't look like there weren't chains on the bed. If he planned to tie me down, he must not want his daughter to see that sort of thing. That had to be a good sign, right?

I sat on the edge of the mattress and kicked off my shoes. I glanced at the pillows with longing and gave in to the temptation to lie down. I'd close my eyes, only for a little bit. I curled into a ball on my side and couldn't hold the tears back another moment. I sobbed silently, not wanting anyone to see me in this moment of weakness. Crying had never solved anything, but I was so damn scared right now. I didn't know what to expect of the man I'd been given to like some sort of prize or object. I only hoped that when he hurt me, I wouldn't scream and scare the little girl. She'd looked so precious, and I never wanted anything to bad or ugly to touch her life.

No one deserved the fate I'd been handed.

Chapter One

Saint

I hated that Torch had asked me to house one of the girls from Colombia. I didn't like having her around Delia, didn't know what sort of influence she would be on my small daughter. I'd heard her crying after I'd pointed out her room, but I hardened my heart and refused to go check on her. I hadn't asked for this, and I didn't want her here. Out of all the men at the compound, why me? I had a kid to think about. Just because I didn't have a woman living in my house, didn't mean I was up for this shit. I hadn't even slept with a club whore since my daughter had come to live with me.

It wasn't that losing her mother was so painful. I'd cared about Rhianon, but we weren't in love. Or at least I hadn't been in love with her. We'd had fun, and that had apparently resulted in us having a kid that she hadn't told me about. When she'd passed, her brother had contacted me. I'd dropped everything and gone up to the Hades Abyss compound to meet my daughter.

Delia didn't remember her mom, even though I'd made sure to keep a picture of Rhianon in Delia's room from the very beginning, and had a few others around the house. I didn't know her mother well enough to share many stories, not appropriate ones anyway, but her Uncle Rocket told her enough that I hoped Delia felt like she knew her mother. If there was anything I could give my little girl, it would be her mom. Even though Rhianon had kept her from me, I liked to think she'd have eventually told me. Delia was the best thing that ever happened to me, even if the only action I'd seen in the last four years was from my own hand. I'd give up women any day to have my daughter here with me. She was the most precious thing to me.

I shifted on my bed, unable to sleep. We were about to start day three with the stranger living in our home, and while Delia was starting to edge a little closer to Sofia each day, I was doing my damnedest to keep the hell away. I was twenty-seven, not some high school kid, and yet every time I looked at Sofia I could feel my body respond. It was starting to piss me off. The club whores tried but never could get a rise out of my cock, but one look at the little Colombian princess and I was hard as a steel post. What the fuck was wrong with me?

A faint noise had me going completely still and straining my ears. Another rustle of sheets and then a whimper. Was Delia having a bad dream? She hadn't had nightmares before, but I knew introducing someone new into our home could change her sleep patterns among other things. It had just been me and Delia since she was an infant, another reason I hadn't wanted the girl here. Girl. Woman. The way my body reacted to her, I couldn't really call her a girl, even though I'd been told she was only nineteen. Hell, I'd been part of this MC before that age so who was I to judge based off some numbers? Age wasn't a big deal around here. Torch was thirty years older than his wife, but she adored him.

I heard the noise again, then a scream that had me leaping out of the bed and racing from my room. The second scream sent a chill down my spine as I opened Sofia's door. She fought against her bedding, speaking rapidly in Spanish. When she switched to English, my stomach knotted and twisted because I had no doubt exactly what was happening.

"No, Pedro. Stop! Please, don't hurt me!" she cried out, grappling with the sheets. "No more! It hurts."

She bucked her hips like she was trying to throw someone off. When her legs jerked apart and her arms went over her head, immobile as if someone were pinning her down, I nearly threw up. Moving farther into the room, I eased onto the bed and tried to gently rouse her.

"Sofia." I brushed my fingers over her cheek, unable to help but notice how soft her skin was. "Sofia, it's a nightmare. You need to wake up."

"No. No more," she begged. "Not again."

Not again? Jesus. How many times had the man brutalized her? I shook her, but she just tossed her head and screamed again. I worried she'd wake Delia, and I wouldn't know what to say to my daughter. She'd never witnessed someone having a nightmare, and it would likely scare her. Hell, it was scaring *me*.

After she screamed again, I decided enough was enough. I lifted her into my arms, wrapping her tight and holding her against my chest. She struggled a moment, but I kept murmuring to her, hoping to snap her out of it or at least calm her enough she could rest easy again and stop fighting off men in her sleep. If felt like forever before she started to relax. Her breathing evened out and her screams turned to whimpers, then soft murmurs. She took a deep breath and rubbed her cheek against my chest before going completely limp.

A knot lodged in my throat as I looked down at her, realizing she looked so sweet and innocent like this. Whoever had hurt her needed to pay. I eased her back down onto the bed, but she clutched at my T-shirt, holding on. I tried to pry her fingers loose, but she just held on tighter. With a sigh, I decided to just hold her until she shifted enough for me to make an escape. I leaned back against the headboard and curled an arm around her waist.

Four hours later, when the sun was starting to peek through the blinds, Sofia hadn't moved, and my eyes were feeling like sandpaper. Delia was still quiet and would probably sleep at least another hour or two. I decided to close my eyes just for a moment, in hopes of them feeling a little less gritty. Sofia mumbled and snuggled closer, and I could feel sleep pulling me down. I must have dozed off because I woke with wide chocolate eyes staring at me in absolute terror. Her grip had loosened on me and I slid out of the bed, holding my hands up to show I meant her no harm.

"You were having a nightmare and when I tried to wake you, you grabbed onto my shirt and wouldn't let go."

She blinked and looked down, her cheeks flushing darkly. "I'm sorry."

"You have nothing to be sorry for." I swallowed hard, an apology on the tip of my tongue, but I couldn't afford to soften toward her. I needed her out of my home and away from my daughter.

"I didn't scare Delia?" she asked, her voice heavily accented this morning.

"She slept through it," I said.

Sofia sighed and nodded.

"I'm going to head back to my room and try to sleep until Delia wakes up. Help yourself to anything in the kitchen."

Before she could say or do anything else, I bolted. Big bad biker, my ass. I snorted at myself. Running from a little slip of a woman. Okay, so it was more of a brisk walk. I knew Sofia had trouble written all over her, and I didn't need that sort of complication in my life, or Delia's. I needed to remain strong for my daughter and do the right thing, even if running out of that room hadn't been the easiest thing I've ever done. It would be better for everyone involved if Torch placed Sofia with someone else, maybe with one of the married brothers. I didn't know why Sofia had to be in my home, but I didn't like it.

I shut my door and leaned against it, feeling like a damn coward. I hadn't backed down from anything in my entire life. Before Torch had found me wandering the streets, I'd left home on my own terms because my mother's latest boyfriend was an asshole who liked to hit people. But I'd stood up to the guy and that's what mattered. Torch had shown me what it was like to be a real man, had given me a home and a chance at a better life. Even though I'd had to leave my sister behind, I'd done what was necessary at the time. I wouldn't have been any good to her dead. Now my twin was the old lady of a club member, and was completely in love with Preacher. She'd brought him back from a dark place, but I think he'd saved her just as much.

I didn't kid myself. That wasn't me. Having an old lady? I might have wanted that at one point, and for Delia's sake I knew I needed to consider it, but I was too worried about letting the wrong sort of woman into her life. The ladies who flocked to the MC were usually more club whore than mom of the year. I wasn't saying they couldn't be both, but I hadn't found one like that yet, and that's what I wanted. A mom who would adore Delia and give her everything she needed from a woman, and a tiger in my bed who clawed the hell out of me and begged for more. I didn't think anyone like that actually existed. Not around these parts anyway.

I walked across the room to my bed and face planted across the mattress. Groaning, I tried to scrub the scent and feel of Sofia from my mind. My cock twitched in my boxer briefs and I wondered if I'd be a completely sick and twisted bastard if I jerked off imagining what she'd feel like wrapped around my dick. I'd never been *that* guy. Yeah, I'd yanked one out plenty of times, and I'd slept with my share of women, but I'd always respected them. The thought of a rub and tug while thinking about the abused woman down the hall didn't seem right. I might not know for certain what had happened to her, but that nightmare had been a bit enlightening, and not in a great way.

I knew there was no way in hell I was going to sleep, not with my thoughts all jumbled and my cock aching. Why the hell did my body have to be interested in *that* woman? With all the ones who'd been flinging themselves in my direction, my dick didn't give a shit. But the one female I shouldn't want, and he's ready to lay claim to her. Fucking figures. I rolled onto my back and groaned as I shifted. It had been too fucking long since I'd been with a woman.

I stripped off my boxer briefs and flung them onto the floor, followed quickly by my T-shirt. Sprawled naked across the bed, I reached into the bedside table and pulled out the lube. Whether it was wrong or not, I needed some relief, and I had no doubt that I'd be thinking of Sofia. I squirted a liberal amount on my palm and slicked it down my shaft. I rubbed my thumb over the sensitive head before gripping my cock tightly and starting to stroke. It felt good, but nowhere near as good as being inside a woman.

I closed my eyes and pictured Sofia, unafraid and reaching for me. Her soft hands, gripping my cock, her lips parted and eyes dark with arousal. I got harder when I pictured her legs parted, her pussy slick with arousal as she begged me to fuck her. I moaned her name as I jerked my cock faster and harder. Soft hands coasted over my chest and abs, making me bite my lip at how real it felt. When thighs encased mine, my eyes flew open and I stared at Sofia, naked and straddling my body.

"What are you doing?" I asked.

She pried my fingers off my cock and lowered herself. I gripped her hips, intent on pulling her off, but Christ she felt so fucking good!

"Sofia." I closed my eyes a moment as she squeezed me with her inner muscles. "Why are you in here?"

"This is what you wanted, yes? To fuck me?"

"You aren't here for this. It's not why my club took you in."

"Of course it is," she said, pulling my hands loose and starting to ride me.

I thought I had better control over myself, but I hadn't been inside a woman in years. I tried to pull her off again, but she clamped her thighs against me and refused to get off. The look in her eyes said she wasn't really here, didn't want this, and I wasn't about to become yet another asshole who has used and abused her.

"Sofia, get the fuck off."

She slid up and down my cock again. "Doesn't feel like that's what you want."

"Damn it. Just because my dick is hard doesn't mean I want you to whore yourself out to me. Get off! You don't want this, and don't lie and say you do."

"It's why I'm here," she said again, seeming insistent. "I'll be good to you."

Fuck. Me. "No, Sofia. Please. I've never hurt a woman, never taken one who wasn't willing. Don't do something we'll both regret." I could throw her off, but I was worried I'd hurt her.

She paused, looking down at me, her brow furrowed and confusion in her eyes.

My heart was racing in my chest, and I had the horrible realization that she hadn't just been raped once or twice. She'd been forced to give herself to anyone who asked.

"Sofia, have you ever enjoyed sex?" I asked softly. "Tell me the truth, not what you think I want to hear."

"No," she said, looking away.

I reached up and turned her chin so that I could hold her gaze. I scanned her body and saw not a single hint of arousal. Her nipples weren't hard, there wasn't lust in her gaze, no goose bumps along her arms. She was just getting me off because it's what she thought she was supposed to do. Son of a bitch.

"Do you want to come, Sofia? Do you want to know what sex *should* be like?" I asked. I should bail and run like fuck, but the thought that she'd never experienced pleasure, had only been hurt had my stomach knotting.

"There's no pleasure in sex," she said. "Only pain."

"Am I hurting you right now?"

She shifted and winced, then nodded a little.

"It's because you aren't ready for me. You don't want this, and your body isn't prepared to take me. If you insist of me fucking you, I'll only do it if I can show you pleasure. Will you give me a chance to show you that sex can be a good thing? Not painful, but something to enjoy?"

She hesitated a moment, chewed on her lower lip, then nodded. I placed my hands on her hips again and lifted her off my cock, rolling us so that she lay under me. Her eyes went a little wide. I braced my weight so I wouldn't crush her, then leaned down and gently traced my lips along her jaw. Her body was tense and I could feel her heart pounding. If she didn't respond, didn't seem to really want me, then I'd get up and walk away. I would never take her, or anyone else, against their will. I might be an asshole on occasion, but I wasn't a rapist and I didn't fucking hurt women.

I pressed my lips to the fluttering pulse in her throat before I slid my hand up her side and cupped her breast. Her body got tighter and her breathing increased. I stroked over her nipple, careful not to hurt her. Pulling back so I look into her eyes, the confusion had increased and she seemed to be struggling with something.

"Talk to me, Sofia."

"It… it doesn't hurt," she said.

"I will never hurt you. It's why I told you to get off me. I knew you didn't want it, and I won't be the kind of guy who takes what's not truly offered." I watched her face as I stroked over her nipple again. It puckered and her eyes dilated slightly. "Do you want me to stop?"

She slowly shook her head, her gaze locked on mine.

"Does it feel good?" I asked.

"Y-yes."

"Do you want more? Am I allowed to put my mouth on you?"

"Please," she said.

I leaned down and took one nipple into my mouth, sucking on the hard tip. She gasped and her fingers gripped the back of my head as she pressed me closer. I took my time, exploring her body with my lips and hands, inching my way down her body. When I spread her thighs and I looked at her pussy, she wriggled a bit and a flush crept up her.

"I can still stop," I said.

"N-no. I th-think I want m-more."

"Think? Or you're sure?"

"I'm sure," she said. "Please, Saint."

She'd either shaved or waxed, and her pussy lips were plump and soft. I lapped at her folds, listening to every little noise she made. My tongue touched her clit, and a loud keening came from her as her hips arched. I flicked the little bud with my tongue until she was whimpering and begging. Sucking on it long and hard, I felt the moment she shattered, crying out her release. Her body trembled and I heard a soft cry. I looked up and saw a tear slip down her cheeks. I quickly moved off her, fearing that I'd scared her or hurt her in some way.

She reached out and gripped my arm. "Don't go."

"I upset you."

"No. The opposite. I never knew it could feel like that. I've never…"

"You've never come," I said. "Not even by your own hand?"

"I didn't want to touch myself after… all I wanted to do was scrub off their touch and their seed."

"How many?" I asked quietly.

"I don't know. When I misbehaved, my father let his men have me. Sometimes they kept me to themselves, taking turns. Other times, they'd let anyone use me."

I closed my eyes, my heart breaking for her. She didn't deserve that. No one did!

"You're only nineteen, for fuck's sake! What kind of monster does that?" I asked.

"I was fifteen the first time," she said.

I leapt from the bed and rushed to the bathroom, throwing up in the toilet at the thought of men raping an innocent young girl. I felt Sofia's hand against my back, and I looked over at her.

"I understand," she said. "I'm dirty and... I'll go back to my room."

"What? No!" I reached for her. "That's not... The thought of all you've suffered made me sick, Sofia. But not *you*. None of that was your fault. How could you let me touch you? After everything you've been through, you should have run from my room when I told you to. Why did you stay?"

"I'm programmed to take whatever men demand," she said, her lips twisting a little. "Defiance means a harsher punishment. Then you said you wanted to show me pleasure, and I... I was tempted. I didn't think what you made me feel was even possible."

My dick certainly wasn't hard now, but I was glad I'd been able to give that gift to her. Now I needed to keep my damn hands, and definitely my cock, away from her. I didn't see her the same as before, didn't worry as much about her influence on Delia, but I knew that I wasn't the right man for her. She needed someone gentle, and I tended to be demanding in bed. It would likely scare her or give her flashbacks of the men who hurt her.

"Go to your room, Sofia. You should stay away from me." I saw the stricken look on her face, and I placed a hand on her arm, halting her flight from the bathroom. "Not because I feel like you're dirty or inferior. I'm not the right man for you. I'm not gentle, and the things I like in the bedroom wouldn't be good for someone who's suffered the way you have."

Her chin shot up a little. "Isn't that for me to decide?"

I wanted to smile at the little bit of fire she was showing. It couldn't be easy, not after everything she'd been through. I liked that she felt secure enough around me to show that little spark. It gave me hope that she'd heal and be able to have a normal life, find love, and enjoy all the things she'd missed out on so far.

"I like to tie up my women, Sofia. I like to spank them. Watching a woman gag on my cock makes me even harder. You don't need that shit."

Her lower lip trembled a moment, but she held out her wrists. "Then tie me up."

I ran a hand down my face, then moved over to the sink, brushing past her. I splashed water on my face and rinsed my mouth with Listerine. She hadn't budged, still offering up her wrists, a look of determination stamped on her face. As tempted as I was to see if she could handle it, because I'd be lying if I said she wasn't gorgeous and didn't make my cock hard, I was also enough of a gentleman to know when I should back away. This was one of those times.

"If you don't take me, show me what it's like to be with someone of my choosing, then I'll have no choice but to think it's because you really do think I'm nothing more than a dirty whore and not worthy of you," she said.

Fuck.

I ran my hand through my hair and tried to think of a way out of this one. I couldn't use her that way, not even if she was asking for it. It was wrong, and I knew I would feel like shit, especially if she started crying or got scared.

The stubborn tilt of her chin told me she wasn't going to be swayed.

"Sofia, if we do this, it's just the one time. It won't change anything between us. I can help you prove to yourself that you're not broken, but we're not going to live happily ever after. Do you understand? It would just be a release for me."

Her lip trembled a little, but she nodded.

She was fucking killing me, looking at me with those big brown eyes. I couldn't be her hero. I had to think about my daughter, put her first. Delia was still so little and demanded a lot of my time. Torch had been great about giving me things to do close to home, and nothing overly dangerous. I felt like I was letting the club down, not pulling my weight. It's why I hadn't fought very hard when he'd insisted that Sofia come stay with me. I'd hated it, wanted to flat-out refuse, but after I'd argued my point about how it might affect Delia, I'd just accepted my fate. It never occurred to me that I might actually *like* Sofia or feel any sort of empathy toward her.

I rubbed the back of my neck. "I, uh, don't have any condoms. It's been a while since I was with anyone."

She didn't look like she believed me.

"My daughter, Delia, was a complete surprise. Her mom died and I've been so focused on her that I admittedly don't make much time for myself. Haven't had an interest in a woman in a while. Even if I did, I wouldn't bring them here," I said.

"It's been four years and my father's men seldom if ever used condoms. Mr. VanHorne insisted on having me tested before I was brought here. I'm clean, but I've never once gotten pregnant. I don't think I'm able to conceive."

I hated that for her. Not just the abuse she'd suffered, or that they'd put her in jeopardy by not using protection, but I would imagine it was painful knowing she couldn't have children. I knew nothing was certain until she'd seen a doctor, but four years and not one time had she gotten pregnant? She was probably right and was likely barren. Just another thing they had stolen from her. As brutal as her nightmare had sounded, I could imagine they'd done a lot of damage to her over the years. Maybe the irreversible kind.

"I'm clean too," I said. "I used to get tested regularly, and I had another done after the last time I was with someone. Even when I used condoms I didn't want to take any chances."

She nodded and fidgeted, shifting from foot to foot.

"Sofia, we don't have to do this. Why don't you take some time to think things over?" I asked.

"No, I want this."

"I --" My sentence was cut off by Delia calling out for me. I sighed, wondering at the relief I felt over hearing my daughter's voice. I'd wanted Sofia, but even I knew this was wrong. "Sorry. My daughter needs me. I'll distract her to give you time to get back to your room."

"All right."

I hurried past Sofia and pulled on my boxer briefs and a T-shirt before dashing down the hall to Delia's room. I'd had to insist that she not leave her room without permission after the morning she'd wanted to make me breakfast and almost burned down the house. Thankfully, she was a good girl and followed instructions pretty well. Most of the time, I amended, as I tripped over the toys I'd told her pick up the night before.

"I'm here, sweetheart," I said as I made it to her side.

Delia flung her arms around my neck and squeezed tight enough I choked a little. I wrapped her up and hugged her tight. There was no one on earth I loved more than my sweet little girl. I'd been scared as hell the first time I'd held her, but she was everything to me now.

"I had a bad dream, Daddy," she said.

"You did? Want to talk about it?" I asked. When she'd gotten old enough to talk, I'd learned that she often dreamed of her mother. I didn't know if the pictures were to blame and a constant reminder of what she'd lost, but it only seemed right that she get to see the woman who had given birth to her and adored her. Rocket had made sure I had plenty of pictures of his sister, and I had a few of him with Delia too, which I'd placed in her room and one in the living room.

"I dreamed that someone was hurting Sofia. She was crying and begging them to stop, but the mean man just laughed," Delia said.

A chill went down my spine. Had she heard Sofia's nightmare and it had filtered into her dreams? I knew that Sofia hadn't said anything to Delia about what had happened to her. Until last night, I hadn't even known the woman had been abused. I knew I needed to say something, but her words were a bit shocking.

"I promise that Sofia is fine, sweetheart. She's in her room just down the hall from you."

"You won't let the bad men hurt her anymore, will you, Daddy?" Delia asked.

"Of course not. Sofia is safe here with us. I'll protect her just like I protect you."

"You should marry Sofia," Delia said, snuggling closer. "If she were my mommy and your wife, then she'd always be safe from the bad men."

My heart stalled a moment. Marry Sofia? What the hell? Delia had never once asked me to give her a mommy before. She knew that she'd had one who loved her above all else, and that had always been enough. Had bringing Sofia here made her long for something she'd been missing? Or was it something else? The little girl in my arms was far too observant, and the way she'd talked about someone hurting Sofia… I didn't believe in any of that psychic stuff, but I did find it eerie that Delia had known that Sofia had been hurt. No, I'd just have to believe that her subconscious had absorbed the screams from Sofia last night. Still… Delia had been rather sheltered all her life. She wouldn't have leapt to the conclusion a man was hurting Sofia.

"I'm afraid it's more complicated than that," I said. "You want Daddy to love the woman he marries, don't you?"

"You could love Sofia. She's nice, Daddy, and I think she's scared."

Damn. My little girl was growing up way too fast. She'd walked before she was supposed to, talked way earlier than she should have, and now she ran circles around me some days. She spoke better than most kids I knew who were older than her, and she was scary smart.

"We'll see, sweetheart. Right now, I'm going to lay out some clothes for you, and I want you to wash your face and brush your hair, then get dressed. You play in here while Daddy takes a shower and gets dressed, then we'll figure out breakfast."

"Okay. Love you, Daddy."

"I love you too." I brushed a kiss against her forehead, then got up and rummaged through her dresser, pulling out one of her favorite outfits.

I went back to my room and found Sofia standing near the foot of the bed, a stricken look on her face.

"What's wrong?" I asked.

"She knows. How does she know?" she whispered.

"Knows what?"

"What the men did to me. You can't let that touch her life, Saint. I'll ask your President to move me elsewhere. Someone like me shouldn't be around that sweet little girl. I don't want her to know about the ugliness in the world."

My heart shattered at that moment and fell to the floor in pieces. Sofia, for all she'd suffered, was worried more about Delia than herself. She didn't know my daughter, or me for that matter, and yet she was willing to put Delia first.

"It was just a nightmare, Sofia. She doesn't know anything for certain." At least, I hoped she didn't. Like Sofia, I didn't want any of that darkness to touch my daughter. I knew I couldn't protect her forever, but I could damn sure try.

Sofia didn't appear convinced, but she left my room and I quickly showered and dressed. I didn't know what to do about Sofia, or my daughter, but first I needed to make sure everyone was fed. We could worry about the rest later.

Chapter Two

Sofia

Hearing Delia speak to Saint had left me shaken. I would do anything to keep her safe, to ensure my father's men never came anywhere near her, even if it meant I put myself in jeopardy. I'd always loved children, and Delia seemed especially sweet. Tears misted my eyes over her request for Saint to marry me. He was right to shut that down. I wasn't anywhere near good enough to marry a man like him, or anyone for that matter. He'd been so honorable, tried to push me away even when I'd insisted otherwise. I'd never met anyone like him before.

If my interaction with him this morning hadn't thawed my heart, then hearing him speak to Delia had done the trick. I had no doubt if I spent enough time with them, I'd fall for both of them, want to keep them and make them both mine. My family. Even though I loved my two sisters, and we were close, I didn't remember my mother and my father had been a monster.

I dashed away the tears that slid down my cheeks and finished getting ready. I could still hear the shower running as I crept down the hallway past Delia's door. I snuck out of the house, and wandered down the road in what I hoped was the direction of the front gates. Maybe I could slip past unnoticed. I'd never been good with directions, and I'd been so scared when I'd arrived I hadn't paid much attention.

As I got closer to the front gates, I saw someone standing guard. He was young, maybe close to my age. I didn't know if that was a good thing or not. Maybe he'd be more likely to let me pass? I could hope at any rate. I didn't want Saint to get into trouble for me leaving, but I also refused to put him and his daughter in any sort of danger. I knew my father had brokered some sort of deal through Mr. VanHorne, but I also knew he'd want us back eventually. His good little whores.

The man at the gate folded his arms and stared down his nose at me. "Are you lost?"

The leather vest he wore said Prospect. I didn't know if that was his name or a title. I knew nothing about bikers, and it didn't seem I'd be learning anytime soon. Not if I could make my way around this guy and through the gate.

"Um, no. I need to go. Please."

He snorted.

"I said please," I pointed out.

"I can't let you leave. Torch would hand my ass to me, and I'm sure Saint would too, even though he didn't look too happy about having you in his home." The man's gaze skimmed over me. "Not much to you from what I can see. I don't know what Torch is thinking, giving you to Saint, but I'm sure he has his reasons."

"You don't understand. Saint and his daughter could be in danger if I stay with them. Please, I need to leave."

He shook his head. "Nope. Not happening. I'm not opening this gate."

A clawing panic filled me as I looked around. I didn't see another person except the one refusing to let me leave. I didn't know how big the territory was, or whether or not there might be a weak place in the fencing. I turned and walked off, heading back in the direction of Saint's home, but I didn't plan to stop. The man at the gate didn't need to know that.

As I passed Saint's house, I didn't see either him or Delia. His bike was still parked in the carport. I picked up my pace, not wanting him to see me. As I rushed farther down the road, following the winding path past more homes, I eventually reached an area that was heavily treed. I tried to hide in the shadows and tested the sections of fencing, praying that I would find a spot where I could slip through.

The stomp of boots made me freeze and hold my breath. I heard some cursing, and when I looked over my shoulder, I saw an older redheaded man who looked more than a little pissed.

"What the hell are you doing?" he demanded.

"I..."

He shook his head. "Saint is going to be furious. If he doesn't tan your ass, maybe I should."

I gasped and hastily stepped back, tripping over a tree root and falling. My ankle turned and pain shot up my leg, making me cry out. The big man came closer and I tried to scramble away.

"I'm not going to hurt you. Just sit the fuck still."

I whimpered as he hunkered down next to me. His touch was light as he pressed against my ankle, but it just made the pain worse. He sighed and picked me up, cradling me against his chest. I struggled to get down, not liking the way it felt to be held by him.

"Would you be still!" he yelled. "Christ. My daughter is close to your age and isn't half this much trouble."

"Daughter?" I asked, ceasing my struggles. Was he the kind of dad like Saint, or more like mine?

"Yes. My daughter, Pepper, is with the club's Treasurer, Flicker. You're safe with me, Sofia. I'm not going to hurt you, but Saint is going to be really damn mad. Why were you trying to leave?"

"To keep him and his daughter safe," I said.

The man froze and looked down at me. "What?"

"My father will want me back. I don't want little Delia getting caught in the middle."

"Jesus," he muttered. "That's really fucking brave of you, and selfless. Probably won't keep Saint from spanking your ass, though. Especially since I saw Torch going in to speak with him. I have a feeling it's about you."

I hoped not. Unless it meant that Torch would place me with someone else, someone without kids. I let the man with *Sarge* stitched on his vest carry me back to Saint's house, and I hoped I could make everyone see reason. It really wasn't safe for me to remain with him and Delia. Not only for them, but I knew it wasn't safe for me either. I'd get attached, fall for them, and then I'd be forced to leave. I couldn't allow any of their warmth to seep into me or I'd never survive when my father wanted me returned.

Sarge kicked Saint's door with his booted foot and when it opened, Saint looked relieved more than anything. He took me from Sarge, holding me close.

"Thank fuck. I thought someone had come into the house and snatched her," Saint said.

"Nope," Sarge said. "She decided to save you and your daughter, so she was trying to find a way out of the compound."

Saint growled and narrowed his eyes as he gazed down at me. "You what?"

"It would be better if I left," I said.

"And that is why I came to talk to you this morning," said the President from over Saint's shoulder. "Casper is also concerned their father may ask for their return, and he wants to make sure it's impossible for Gomez to get his hands on them."

"I don't understand," I said. "How can you keep him from taking us back? If he demands our return, refusing will only put a target on your men and their families."

"Not if you're legally a US citizen and married to someone here," Torch said.

My breath froze in my lungs as I blinked at him, knowing I couldn't have heard that right. "Is that possible? To be a legal resident here?"

I wasn't about to mention the second part. Marrying anyone wasn't the best of ideas, especially if the man he chose had a child. While part of me would love to live with Saint and Delia for the rest of my life, I knew it was just a dream that could never happen.

"With Wire on the job, anything is possible," Torch said.

"Breakfast, then we'll talk," Saint said. "I promised Delia waffles so she wants to go to the diner."

"And I'm out," said Sarge as he turned. He paused in the doorway. "Your girl turned her ankle. She needs to ice it."

Before anyone could respond, he walked off.

"What's that about?" Saint asked.

"I think it has to do with a certain waitress there," Torch said. "He'll get it figured out. Eventually. If he doesn't, Pepper may decide to handle the matter herself, and none of us want that."

"You can put me down," I told Saint, liking it a little too much that he was still holding me. Even though my ankle was still throbbing, it wasn't like he could carry me everywhere. I'd have to put weight on it eventually.

"Nope. Now that I know you're a runner, I'm holding on," he said.

"Since Delia's seat is in your SUV, we'll take that," Torch said. "I'll have Wire meet us there."

Saint carried me out the door and placed me in the back seat of an SUV I hadn't even noticed before now. It was a dark gray and was hidden in the shadows on the other side of the carport. How I'd missed it, I didn't know. It wasn't exactly small. He buckled my belt, flipped a switch on the inside of the door, then shut it.

Torch slid into the front passenger seat, chuckling.

"What's funny?" I asked.

"He just activated the child locks so you can't escape. He didn't handle it well when he realized you'd vanished."

Why had Saint even cared? If I was gone, his life could go back to normal. I would think he'd be glad to be rid of me.

He brought Delia out of the house and buckled her into her booster seat, pressed the child lock on her side, while staring me down, then got behind the wheel of the SUV and started the engine. Everyone was quiet on the way to the diner, except Delia.

"You don't like us?" Delia asked me.

I blinked at her a moment. "Of course I like you."

"Then why did you leave?" she asked.

"Because I thought it would be better. Safer. My father is a very bad man. I don't want him to try and hurt you or your daddy."

She nodded and seemed to think it over, her brow wrinkled and her lips pursed. Adorable. "My daddy can keep both of us safe. He's good at keeping people safe."

"Isabella is going to meet us at the diner with the kids," Torch said. "I thought Delia might like to sit with them. At another table. Far from the grownups talking."

Saint nodded and my stomach knotted. That meant we would likely discuss my father, and whatever plan Torch had for me to marry someone. I wanted to prolong things as long as possible. I'd make them see reason. I didn't have a choice, but I also loved spending time with Delia. She was so sweet and innocent. Most kids were, unless they'd been exposed to the horrors of the world far too early. I hoped that Delia never had to see that side of life.

At the diner, a woman with long black hair smiled warmly at Torch, an infant wrapped in a blue blanket was cradled in her arms, and a cute little girl stood next to her. I assumed that was Torch's wife and kids, the ones he'd mentioned in the car. He was a lot older than her, which surprised me, but no more so than the look of complete love on her face when she watched him. Despite the age difference, it was obvious she adored him.

I couldn't remember any of the women back home looking at my father, his men, or his associates like that. They respected their men, mostly out of fear, but there was definitely no love between them. It amazed me to see such a tough man have a gentle touch with his wife and kids. It also made me yearn for a life like that one day. If he forced me to marry someone, then I'd likely never have that. What man would love a woman he'd had no choice in marrying?

Delia took my hand as we got out of the car and walked over to the little family. I fought not to wince or show any discomfort. Saint was just behind me, the heat of his body pressing against me. Isabella smiled down at Delia.

"This is Sofia. She's going to be my new momma."

I sucked in a sharp breath and ended up choking. Saint patted my back until I was able to breathe normally again. "What?"

"I want you to be my new momma," Delia said. "My other momma is in heaven, so she can't be here. But you can."

I opened and shut my mouth several times before Isabella reached for Delia's hand, tugging her along with her own children. The woman looked over her shoulder and winked at me, making me wonder if she knew something I didn't.

Saint placed his hand at my waist and led me into the diner in Torch's wake. I tried to hide my limp, but his grip on me tightened and I knew that he'd noticed. Isabella and the children took a booth at the very back, but Torch chose one nearer to the door. He placed his back to his family so Saint and I sat across from him. A moment later, a ginger-haired man slid into the booth next to Torch.

"Sofia, this is Wire," Torch said. "There isn't anything he can't do on a computer."

Wire smiled and gave me a little wave, setting me at ease immediately. He seemed friendly enough. Saint patted my thigh and I relaxed back into the booth, realizing I was on the edge of my seat like I would flee at any moment. Not that I could get past any of the men sitting with me. For one, I'd have to go over Saint to get free.

Wire pulled out a manila folder he'd stuffed inside his leather vest and set it on the table. The first paper he pulled out and placed in front of me just left me confused. I could read English well enough, but it didn't make any sense.

"I don't understand," I said.

"As of this morning, you're a legal citizen in this country," Wire said. "If your father tries to take you back to Colombia, then the US Embassy over there should be of some assistance. If we go about things the legal way when it comes time to retrieve you."

Retrieve, like a dog toy. Wonderful. I swallowed hard. The thought of my father getting his hands on me again was the scariest thing I'd ever faced. I didn't understand why he'd let us go. I mean, it sort of made sense. He wanted to work out a deal with the clubs here in the United States, but why not just loan out me and my sisters for a few weeks or months? Or purchase other girls for them. He'd made it sound like we would be living here from now on, property of the clubs. I knew better.

"I also have something else for you," Wire said, pulling out another piece of paper.

"A marriage license?" Saint asked. "Really?"

"Who's Jonathan?" I asked, looking at the names listed.

Saint cleared his throat. "That's me, but I go by Saint these days and Johnny prior to that."

"It's a marriage license for me and... you?" I asked, looking at him.

"So it would seem. Torch believes if we're married, then it will give you an added layer of protection from your father. I can't say that he's wrong, but I also have Delia to consider, which I've pointed out to him. Several times."

Torch waved him off. "Delia obviously likes Sofia. If Sofia was willing to put herself in danger in order to save your daughter, do you really think she'd do anything to hurt the girl?"

"No," Saint said. "But if Gomez does come for Sofia, it's going to put a target on my daughter. It's not that I don't want to marry her, I'm just concerned about Delia. I have to put her first."

"I agree," I said. "I won't do anything that could hurt Delia."

"If Saint won't marry you, then I'll have to find someone else," Torch said, pulling the marriage license from my hand. Panic shot through me. *Someone else.* A stranger. It felt like the walls were closing in on me, and I couldn't seem to breathe. Everything started to spin.

"Shit," Wire said. "She's having a panic attack."

I felt an arm go around my shoulders, but there was a loud buzzing in my ears as the room started to get dark. Someone turned my face, then warm lips pressed against mine. My breath caught and my lashes fluttered. When the contact was gone, I blinked at Saint. He was gazing at me with concern.

"Better? You back with us?" he asked.

"Sorry."

Torch leaned back in the booth. "What triggered that response?"

"The thought of marrying a stranger," I admitted. "But I'll do whatever you want."

"We'll just have to hope your dad doesn't press for us to return you," Torch said. "I'm not about to force you to marry someone if that's your reaction. I'd thought Saint would be the least threatening of all of us, but that's apparently not going to work."

"Would you put Lyssa, Portia, and Hadrian in danger?" Saint asked.

"You have three kids?" I asked. "I only saw two."

"Portia wasn't feeling well, so Ridley offered to watch her," Torch said. "Ridley is with my VP. You'll need to meet everyone if you're going to make your home here."

But would I be staying here? Just because Mr. VanHorne had made arrangements for me to live with the club, it didn't mean it was a permanent thing. I'd thought I was here to be their whore, but Saint had seemed horrified when I'd tried to get him off. If that wasn't why I'd been brought here, then...

Torch cleared his throat and looked at me, then Saint. "Got an interesting call from Spider. It seems Luciana stripped naked and offered herself to him. Anything I need to know?"

My cheeks burned and I dropped my gaze, but Saint reached over and squeezed my hand. It was humiliating to know that our father had done that to us. Made us feel like we weren't good for anything but spreading our legs. If I hadn't been given to Saint, would someone else have taken me up on the offer? Would they have used me and not even noticed I wasn't into it? Or would they have cared at all?

"There was a slight misunderstanding this morning," Saint said. "It's been cleared up."

"Not really," I muttered.

"You think you're here to service the club?" Torch asked.

"If not that, then why am I here? It's all I'm good for."

Saint's hand squeezed mine tighter and he glared at me, anger flaring in his eyes. "That's not all you're good for, Sofia. Knock that shit off."

"What do you know of Casper VanHorne?" Torch asked me.

The conversation was put on hold as a harried-looking waitress made her way over. She huffed and puffed like she'd been running all morning. "Sorry it took me so long to get over here," she said. "What can I get you folks to drink?"

We placed our drink orders and she rushed off.

"I just know he was brokering some sort of deal for my father," I said after she was out of earshot.

"Not entirely," Torch said. "That's what your father thought. Casper is trying to take down your father and his organization. But first he wanted to make sure the three of you were safe. He brought you here to me, and sent your sisters to Hades Abyss for protection. Neither Luciana or Violeta are being harmed in any way. They aren't being forced to have sex with anyone."

Wire snorted. "No, but from what it sounded like, Luciana and Spider might end up together. I think he's going to claim her."

"*Claim?*" I asked.

"She'll be his, his woman. No one would dare touch her," Saint said. "He's the President of Hades Abyss. Being his old lady or wife would put her in the safest position of all. Every last man in that club would lay down his life for her. And Violeta, by association, since she'd be Spider's sister-in-law. It means they'd protect you too, if you wanted to join your sisters."

The waitress returned with our drinks and took our food order before rushing off again. Saint's words weighed heavily on me. I stared at him. He wanted me to leave. Of course he did. He'd pointed out repeatedly what a bad idea it was for me to be around his daughter. I knew he was right, and it would be better for me to be far away from them, but the thought of never seeing him again made my chest ache.

"Sofia is staying here," Torch said. "If you really don't want her in your home, I'll find a spot for her."

Wire winked at me. "She can come stay with me."

Saint stiffened next to me. "I don't think…"

"You don't think what?" Torch asked, his voice going hard. "You don't want her under your roof. Fine. She won't be. It doesn't give you a say in where she lives."

"Pardon me for being worried about my daughter," Saint said, his jaw clenching.

"It's fine," I said. "I don't have much to move. He's right to be concerned about Delia. My father wouldn't hesitate to use her in order to get to me, or keep me in line. He's done it before."

Saint focused on me. "What's that mean?"

I looked away, wishing I hadn't said anything. The fact he'd heard my nightmare and had an idea as to what I'd been through was bad enough. Telling him that my father threatened to hurt little kids if I didn't obey? No, I wasn't going to tell him that.

"Sofia. Damn it. Speak to me," he said.

"You don't want to know, okay? Just leave it alone," I said.

"Sofia…"

"What do you want to hear, Saint? Do you want to hear that my father will find small children and threaten to send them to his men instead of me if I don't fall in line? Do you want to hear about how he tortured one in front of me before I realized what sort of man had sired me? Is that what you want?" I demanded.

"We need to put that fucker in the ground," Wire said.

"Agreed," Torch said. "And I think Casper is working on it."

"You sacrificed yourself for those kids," Saint said softly. "Did whatever was asked of you so they wouldn't suffer. Sofia, I…"

I shook my head, not wanting to hear it. I wasn't some angel or anything. Any decent person would have done the same thing. At least, that's what I told myself, but after being around so many monsters, I'd started to wonder if there were any decent people in the world. Then I'd met Saint and now I knew there were. I wondered what my life would have been like if I'd had a father who loved me, had met a guy like Saint and fallen in love. Not that playing the "what if" game would get me anywhere.

"She can stay with me, but I won't marry her," Saint said.

It felt like an arrow had pierced my heart. Of course he wouldn't want to marry someone like me. I was just trash, a whore, thanks to my father. Saint would pick a woman who was sweet and hadn't been used so thoroughly. The perfect mom for Delia, and the perfect little wife for someone like him.

"I don't think I'm hungry," I murmured. "Can I go home?"

Saint looked across the room at Delia, and I saw that she was chatting with Torch's daughter and having a good time.

"You can stay," I said. "I'm sure I could find my way back."

Wire stood. "I'll take her. Someone bring the breakfast special back to the compound for me. I'll pay you back."

Saint's jaw tightened, but he nodded his agreement and let me out of the booth. I needed space, and time to think. I followed Wire out of the diner and gripped his waist as I climbed onto the back of his motorcycle. The wind dried my tears as they fell, and by the time we'd reached the compound, I knew what I had to do. It would hurt, but in the end it would be for the best. No matter how tempting I found Saint, or how much I wanted to hug his little girl, I knew I needed to keep my distance. I just hadn't realized how difficult it would be.

Chapter Three

Saint

The look on Sofia's face when she left the diner had gutted me. It wasn't that I didn't want to marry her, or have her in my home. It was that both of those were entirely too tempting. If I didn't have Delia, then I wouldn't have hesitated. But the fact was that I was a father first, a Dixie Reaper second, and anything else had to take third place in my life. It wasn't fair to Sofia to not give her all of myself, and I knew I couldn't do that. If anyone deserved a happy-ever-after, it was her. I hoped she'd get her fairy-tale ending someday. I just knew I couldn't be the one to give it to her. I hated that Torch and Wire had pulled that shit, showing her a marriage license with our names on it. It was cruel. I'd never once argued with Torch over anything, but for the first time, I'd wanted to rip into him.

I'd held my tongue. Barely.

I dropped Torch off at his home, and he pulled Delia from her booster seat. Lyssa had asked if my daughter could go to the playground with them, and I'd thought it would be the perfect opportunity for me to speak with Sofia. Lay everything out, without worrying about being interrupted.

I pulled into the driveway, parked under the carport, then shut off the vehicle and blew out a breath. Looking at the house, I felt my stomach knot. I wasn't looking forward to going in there, knowing that Sofia could very well be crying. I hated that I'd made her upset enough she'd wanted to leave the diner, and with Wire of all people. He was single, the ladies loved him, and I knew he'd be good to her. I hated the fucker right then.

Sitting in the car wouldn't accomplish anything, so I made myself go inside. I didn't hear a single sound and frowned as I went room by room. I found Sofia in my room, gathering the dirty laundry into a hamper that she was dragging behind her. The damn thing was almost as tall as her. Well, maybe not quite, but it did go up past her waist. She looked like a little pixie standing next to it.

"What are you doing?" I asked.

She shrieked and knocked the hamper over. "You scared me!"

"Sorry, but seriously. What are you doing?"

She waved a hand. "What's it look like?"

"Gathering my dirty clothes?"

She nodded. "Good. Because that's exactly what I'm doing. Might as well keep busy, so I thought I'd do some laundry. The housekeeper back home made sure we all knew how to use a washer and dryer, and I learned to cook some basic things. I'm not very good, though. I tend to burn most everything. Even using a toaster."

"Sofia, you aren't my maid. You don't have to do this."

"Not your maid. Not your whore. Not your wife. I'm not anything, Saint. Just let me do this so I can at least feel like I'm contributing in some way."

"What the fuck?" I demanded. "Seriously?"

"Am I wrong?" Sofia asked.

"Of course you aren't my maid or a whore. It wouldn't be fair for me to marry you, Sofia. I can't give you a fairy tale, and that's what you deserve. I didn't refuse just because of Delia, although her safety is a huge part of it."

Her gaze softened a little and she gave a slight nod before she turned to pick up more clothes. I watched her, my hands clenching and unclenching at my sides. I wanted to reach for her, kiss her, promise her that everything would be fine. Somehow, I managed to hold myself back. Kissing her would lead to other things. The brief brush of my lips against hers at the diner had been enough to make me hard as a damn rock.

I couldn't deny that I wanted her. If I were honest with myself, I was more intrigued by Sofia than the woman who had given birth to my daughter. Rhianon had been sweet, and we'd had fun, but I'd never wanted forever with her. I'd have given it to her if I'd known we had a kid together, but she'd kept that from me. If Rocket hadn't called me after her death, I'd have never known about Delia.

I should walk away, give Sofia her space. But we were alone, and… I didn't think I was strong enough to resist her for long. If she told me no, pushed me away, then I'd leave. If she didn't, though… that's the part that had me rooted to the floor, wondering if I should pull her into my arms and kiss her the way I wanted. She'd wanted me, wanted more until Delia had interrupted us. At the time, I'd be grateful, but now I was wishing that we'd had more time. I was so fucking conflicted. I wanted Sofia, wanted to keep her, but I knew that wasn't what was best for her or for Delia. Was it?

"You're staring," she said, not even turning around.

"I'm watching a beautiful woman. Kind of hard to look away."

She dropped the shirt in her hand on top of the pile in the hamper, then faced me. There was a cautious sort of hope on her face, but she shuttered her gaze and tightened her jaw. "You were right. We can't be together," she said. "It's best if we keep our distance."

Right. She was right, and I knew it, but... I moved closer and reached out, wrapping a loose curl around my finger. Her hair was soft, just like the rest of her. I was going to hell. I knew it, but I leaned closer anyway, not stopping until my lips brushed against hers. Sofia gasped and stiffened a moment before melting against me. I wrapped my arms around her and held her close, my mouth devouring hers. My cock pressed against the zipper of my jeans and I rubbed against her.

Sofia made the softest, cutest sounds as I explored her curves and tasted her sweet lips. Her hands slipped under my shirt and pressed against my bare skin. I shuddered, my cock starting to throb. Jesus. I'd never wanted anyone as much as I wanted her, and it scared the fuck out of me. Sofia was the last woman I should crave, and yet I couldn't deny that I wanted her as badly as a junkie wanted their next hit.

"Tell me to stop," I murmured against her lips. "Yell at me and tell me this is a bad idea."

"It's a bad idea," she said, then kissed me again.

"We shouldn't do this," I said, drawing back to catch my breath.

"No, we shouldn't," she said, and tugged on my cut until I pulled it off and set it on the dresser, then yanked my shirt over my head.

"Christ, Sofia. I don't know that I can walk away."

"Then don't. Maybe we can have just this one moment."

One moment. I could do that. She started to shimmy out of her clothes, and I kicked off my boots before reaching for my belt. She was already naked before I'd even gotten my jeans all the way off. I hadn't felt this damn eager since my first time.

Sofia reached for me, and we fell onto the bed in a tangle of limbs. She smiled so brightly that my breath caught for a moment. I reached up and smoothed her hair back from her face, then kissed her softly and slowly. As eager as I was to be inside her, I also wanted to savor the moment. If this was our one and only chance to explore one another, then I wanted to take advantage.

I licked and kissed every inch of her body, loving the way her nipples hardened as I blew across them. She squirmed beneath me and clutched at my shoulders as I worked my way down, parting her thighs to settle between them.

"Saint." She threaded her fingers through my hair and tugged. "I don't want to wait."

"Patience." I grinned up at her. "I'm not in a rush."

"Maybe I am."

I leaned down and traced her slit with my tongue, making her gasp, and she clenched her thighs against me. I parted her pussy lips and thrust my tongue inside her tight channel before teasing her clit. Sofia was so damn responsive, I just wanted more and more of her. I sucked on the little bud and eased two fingers inside her, thrusting slowly. As much as I wanted to make her come, I knew we had some time to play, and I wanted this moment to be memorable for both of us. Not that I thought I'd ever forget a single moment spent with her.

Sofia lifted her hips, pressing closer. I could hear her panting as I worked her pussy with my lips, tongue, and fingers, pushing her closer to an orgasm. I wouldn't take her until she'd come, worrying that I wouldn't last long once I was inside her. It had been too fucking long, and she was too damn tempting.

"Saint, please," she begged.

I growled softly and doubled my efforts, loving the sounds of her screams as she came apart. I made her come a second time before I kissed my way back up her body, my weight settling over her. She looked dazed, but her eyes were shining brightly, and her cheeks were flushed. Gorgeous. That's what she was, absolutely gorgeous.

My gaze stayed locked on hers as I sank into her, the wet heat of her pussy clasping me tight. I groaned and fought not to close my eyes. Sofia felt incredible, better than anything I'd felt before. Now that she was ready for me, willing, even eager, everything felt a million times better. She was perfection.

Her legs went around my hips, and she gripped my biceps, her nails biting into me. The trust in her eyes, the total surrender as she gave herself to me, made the walls around my heart crack even more. If things were different…

I kissed her, long and deep, as I started a steady thrust that soon had my skin humming and my balls drawing up. I couldn't remember ever taking a woman bare before, not even Delia's mom. But Sofia wasn't just any woman. Sweat slicked our skin as I took her harder and faster. It had been long before Rhianon since I hadn't felt the need to tie up a woman before fucking her. Even though Sofia had begged me earlier, it didn't feel right. Not in this moment. Next time…

My chest ached when I realized there wouldn't be a next time. This was it. Our one moment.

"I'm losing you," she said.

Damn. I knew she hadn't meant it like that, but the words definitely had a double meaning right now. I focused on Sofia, on the here and now, and blocked out all thoughts of what tomorrow, or even later today would bring. I cupped her breast and pinched her nipple, rolling it between my fingers. Her pussy clenched down on my cock, and I could feel how close she was to coming. On the next stroke, I ground against her clit and tugged on her nipple. Sofia came, her body going tight, and her pussy milking me dry.

I grunted with every thrust as I filled her up, jet after jet of cum shooting into her. Damn. My chest heaved as I tried to catch my breath. Sofia reached up and cupped my cheek, a look of complete devotion on her face, a look that gutted me since I knew nothing could come of it.

"Maybe we can have one more moment," she murmured.

"One more," I agreed.

She crossed her wrists in front of me, looking up at me expectantly.

"You want me to tie you up?" I asked.

"It's what you like, right? You don't have to hold back with me, Saint. I can take whatever you want to give me. I want you, all of you, whatever that entails."

I swallowed hard and nodded before withdrawing from her body. I got up and walked over to the closet and pulled down a box off the top shelf. They were things I'd purchased years ago, before finding out about Delia. The container was airtight, so no dust had gathered on the items. A pair of padded cuffs were at the bottom and I pulled them out, then carried the box over toward the bed, setting it down on the nightstand.

"Turn over. On your knees, ass in the air," I said. "Put your hands up by the headboard."

She quickly got into position, and held her hands by the spindles that ran along my headboard, just as I'd demanded. I fastened the cuffs, making sure they weren't too tight, and yet snug enough she couldn't escape. If she got distressed or wanted me to stop at any time, I'd release her immediately. I still worried that it would be too much for her.

"What else is in the box?" she asked.

"Some things I bought and never used," I said vaguely, not sure I wanted to use any of those things on her.

"Like what?"

Christ. It figured she'd push the issue. I reached into the box and pulled out a package with a small, pink vibrator. It was shaped like a cock, but only five inches long. Well, maybe not small, unless it was compared to my dick. I showed it to her, and fuck me if her eyes didn't light up with interest.

"Do you have batteries?" she asked.

"Yeah. Sofia, I don't know that…"

She arched an eyebrow as she stared at me over her shoulder. "I want the full experience, Saint. Don't treat me like I'm made of glass. It's just you and me in this room. I'm a woman who needs to be fucked by the greatest guy she's ever met."

I nodded and reached into the bedside table drawer. I always kept a variety of battery sizes in there. Hadn't realized I'd be using them for this particular purpose, not with a kid in the house. I'd figured those days were long gone, unless I decided to settle down. I ripped open the package, and the vibrator fell out onto the bed. I grabbed the bottle of lube and the AA batteries, inserted them, and hit the power button. The toy whirred to life, and I was honestly a bit surprised the damn thing worked after sitting in the closet for so long.

"Spread your legs, Sofia. Wide."

She shifted and did as I'd commanded. I ran my hand down her back.

"Good girl."

Setting the toy on a low speed, I rubbed small circles against her clit. She moaned and lowered her head, lifting her hips more and giving me better access. I caressed the cheeks of her ass as I slid the toy higher up and plunged it inside her pussy. I fucked her with it a few times before teasing her clit some more.

"You're going to come like this," I said. "Then I'm going to fuck you good and hard."

"Please," she whimpered.

I turned up the speed and she cried out, her body going tight. As she started to come, I backed off. Using our mingled release to coat the toy, I pressed it against the tight ring of muscle between her ass cheeks, just lightly circling. She gasped and twisted, her legs trembling.

"Hmm. It seems you like that, maybe a little too much."

"Saint. I... I need..."

"You need what?" I asked.

"Please. I need to come."

I put the toy against her clit again, turned it all the way up, and she was screaming her release within seconds. I kept it pressed against the hard little bud, making her come multiple times. Sofia was crying and begging, nonsensical words coming out of her mouth as she rode wave after wave of pleasure. When my cock was leaking all over the damn bed, I knew I couldn't wait another moment.

I thrust deep and hard, fucking her through another orgasm. Her body twitched and her pussy grabbed me tight. I removed the toy from her clit. Grabbing the lube, I squirted a liberal amount down the crack of her ass, then pressed the toy against that forbidden spot again. Sofia cried out and bucked, my cock sliding in deeper. I grunted and helped reposition her. With her ass higher and her shoulders flat on the bed, I was able to slam all nine inches into her until the head of my dick kissed her cervix.

I slowly worked the toy into her ass, fucking her with it as I pounded her pussy. Fuck but she felt incredible! I growled as I came, but even then my dick didn't deflate. I kept thrusting and fucking her with the toy. Sofia grew hoarse as she came twice more. I felt possessed, taking her like some crazed beast, but I couldn't stop. Didn't *want* to stop. I'd never come so much so close together in my life, but I came again. My cock twitched and throbbed as I emptied myself into her tight pussy.

"Fuck!" I panted for breath, my legs shaking from the force of my release. I ran my hand down her back. "You okay, baby?"

She whimpered and I eased out of her, then slowly removed the toy. I shut it off and unfastened the cuffs. Sofia collapsed onto the bed and I lay beside her, pulling her into my arms. Her body shuddered and she sucked in a big breath before she turned to face me.

"I never knew it could be like that," she said.

"Me either," I admitted.

"I find it hard to believe you've never done that before, since they were your toys."

"No, I mean… it was different with you. I've never lost control like that, or come so damn much. I didn't hurt you?"

"I'm good." She smiled softly. "More than good."

Then the smile slipped from her face, and I knew what she was thinking. This was our one and only. There wouldn't be more moments like this one. No more fucking between us. My dick wanted to protest, and so did my damn heart. Figured the one woman to come along and completely captivate me was the last one I should want.

"Rest, sweetheart. We'll shower before Delia comes home."

She ran her fingers down my chest, a wistful look on her face. "It's not fair."

"What's not?"

"I never knew men like you existed. I finally find one, and I can't keep him."

I closed my eyes, my heart breaking a little at her words. If I were a selfish bastard, then I'd say to hell with it and make her mine in every way possible, but I couldn't do that. The day Rocket had placed an infant in my hands, my life had changed. I could no longer do things because they were what *I* wanted. I had to put Delia first, and think of what was best for Sofia, even if it meant forgoing my own happiness. We were in a shitty situation, and I didn't see a way out. Not as long as her father and his men were breathing. I hoped Casper worked fucking fast on whatever he'd planned. If there came a time that Gomez wasn't a threat, then things would be different. If Sofia was still speaking to me by then… I wouldn't hold it against her if she didn't want anything to do with me as time passed.

"I think I could love you," she whispered.

"Me too, baby. I could easily love you. Maybe we'll get our chance."

"He'll never let me go," she said. "Without us, he'll lose out on business. It's common knowledge that anyone who deals with my father gets…"

I placed my fingers over her lips, not wanting to hear another word. The thought of anyone touching her without her permission made rage fill me, especially now. Now that I felt like she was mine.

She pulled away and got out of bed, padding into the bathroom. I stared up at the ceiling a moment before following her. I knew it would be best to keep my distance, to start building the wall again, locking my heart away. And yet I couldn't. I wanted as much time with Sofia as I could get. I'd squeeze as much enjoyment out of however many minutes or hours we had left as I could, and hope that it was enough until I could figure things out, find a way for us to be together without putting my daughter at risk. I wanted us to be a family, for Sofia to be a permanent part of our lives. It was dicey enough, just having Sofia in the house with us if her father wanted her back, but if I married her, then it would put a bigger target on us.

"There has to be a way. I don't know what it is yet, but whatever this is between us can't be doomed from the start."

I stepped into the shower, pulling her against my chest. "My club, the Hades Abyss, or Casper VanHorne, will take care of your father, and then we can be together. Give me time, Sofia."

She cuddled against me, but she didn't confirm or deny that she would be with me when all this was over. I understood her hesitation, but I hoped it was unfounded.

I prayed for the first time since I was kid, hoping that we would get a miracle. I hadn't had one in so long that I'd stopped believing in them, but I needed one now. We all did.

Chapter Four

Sofia
Six Weeks Later

I stared at my sister as she walked into Saint's house, unable to believe that Luciana was really here. I'd heard that our father was trying to reclaim her, and if that failed he wanted either me or Violeta. I'd go back before I'd let him hurt my baby sister. I'd endured the pain and humiliation longer than Violeta, and I worried about her gentle spirit being broken to the point she would never recover.

I looked at Luciana again, really looking this time. Despite the worry in her eyes, she fairly glowed and I wondered if she'd been doing well with Hades Abyss. A flash in the sunlight caught my attention and I noticed she was wearing a wedding ring. My gut churned. Not because I begrudged her any happiness, but because I'd started to fear I'd never have that for myself.

The day Saint had thoroughly ruined me for any other man had been the beginning of the end. When Delia had run home and hugged me before her dad, it had been the final nail in the coffin. Saint had not only distanced himself, but he'd frozen me out completely, of both their lives. Delia still talked to me, and we watched cartoons together, but if her daddy was around, she ignored me. Even though I knew she didn't want to, it was painful. On some level, I could understand his reasoning, but my heart still ached for what I would never have.

I lived here, and yet I could tell I wasn't really welcome. It hurt. So damn much. I looked longingly at Saint and Delia, but quickly turned away.

"They won't stop," I said. "We'll never be safe."

And that also meant I'd never have Saint or Delia. He'd been right to put up a wall between us, no matter how much pain it caused me.

"We're not going back, Sofia. Never," Luciana vowed.

I nodded, knowing she meant the words, but I didn't think she could make them an actuality. Just because she decreed we would be free and never suffer at our father's hands again didn't make it so.

"I miss you and Violeta," I said. I'd been so lonely.

"We miss you too. They're treating you well here, aren't they?" Luciana asked.

I cast a glance toward Saint and my cheeks flushed a little. "I'm good. I don't think he likes me, though."

I knew that wasn't entirely true. It wasn't that he didn't like me, it's that he feared letting me get too close. He had every right to be concerned for Delia.

"And the little girl?" Luciana asked.

"She's great. Delia is so much fun, and so sweet. We get along fine. She's four, but she's so smart. I think she's ahead of the other kids her age."

Luciana gave me a knowing look, and I worried that I'd let her see too much. Yes, I loved Delia, and her daddy too. Sometimes loving someone wasn't enough. They had to love you in return, and my parentage alone was enough to keep a wedge between me and Saint. Possibly forever. Unless my dad succeeded, and I was returned to Colombia. There were times I wondered if that would be better. At least I knew where I stood back home. Being in limbo with Saint and Delia was confusing. Even worse, knowing the pleasure and tenderness of his touch only to have it taken away left me feeling ice cold deep down.

The man who had arrived with Luciana came over, his hands shoved in his pockets. I noticed his vest, which I'd learned was called a cut, said *Prospect*. "So, I'm going to stay with you at another house. Rocket will be staying there too with Violeta. Saint said Sofia was welcome to go with us."

"Thank you, Teller," Luciana murmured.

Of course he said I could go. I swallowed hard and fought hard not to cry like a damn baby. I'd been more emotional than usual lately, and I hated it. My periods had never been regular, and it was common for me to miss a month or two at a time, but the way I felt the last few weeks, I figured I was due any day. Just what I needed. Cramps on top of dealing with a broken heart. At least ice cream helped with both issues.

"Delia doesn't want her to go," Teller said.

I felt lighter, happier at the mention of Delia. "She wants me here?"

He nodded. "I told Saint it would be best for you to stay since you're already set up here. I mean, this isn't my club and even if it were, he outranks me so… If he says you have to go, then you'll have to go."

I sighed and slowly stood. I walked over to Delia, who still clung to her daddy's leg, and knelt down.

"Delia, my sister is here and my other sister is coming too. I think it's best if I go with them for now, but I'll still be close by."

"She doesn't need you," Saint said.

His words were like a dagger to my heart and I didn't think I could hide my tears. I turned away quickly and headed for the front door. Luciana came out and wrapped her arms around me, glaring over my shoulder, no doubt at Saint. Despite the pain at being so easily dismissed, I refused to crumble. After all I'd faced in my life, I wouldn't let Saint break me. I'd looked evil in the face and I was still standing. A broken heart wouldn't be the thing that took me to my knees.

"Come on, Sofia. We'll find somewhere else to go until the house is ready for us. And Saint can have your belongings packed," Luciana said. "You've been through enough without remaining in a hostile home environment."

"Spider chose well," Saint said. "I'm sure you're the perfect wife for the President of Hades Abyss. Ryker didn't have too many nice things to say about you, but don't worry. He'll come around."

Luciana glanced from him to me and back again. "The question is whether or not you'll come around. Don't let fear hold you back."

I looked over and saw him smile faintly and lift his daughter into his arms. "If things were different... but they aren't. I'm not a bad guy, Luciana. But I will die before I let any darkness touch my daughter, and you and your sisters have trouble written all over you. It follows you, stalks you from the shadows, and I don't think it's backing down."

I let Luciana and the Prospect help me into an SUV and we drove to another home inside the compound. There was another man there, one wearing the Hades Abyss cut, and our sister. I'd missed Violeta so much! Despite the fact she looked a bit banged up, I smiled, a true smile, for the first time in a while, and rushed out of the vehicle to go hug her. The man beside her frowned, a flash of something in his eyes. I didn't know who he was, but it was clear that he was protective of Violeta.

"Sofia, this is Rocket," Violeta said. There was a hint of hero worship in her voice, and I wondered if he noticed. A quick glance at Rocket showed that he didn't seem completely oblivious to Violeta, but I didn't see lust either, which was good since she was still young.

"It's nice to meet you," I said.

Luciana pushed me out of the way so she could hug Violeta too. I thought it odd she seemed to excited to see our sister when they lived at the same place. Didn't they? I'd been told both my sisters were with Hades Abyss. Were they not allowed to visit one another? Had I been wrong about them being good guys? I didn't get an evil vibe from them, but that didn't exactly make them angels either.

Rocket gave me a nod. "All right, ladies. Go find your rooms. The Dixie Reaper women are gathering some things you might need. Except you, Sofia, since your things are already here."

"Thank you," Luciana said, holding Violeta a little tighter.

"She's not getting taken on my watch," Rocket said.

We moved into the house. There were plenty of rooms for everyone, and I picked one closer to the back. I'd barely had time to sit down before I heard Luciana screaming for someone named Teller. The Prospect, I assumed, but it was the tone of her voice that had me racing out of the room. Blood soaked Luciana's pants and I gasped, my gaze locking with hers. Terror stared back at me, and I knew that even though she hadn't asked to be pregnant, that she loved her baby. And I'd been the one to wish she'd have a miscarriage. I felt horrible, as if my thought had brought this moment into existence. If she lost the baby...

"Teller, something's wrong. The babies…" She gasped and held her belly.

Babies? More than one?

"Hospital. Now," Teller said. "Rocket, stay with Violeta and Sofia. They're safer here at the compound."

"But I want to --"

Rocket placed a hand on my shoulder. "Let Teller take her to the hospital, Sofia. She'll only worry if you're outside the gates, and she needs to focus on her children."

I nodded, knowing he was right.

"Stay safe," I told Luciana, wanting to hug her, but there was no time. Teller had already lifted her and quickly carried her from the house. As the door slammed shut, a spike of fear filled me. I hoped Luciana and the babies would be okay.

"If she loses the babies, she'll still be all right, won't she?" Violeta asked.

Rocket put his arm around her, drawing her close to his side. "I'm sure she'll be fine, Violeta. Teller will make sure she's taken care of and kept safe."

"Do you really think Spider didn't make it?" she asked.

"Spider's a tough bastard. He'll probably walk through the front door at any moment," Rocket said.

"Shouldn't he have called? Wouldn't he be worried about Luciana?" Violeta asked.

"Spider's her husband?" I asked. "The President of Hades of Abyss?"

Rocket nodded. "Never seen him act like that around a woman, but he's head over heels for Luciana, and I know she feels the same."

"So we just sit and wait?" I asked.

"Not much else we can do. Spider was going to take care of Gomez, but something went sideways if

Luciana and Teller are here, and I got word to come straight here without any stops. I don't have all the details yet," Rocket said. "Whatever went down, the Pres can handle it. He's a tough bastard."

"Will he be angry?" I asked, worried about Luciana. What if her husband became furious that she'd lost the babies? I knew they weren't his, but maybe it had been a factor in their marriage? Luciana and I hadn't seen nor talked to one another since I'd stepped off Casper VanHorne's jet. I knew nothing of her new life with the Hades Abyss.

"Angry?" Rocket asked.

"Because she's losing the babies," I said.

"No. Spider will be more worried about Luciana. As long as he has her, that's all that matters. He'd have loved the kids, but he won't love her less because she miscarried."

He sounded like a wonderful man, and anyone Luciana loved would have to be rather remarkable. It made me long for that type of relationship, but I didn't want just anyone. I wanted Saint. I wondered if Luciana's husband had managed to kill my father, or was Mateo Gomez still out there, waiting to strike? Would he come for me and Violeta now? If my father was no longer a threat, would I be welcomed back into Saint's home? I'd felt close to him the one day we'd shared. Even though I understood the walls he'd put up, it didn't mean I had to like it. He should fight for me, for us. Shouldn't he?

My stomach clenched, and then I felt acid rising up the back of my throat. I scrambled for the nearest bathroom and fell to my knees seconds before I threw up. I flushed the toilet, but just ended up throwing up again twice more. When I was finished, I lay on the cool tile and focused on breathing. My stomach gurgled and I worried I'd get sick again. Too much stress.

"You okay?" Rocket asked, leaning against the doorway, a frown on his face. "You sick?"

He couldn't be that worried since he stayed out of reach. Or maybe he was worried about scaring me. I knew Violeta jumped at shadows most of the time, and if he'd been around her, then he might expect the same of me. I wanted to hate the men keeping my sisters from me, but they seemed like decent guys. Not once had Rocket been harsh with Violeta. If anything, he was tender with her, and sweet. Maybe he was exactly what she needed. I hadn't had a chance to spend much time with them, but I didn't see evil lurking in his eyes. The way he protected her, watched her, was touching.

"I don't think I have anything contagious. My stomach just cramped and I knew I was going to be sick. I think I'm fine now."

Violeta eyed me from beside Rocket and nibbled her lower lip. She cast a glance up at him before coming into the bathroom and kneeling in front of me. Her hands trembled as she reached out and ran her fingers through my hair. Fear filled her eyes, and worry. Had my throwing up scared her? It wasn't like I'd never been sick around her before.

"Sofia, did anyone hurt you since we left Colombia? Like before?" she asked softly.

Hurt me? My brow furrowed and I tried to... Oh. She was worried someone here had forced themselves on me. "No, Violeta. No one hurt me like Father's men."

She stared at me as if she didn't quite believe me. Did she worry that I would lie out of fear or to protect someone? Since when had my little sister turned into a protector? It was my job to watch over her, not the other way around.

"But you threw up," Violeta said. "I threw up a lot the first two months of my pregnancy. What if you're pregnant? If someone hurt you... Rocket will help you. All the Hades Abyss men will."

Pregnant? I snorted. In all the years of abuse I'd suffered, not once had I ever conceived. No, it was doubtful I was pregnant. I was just scared and worried. That's all it was. I struggled to sit up, but the room spun.

"Rocket, help her," Violeta said, rising to her feet. "She needs a doctor."

Bossy. Little Violeta was getting bossy, and it made me smile. It was nice to see this side of her. It had been so long since she'd spoken up. I wanted to argue that I was fine, but I wasn't really feeling all that great at the moment. Maybe a doctor wasn't the worst idea ever.

"The Reapers have a doctor they use on a regular basis," Rocket said. "We'll get her back to her room, then I'll have someone call him."

Rocket picked me up and carried me to the room I'd chosen earlier. He eased me down onto the bed and slipped off my shoes. Violeta sat in the chair next to the bed. Rocket gave her a tender look before he pulled his phone from his pocket and stepped out of the room. It didn't escape my notice that Violeta watched him, her heart in her eyes. I hoped she didn't have a heartache in her future. There was quite the age difference between them. Violeta had grown up fast, she'd had no choice. None of us had. But there were still laws to follow, and I was fairly certain it was illegal for a man of his age to be with a seventeen-year-old girl.

"You like him," I said.

"Yes, but I'm too young. He won't touch me since I'm not eighteen. He keeps insisting he doesn't think of me that way, but I know different. I've heard him, when he thinks I'm asleep." Her cheeks flushed. "He sometimes calls out my name and I can tell he's pleasuring himself. The next morning, he always looks guilty. It weighs on him, to be attracted to someone my age."

"You won't be seventeen forever, Violeta. The fact he wants to wait means he's an honorable man."

Violeta nodded and reached for my hand. I gave hers a squeeze while we waited. I didn't know how much time passed before Rocket came back into the room with a man in a lab coat following.

"Sofia, this is Doctor Myron. He treats the ladies here at the Dixie Reapers' compound," Rocket said.

Doctor Myron smiled. "Hi, Sofia. Do I have your permission to look you over and make sure everything's okay?"

"Yes," I said, releasing Violeta's hand.

She scurried out of the way, plastering herself to Rocket's side. I noticed she was trembling, and I hated that she was scared of the doctor. I answered Doctor Myron's questions, my cheeks flushing when he asked when I'd last had sex and about my last period. I saw Violeta's eyes go wide when she heard I'd had sex with Saint about six weeks ago, and Rocket led her from the room. I hoped she didn't think Saint had forced me, because he hadn't, not even a little. I'd told her as much already, but I knew she was worried. I'd wanted him, still did for that matter.

"And you haven't had a period since then?" the doctor asked.

"Well, no. But it's not unusual for me to be late or skip a month completely. I've never been regular."

He hmm'd and listened to my heart and lungs, checked my eyes and ears, and seemed content that I was in good health. He couldn't find anything out of the ordinary. The look in his eyes said he suspected that my sister was right and I most likely carried Saint's child. I didn't see that going over well.

"Without a urine or blood test, I can't say for certain, but I think you're pregnant," Doctor Myron said.

"But I never conceived before," I said. "I've been... sexually active for about four years. Why now?"

I'd barely gotten the words out. Sexually active? That was one way to put it. The wrong way, but I didn't want to delve into my past right now. I didn't know how much he knew of me and my sisters. Discussing the dark years of my life wasn't a fun pastime, even if it was for medical purposes.

"Maybe it was just meant to be," he said.

Meant to be? No, I couldn't accept that. When Saint found out, he'd be so angry. I'd told him I couldn't get pregnant, so he hadn't bothered with a condom. Now I was carrying his baby, and he'd think I'd lied. Oh, God. I might be sick again. My stomach felt like it was bubbling, and I fought back a whimper. I didn't know anyone who enjoyed throwing up, but I especially didn't. I could handle broken bones, headaches, anything other than nausea. That was the one thing that would kick my ass and put me in bed until it passed.

"I can take the blood now and have the lab run it when I get back to my office. I'll call as soon as I have the results," he said.

"Okay."

Doctor Myron drew some blood, then packed up his things. "I'll be calling within the hour. Try to rest. I know there's a lot going on right now, but stress isn't good for you. Anything upsetting doesn't have a place in this house or in your room. Understood?"

"Yes, Doctor Myron. Thank you for coming."

"I won't say anything to anyone," Doctor Myron said, "and I know it's not my place, but I consider the Dixie Reapers to be friends. I think you should tell Saint. He might surprise you. Planned or not, he'll love the baby."

It hadn't escaped my notice he'd said Saint would love the baby, not me. I didn't fear Saint being a good dad. I already saw how amazing he was with Delia. What concerned me was how he'd feel about me. I'd hoped things would go back to the way it had been the day we'd conceived this baby, but now I doubted that would happen.

I shook my head, a tear slipping down my cheek. "No. He'll hate me."

What the hell? I seldom cried. Yes, I'd bawled my eyes out when I'd arrived here from Colombia, but I didn't do that often. I'd learned early that tears didn't solve anything. Every now and then, it was a good way to do an emotional purge, but otherwise tears had no place in my life.

"I doubt that very much, but I'll leave the decision up to you. Rest, Sofia."

He let himself out of the room and I rolled onto my side, crying into my pillow. I'd screwed things up so badly this time. The one man I wanted more than anything would be so angry with me. Even though he'd never hurt me, I didn't know what to expect if he found out I was pregnant. I tried to calm down, breathe, and focus. Just because the doctor thought I was pregnant didn't mean I was. The test could come back negative.

Was the pregnancy the reason my emotions had been so scattered lately? I'd felt like someone was jerking me from one end of the spectrum to another with one quick tug. I knew that pregnancy could cause hormonal and emotional changes, just from what I'd witnessed with Luciana and Sofia. It had never occurred to me that was what was happening to me, though.

Violeta quietly came into the room and sat beside me, reaching out to take my hand. I held on, needing the comfort she offered.

"You said you weren't hurt," she said softly. "Why did you lie?"

This again? I guess I could understand her concern. After everything we'd suffered, she probably had a hard time picturing me sleeping with a man voluntarily. Even though she seemed to like Rocket, I wondered if she'd have trouble with intimacy if anything ever developed between them after she grew up a little more.

"I wasn't hurt," I said, wiping the tears from my eyes. "I agreed to be with him."

"Like before? Did you have to agree so things wouldn't be worse?" she asked.

"No. I wanted him. Saint is different from anyone I've met before, and I..." I swallowed hard. "I thought I could handle just one time. I wanted to experience how things are supposed to be between a man and a woman, but it just made me want more, more of him. Once wasn't enough. Not for me, but he doesn't want me. He made it clear that he and Delia don't need me."

"That's not what I hear," Rocket said from the doorway. "It's not what Teller said he witnessed earlier. Saint cares, but he's worried about his kid. And I think he's worried about you too. I don't think he pushed you away as a way to punish you. He's trying to keep his kid and you safe the only way he knows how."

"He has a child?" Violeta asked, her eyes going a little wide.

"He's not like our father," I assured her. "Delia is Saint's entire world, and he would do anything for her. I know that letting me into their lives isn't a good idea. At least, not while Father is around. You know he'd use Delia against me if he ever got the chance. It doesn't stop me from wanting Saint, wanting to be a part of his family."

"If Spider is able to handle Gomez, then that might not be an issue anymore," Rocket said.

"What if he's dead? What if he died and my father is coming here next?"

Violeta's hand trembled in mine. I hated scaring her, but we needed to face reality. Our father would never let us go. I'd known it the moment we were loaded onto that jet. The only way we'd ever escape is if we were going to a worse fate. The fact we all seemed to want to stay in our new homes meant that we were on borrowed time. I knew to some I would seem negative, but I was being realistic. We'd never been allowed happiness, so I didn't expect that to change now. I'd fight to keep Saint and Delia safe, in my own way. Struggling against my father wouldn't do anything, but if I went quietly… maybe that would be enough to make him leave everyone else alone. I'd do it, go back to that horrific life, if it meant that ugliness never touched little Delia.

"I'm stepping outside, but I'll be close," Rocket said. "Sofia, I can't tell you what to do, but I think Saint needs to know if you're pregnant. Saint already had one kid kept from him. Don't make the same mistake my sister made."

Sister? I blinked at Rocket. "What does that mean?"

"You didn't know?" he asked, cocking his head to the side.

"No."

"Delia's mother was my sister, Rhianon. She died in a car accident when my niece was still a baby. Rhianon never told Saint they had a kid together, no matter how many times I told her it was a bad idea. He found out after she'd passed, when I called and told him to come get his daughter. Don't screw him over the way she did. The guy was scared shitless over raising an infant, but I've never seen someone love a little girl more than he loves Delia. He'd be the same with any kids the two of you had together." Rocket turned and walked off, leaving me feeling as if world were tilting.

Saint had been with Rocket's sister, and Delia was their child. Why hadn't she told Saint about the baby? He was wonderful with Delia, and I knew he loved her more than anything in the world. It wasn't that I doubted that he would love any child he had, but I was scared that he would hate me. Would he try to take the baby away? And could I honestly stop him? Would I want to? Here with the Dixie Reapers, that child would have a safe haven, a barrier to keep away the darkness. It was more than I could ever offer. As long as my father or his men were alive, I would always have to look over my shoulder, and I'd do anything to keep them from getting their hands on a child.

Bile rose in my throat and I rushed to the bathroom again. My stomach had nothing left and all I could do was dry heave. I hated throwing up, but I'd heard it was common during pregnancy. As Violeta had said, she'd been sick often enough during the first part of her pregnancy. I didn't remember Luciana experiencing this part, but she could have kept it to herself. Although, as much as I would love to have Saint's baby, I was hoping I'd just contracted the flu or something. The last thing I needed to do was bring a child into the chaos and pain of my world.

"I bet Rocket would let you come stay with us," Violeta said as she came into the bathroom.

"No. I'll figure something out," I said. I could tell my sister adored the biker, and I didn't want to intrude. They might not be able to have the type of relationship she would like, at the moment, but in time that could change. She deserved to be happy, to find love. And since Luciana was not only married but dealing with her own issues -- like a possibly deceased husband and miscarriage -- I wasn't about to be a burden to her either.

I heard voices from the front of the house. Rocket, and two other men. I splashed water on my face, rinsed out my mouth, and decided to be brave and find out what was happening. If it involved me, then I might as well face whatever fate had in store for me now. Violeta kept pace with me, and we drew to a halt when the President of the Dixie Reapers glared in my direction. Oh, hell. Had he found out? Did he think I'd tried to trap Saint? Doctor Myron must have already gotten the results and called someone. I had a feeling that doctor-patient thing didn't exist in this world. Probably the only thing they had in common with my father.

The room spun and I threw my hand up, bracing myself against the wall. I felt hands at my waist and looked up at a man I didn't recognize. His patch said *Venom* and that he was the Dixie Reapers VP. I hadn't had a chance to meet everyone, but there was kindness in his eyes so my fear subsided. Thanks to my time with Saint, I no longer had the gut reaction to run from every man who looked my way.

"We're not angry with you," Venom said. "We're pissed at Saint."

Torch came closer. "Doctor Myron called and confirmed you're pregnant. Before you get upset that he told me, you should know that doctor-patient confidentiality crap doesn't mean shit in this club. You live here which makes you my responsibility. Since you've only been alone with Saint, I knew it had to be his."

"Don't tell him. Please. He'll be so angry, and..." A tear slipped down my cheek. Damn hormones! "I don't want him to hate me."

"Hate you?" Torch asked. "Why would he hate you?"

"We know the boy well enough that I doubt he'd force himself on you," Venom said. "But if you didn't ask for his attentions, then..."

I shook my head. "I wanted him. We agreed it would be the once."

"The condom break?" Torch asked. "I know he knocked up Delia's mom years ago, but I'd have thought he'd learned a lesson. He's been so damn cautious that as far as I knew, he'd been celibate since bringing Delia home."

My cheeks burned and I dropped my gaze. "We didn't use one. He said he didn't have any, and instead of asking him to go find one, I told him it was fine. I've never conceived, and thanks to the test that was done before I came here I knew I was clean. I told him I couldn't have kids."

"How long?" Torch asked softly. "How long did they hurt you like that?"

"Four years," I said. "And I never once got pregnant. I really didn't think I could have a baby. I didn't mean to trap him. I just…"

I clenched my hands at my sides and ground my teeth together. I hated feeling like this. Having a baby should be a reason to celebrate, not worry that the father would think you'd tried to trap him, or not even knowing who the father was. My sisters and I hadn't had the best of luck when it came to this sort of thing. I wanted that happy moment I'd seen in movies and read about in books.

Would Saint think I'd done it as a way to remain here? Being with the Dixie Reapers was better than anything I'd experienced before. I'd felt safe for the first time since I realized exactly who and what my father was.

"This is a fucking mess," Torch muttered. "Saint still should have used a damn condom, or kept his dick in his pants, but she's right. It's not entirely his fault, nor is it hers. I'm not sure how he's going to react."

"The levelheaded, sweet kid we knew grew up," Venom said. "Now he's an overprotective dad, and after the shit with Rhianon he's probably trying to protect himself as well."

Rocket looked between the two of them. "He was pissed when he found out Rhianon had kept Delia from him. You two can't seriously think he won't adore this kid too. Just because the pregnancy wasn't planned doesn't mean --"

Torch cut him off. "It's not the baby we're worried about. I don't know how he'll act with Sofia when he finds out. As heartbroken as he was that Rhianon had died, he was also really fucking pissed that she'd kept their kid a secret."

"You can't tell him," I said. "What if my father comes here? What if I go back to Colombia? It would destroy Saint to know his kid was subjected to that kind of abuse. And I won't have him running off to save me, not at the risk of Delia losing her dad."

"Your father isn't going to come for you," Torch said. "Mateo Gomez and his men are dead. I'm not sure yet who the casualties and wounded are from our side yet, so don't say anything to Luciana. Better for her to have some hope than none. I've been trying to call Spider's cell, as well as Fox's and a few others, but none of the calls are going through. Might be an issue with a cell tower. The landline at the clubhouse was busy the few times I tried."

"Then how do you know about our father?" I asked.

"Casper VanHorne. He hung up before I could get more details, and now the fucker isn't answering."

"If Mateo Gomez is no longer a threat, then maybe it's safe for Sofia to tell Saint about the baby," Rocket said. "His reason for keeping his distance was that he feared Gomez would hurt Delia. That's not an issue now."

"No, it's not," Venom agreed. "But the decision is Sofia's. If she's not comfortable telling Saint right now, then we'll find a safe place for her to stay. I'd imagine you'll be returning home once Luciana is in the clear?"

"As far as I know," Rocket said. "Unless Spider shows up before she gets back. He may want her home as soon as possible. Not sure if she'll be able to travel if she's having a miscarriage."

I placed a hand on my belly and cast a fearful look at Violeta. She'd mentioned she'd miscarried and now it seemed Luciana might as well. What if I did too? No, telling Saint wouldn't be a good idea, not until I knew for sure that the baby would survive. Maybe there was something genetically wrong with us, or maybe our bodies had been too badly damaged over the years to carry a pregnancy to term. No sense telling him anything if something bad was going to happen. No matter how he felt about me, I didn't want him to suffer the loss of a child if he didn't have to.

"Do you remember Wire?" Torch asked.

"Yes," I said.

"I'm going to have you stay with Wire for a little bit. He lives on the opposite end of the compound from Saint, so if you stay close to the house, you probably won't see Saint. You'd be comfortable with Wire?" Torch asked. "I can promise that he won't make any advances."

"I think so."

He nodded. "Then pack your things and I'll walk over with you now. I rode my bike and I don't think it's a good idea for you to be on a motorcycle. If I'd realized we were moving you to a new location, I'd have brought a different vehicle."

I didn't have anything to get. Saint hadn't packed up my things yet, and I hadn't been permitted to get anything before moving to this house. Torch stared at me, probably waiting for me to move.

"I don't have anything here," I said.

"Saint hasn't sent her stuff over yet," Rocket said.

"I'll handle it," Venom said. "Just get Sofia to Wire's place."

Torch gently took my arm and led me out of the house. I cast a glance at Violeta over my shoulder and she gave me a little wave. I knew she was in good hands with Rocket, so I didn't worry about her. Now that our father was dead, we would be safe. Or at least, we'd be safe from him. I still wasn't so sure I'd be safe from Saint when he found out I was pregnant.

Maybe one day I'd have my happy-ever-after, the fairy tale that Saint had said I deserved, but it didn't look like it would be today. He'd said he wasn't the type of man to give that to me. I had to wonder if I wasn't the only broken one.

Chapter Five

Saint
Three Weeks Later

I'd thought it was strange when my VP came to get Sofia's things from my house a few weeks ago. It didn't seem like the sort of thing he'd handle himself. I hadn't questioned it, and just packed up her shit and handed it over. But now that I was staring at the home where she'd been taken, or so I'd thought, I was left even more confused. It was clearly vacant now that Spider had come for Luciana and the Hades Abyss crew was back in Missouri. So where the fuck was Sofia? Had she decided to go with them? No one had said a damn word about it to me. They'd been gone nearly two weeks now, and I'd thought Sofia would have come home. I waited, giving her time. Now I was wishing I hadn't.

I'd asked Darian and Bull to watch Delia for me, but I hadn't explained why. Just said I had an errand to run. If Delia had heard I was looking for Sofia, she'd have begged to come with me. I loved that Delia wanted Sofia in our home as much as I did, but I needed a moment alone with her first. Needed to convince her to come home, where she belonged.

"Problem?" Flicker asked.

I turned to face him. "Where the fuck did you come from?"

He pointed in the direction of the clubhouse. "I was walking home. Had to leave the bike at the house earlier because Pepper insisted it needed to be washed."

I wasn't even going to mention how that woman had pussy whipped Flicker in no time. Honestly, he didn't seem to mind. Anyone could see he adored her, and considering how long he'd waited to find the right woman, I couldn't blame him. Besides, now wasn't the time to give him shit over the fact he fell in love with a woman who loved bikes as much if not more than he did. No surprise her nesting during pregnancy included washing the damn motorcycles.

"Sofia was supposed to be here."

"They all cleared out," Flicker said.

No fucking shit. The big empty ass house had been my first damn clue. "So I see, but where's Sofia? Why didn't she come back once it was safe?" I asked.

"Are you really that fucking stupid? You pushed her away, told her that her presence put Delia in jeopardy. You think she'd come running back to you when her life wasn't in danger anymore? Maybe she wised up and found someone man enough to claim her. You think I backed down when Pepper had the fucking mob after her? Hell no. Did Tank run when Emmie was up on that auction site? Nope. But you? Saint, I'm starting to think you don't have balls anymore. Should I go buy you a dress?"

What. The. Fuck.

"Is that what everyone thinks? That I'm a dickless guy who won't go after what he wants?"

Flicker shrugged. "Well, you haven't exactly proven otherwise. We all adore Delia, you know that, and while it's important to keep her safe, you have to make a life for both of you and not just her. But what happens when she grows up and starts her own family?"

I ground my teeth together. Not only because he was right about me playing it too damn safe, but I also didn't like the idea of my little girl growing up and meeting some asshole who would take her away from me. Dickhead better treat her right or I'd bury him.

But first, I needed to find my woman and bring her home. Never should have made her leave. I'd been a complete shit. No, whatever was worse than that, that's what I'd been. I'd had my reasons, and it wasn't just to protect Delia, but I needed to explain that to her. I hoped she could forgive me, give me a second chance. My life had been shit without her. I couldn't sleep, and every time I closed my eyes, I could see her face as she'd come, begging me for more. "Who claimed Sofia? Where is she?"

Flicker rubbed a hand down his beard. I could tell from the look in his eyes that the fucker wasn't going to tell me a damn thing. My hands clenched at my sides and I fought the urge to put my fist through his jaw. Punching an officer of the club wasn't my brightest idea, no matter how tempting.

"Here's the thing. Pepper is rather fond of Sofia. So are the other wives. If I tell you where Sofia is, then my sweet Pepper is going to make my life hell. With her due any day now, I'm not going to piss her off. Sorry, kid. You're on your own."

Great. I stared at the house again. The only clue I had right now was that she was somewhere inside the compound. There was no way she'd gotten close to the Reaper ladies if she'd left. During her stay at my home, she'd seldom left or spoken to anyone, and her sisters had barely been here a week. Short of going door to door, and pissing off all my brothers, I wasn't sure where to go from here.

I heard Flicker walk off, and I turned to face the road that wound through the compound. I hesitated. Instead of going home, I got on my bike and drove to Torch's house. If anyone here would tell me how I could find Sofia, it would be Isabella. We'd gotten close over the years. If I had to pick a best friend among the

Dixie Reapers and their old ladies, it would be her. I'd do anything for Isabella, and she knew it. I only hoped she felt the same in return.

Coming to a stop in the driveway, I put down the kickstand and killed the engine. I swung my leg over the seat, but before I could approach the door, it flew open and Lyssa barreled down the steps, launching herself at me. I laughed as I caught her, spinning her in a circle before setting her down. "How's my girl?" I asked.

"You haven't been over in forever," she complained.

"I'm sorry, Lyssa. I'll do better. You've gotten a chance to play with Delia, though, and I know how much you love that."

She nodded. "Momma's inside making cookies."

"Um." I glanced back at my bike.

"Saint, don't you dare ride off," Isabella yelled from inside the house. "Get in here!"

I sighed and followed Lyssa into the house. The smell of burning cookies filled the air. I loved Isabella like a sister, but damn. The woman hadn't been able to make a decent cookie since she'd gotten pregnant with Hadrian. It was like her baking skills just vanished overnight. I almost felt sorry for Torch.

"You were going to leave without coming to say hi," Isabella accused as I pulled out a kitchen chair and sat.

"Maybe."

"I told him you were making cookies," Lyssa said.

Isabella groaned and rolled her eyes. "I swear. I've heard of baby brain before, but this is ridiculous. Even if I set the damn timer, I still burn them. Every. Single. Time."

"Where is Hadrian anyway?" I asked, looking around. Usually she'd have him nearby, but I didn't even see the baby monitor.

"Torch has him." She tossed the burnt cookies in the trash and set the baking sheet aside. "He's been fussy all night and all morning. I was reaching my breaking point, so I handed him to his daddy and pointed to the door."

I couldn't help but laugh. Isabella's kids were adorable, but I could see where she'd want a break. I only had Delia and there had been plenty of times I wanted to pull out my hair. With three, I think I'd have been committed by now. Thankfully, she had Torch to help her out, and I knew the other old ladies took turns with the kids too.

"Since I know you didn't stop by for my stellar baking skills, why are you here?" she asked.

"I need some help."

She crossed her arms and arched an eyebrow, something she'd picked up from Torch and perfected over the years. Not that she looked the least bit intimidating with her tiny stature. Even with the baby weight, I could probably still lift her with one arm.

"With what?" she asked.

"I need to find Sofia."

She shook her head. "Nope. Not happening."

"Why the hell not?"

"Because she's suffered enough, Saint. Do you have any idea what you did to her? She was completely shattered when you sent her away. You might as well have ripped her heart right out of her chest and stomped it into the ground. I don't know what the hell has been going on, but I can't let you anywhere near Sofia. Especially not now."

Not now. Right. Because she was shacked up with someone else, someone who apparently wasn't as stupid as I was and had decided to hold onto her. I was a fucking moron, and I could admit it, but I wouldn't give up. Sofia was mine and she belonged in my home, in my bed, and riding my cock. I shifted in my seat and tried to think of anything other than Sofia, naked and spread across my bed. Damn. My hand hadn't been enough, not after being inside her -- bare. It broke my heart that we'd never have kids together, not the conventional way. We could always adopt, if she were willing. Even when she'd thought I was ignoring her, I'd watched as she played with Delia, and she was a natural at being a mom.

"I fucked up," I said. "I'm sorry, but I need to tell Sofia that and not you. I can't apologize if I don't know where she is."

"She's safe and she's being cared for. I think that's all you need to know."

"Damn it, Isabella! Now isn't the time to be stubborn."

"Did you just cuss at my woman?" asked a gravelly voice from behind me. I winced and turned to face Torch.

"You know I adore Isabella, and your kids, but I really need her help and she's refusing."

Torch stared at his wife, and I saw her shake her head from the corner of my eye. Torch sighed and ran a hand through his hair. Hadrian lay in the crook of his other arm.

"The boy deserves to decide for himself," Torch told her. "I'm not sure we're actually protecting her. What if we're just making things worse?"

Worse? Protecting her? What the fuck was going on?

"Fine." Isabella huffed, and I knew she didn't really agree with him. "She's at Wire's place."

Wire? I shot out of the chair and ran from the house. It wasn't that I didn't trust Wire with Sofia, but… yeah, I didn't trust the fucker. All the ladies loved Wire. They thought he was harmless since he spent so much time behind a computer screen, but he was probably one of the scariest motherfuckers in the club. With a few keystrokes, he could wipe out your entire existence. Well, maybe more than a few, but he could make it happen just the same and never have to leave the comfort of his home.

I revved the engine on my bike, and my tires spit gravel as I took off down the road. When I reached Wire's house, he was on the front porch, hands in his pockets, and looking in my direction. Had he been waiting for me? I wouldn't put it past Isabella or Torch to have called him. I only hoped I wouldn't have to hit the fucker just to get to Sofia. If she cared for him even a little, that wouldn't win me any points.

"Need to have a word before you go in there," Wire said.

"You claiming her?" I asked.

He snorted. "No. She's a sweetheart and I'd do just about anything for her. But not that. She's not my type."

"Then what do you want to tell me?"

He rubbed the back of his neck, looked over his shoulder, then lowered his voice. "She's had a hard time of it. Not just you kicking her out, but she misses her sisters, and… she hasn't been well. She's losing too much weight. Doc Myron is worried about her."

My stomach dropped. "She's sick?"

"Not exactly."

"Then what the fuck?"

He nodded toward the door. "Go on in. She's probably in her room. First bedroom on the right. Try not to startle her. Doc Myron said to keep her calm."

My heart was racing as I entered the house and slowly made my way to the back. The first bedroom door wasn't completely closed and I tried to peek inside without opening the door. I could see Sofia on the bed, curled up with her back toward me. The way her body jerked, I realized she was crying, and I felt like shit. Were the tears because of me? Or was it due to whatever illness she had? No, not illness. Wire had said she wasn't exactly sick, but something was obviously going on.

I pressed the door open and went inside. "Sofia."

She tensed and I heard her suck in a breath.

"I'm so damn sorry, Sofia. I should have never made you leave."

She didn't turn to face me, didn't even acknowledge my presence. It hurt, but I deserved it. No, I deserved worse. I hadn't meant to make her feel like I didn't want her. I'd pushed her away not just for Delia's sake but for her own as well. If her father's men had managed to get inside the compound, made it inside my house, I would have been split trying to keep them both safe, and I could have failed one or both of them. And if her father had used kids against her before, he could have done the same with Delia, forcing Sofia to go with him to spare my daughter. I couldn't let that happen, not when they both meant so much to me.

"I fucked up, Sofia. I never meant for you to feel that you weren't wanted. I didn't have a choice but to push you away."

"For Delia," she said softly. "I understood."

"No, not just for Delia. I did it for both of you."

She turned to face me, her eyes red and swollen from crying. It felt like someone had punched me in the gut. I didn't like seeing her so upset, and then I remembered Wire's words. Calm. I needed to make her calm down. I didn't understand why, but if the doctor had said she didn't need to be stressed, then I needed to find a way to fix this fast. I motioned toward her. "May I come closer?"

She didn't say yes, but she didn't say no either. I crept a little farther into the room and kept going until I was able to sit on the bed, I stretched out my legs and reached for her, tugging her against my side. Sofia clung to me, her hand fisting my shirt. For a moment, I thought maybe everything would be fine. Had she missed me as much as I'd missed her?

"I never meant to hurt you, sweetheart," I murmured as I stroked her hair. "I'm so fucking sorry. I thought I was doing the right thing, for both you and Delia."

She held onto me tightly, then pushed away, putting space between us. Sofia looked over at the door, a look of resignation crossing her face and a spark of anger lighting up her eyes. "You should go," she said.

Go? But... "You want me to leave?"

"Yes. It's for the best."

I stared at her, willing her to look at me again. I knew I'd fucked up, but I hadn't expected this reaction from her. I'd hoped she'd understand, that she'd forgive me. Had I lost her because I'd been too damn scared of losing both her and Delia?

"Sofia, I really didn't mean to hurt you. I was trying to keep you both safe."

Her jaw tightened and she turned her back to me. It felt like someone was ripping my heart out of my damn chest. Even though it was clear my brothers had tried to hide her from me, it wasn't until this moment that I realized I might have lost her forever. I got off the bed and slowly walked toward the hall, stopping in the doorway. Glancing at her one more time, I saw the tension in her body and knew that pressing the issue wouldn't get me anywhere right now.

I went back out to my bike, but Wire stopped me on the porch.

"Give her some time," he said. "She thinks that pushing you away is what's best. Sound familiar? You tried to keep her and Delia safe, and maybe yourself too. Now it's her turn to keep everyone safe. At least, that's what she thinks she's doing."

Yeah, too fucking familiar, but I didn't understand what Sofia was saving me from. Or was she trying to save herself from more heartache? "What did you mean she's not exactly sick?" I asked.

"That's for her to tell you. I shouldn't have even let you in the house, but I'd hoped that seeing you might change her mind. Seems that woman is every bit as stubborn as you."

Change her mind. That didn't sound good.

"I can't fight what I can't see," I said. "How do I win her back when I don't even know what I'm up against?"

"Part of what you're fighting is the wall she built when you threw her out. I know you didn't really want her gone, but she didn't. She thought you didn't want her, regretted what happened between you, and now she's determined to give you the space you wanted. She said she understood why you did it, but that doesn't mean it hurt her any less."

"I don't want fucking space. I just want *her*."

Wire nodded. "Maybe you need to show her that. Don't tell her. Words can only do so much, Saint. Man the fuck up."

Show her. How the fuck did you show... Oh. I ran a hand through my hair. Flowers. Dates. All that shit I've never done. Watched enough of those damn romantic movies with my twin, Kayla, that I at least had an idea. Thank God she had Preacher to torture with that shit now.

"Keep her here. I'll be back in an hour." I hesitated thinking of everything I needed to do. "Maybe longer. Just don't let her leave."

Wire smiled and went back inside. Guess that was the answer he'd wanted, which meant he really didn't have the least bit of interest in Sofia. I didn't see how he could have her under his roof and not want her. She had to be the sweetest, sexiest woman I'd ever met. I got on my bike and stopped by Bull's house to ask them to keep Delia a bit longer, maybe even overnight.

"You found Sofia," he said, leaning against the doorframe.

"Yeah, but it seems I have some making up to do, which means I need to know that Delia's taken care of for a little bit."

He nodded. "We can do that. The kids love her. Leave the door unlocked and Darian will head over to get some clothes for Delia."

"I have a few errands to run, then I'll need to shower before I go back to Wire's place."

"Trying to convince Sofia to go anywhere with you won't be easy. And I'd suggest taking the SUV."

"You don't think she liked riding on my bike?" I asked, my brow furrowed. I'd looked forward to feeling her wrapped around me as we rode through town.

"Just trust me. Take the SUV."

I nodded and thanked him again before getting back on my bike. I left the compound and went to the men's shop in town. Since I'd never done the dating thing, all I owned were T-shirts and jeans. I wasn't giving up my jeans, or my cut, but I did want to get a nice shirt for my date with Sofia. The woman who rushed over to help me nearly made me turn around and run back out of the store. I'd seen that eager look before, and I didn't think it was the sale she was drooling over.

"What can I help you with today?" she asked, her smile overly bright.

"I need a dress shirt." I looked around the store, but I honestly didn't even know where to start. I'd never seen so many colors or patterns.

"Do you want a collar?" she asked.

"Yeah." I narrowed my eyes as I looked around again. "I think so. Never really worn a dress shirt before."

"I bet you'll look fantastic in one." She practically purred and I turned to look at her again, just in time to see her scanning my body with a hungry expression. Fucking great. Why couldn't it have been some guy or little old lady working here? At least if a guy hit on me, I could just tell him I didn't play for that team and he'd be fine. But turn down a woman like this one and all hell could break loose. I'd seen her type plenty of times.

"Maybe I could just look around a bit and see if there's anything I like." I edged away from her and started toward a wall of shirts in a variety of colors and styles. I didn't lose the blonde-haired pit bull, much to my chagrin. She stuck to me like fucking glue, even had the audacity to reach out and run her hand down my arm. I moved out of her reach, but determination flashed in her eyes. Fuck. Me.

"Look, lady, I appreciate the help, but I just want to look without you slobbering over me like a bitch in heat." I glared at her. "Unless you want me to call the store manager, stop touching me. I'm not interested. I'm picking out a damn shirt so I can take my woman on a date. I'm taken."

Her lips thinned and her nostrils flared. I seriously expected her to lose her shit, but a throat cleared from across the room and she immediately scurried off. A man in a charcoal suit came over, holding out his hand.

"I apologize for Bitsy. I'm Charles Bowman. The owner of the store."

I shook his hand. "Nice to meet you, Mr. Bowman. Might want to put your employee on a leash."

He smiled faintly. "She's been warned several times. This was her last strike. While you browse a moment, I'll take care of Bitsy, then we'll find you the perfect shirt."

He walked off, or more like glided away, and pulled Bitsy into the back room. I could hear her screaming and cussing as I flipped through some of the shirts. I hadn't even realized men's shirts could have so many different styles. Just the variety of collars was enough to make me anxious. I'd thought I'd just walk in, find a shirt my size, and walk out. This looked way more difficult. Should have just gone to one of the big box stores. It's where I usually bought my jeans, and those places seemed far less complicated than this.

Mr. Bowman returned, his hands behind his back. "Do you have a particular type of shirt, or color, that you need?"

"I honestly have no idea. I just wanted something nice so I could take Sofia out to dinner. All I own are T-shirts, but I wanted tonight to be special."

He nodded and pulled out a measuring tape. "May I?"

I held out my arms. "Go for it."

After he took my measurements and asked a few more questions about my plans for the evening, and what I would be wearing with the shirt, he pulled out a few and showed me to a dressing room. My favorite was a blue-gray with a pointed collar that didn't have pockets. The two I'd tried with pockets felt strange under my cut. The blue-gray also allowed for more movement, which was ideal in case trouble found us. Not that I thought trouble was lurking around every corner. With Sofia's dad and his men gone, things had been quiet the last few weeks.

"That one?" Mr. Bowman asked as I stepped out of the dressing room with the shirt clutched in my hand.

"I like the feel and fit of this one the best."

"Since you plan to wear your jeans and your... cut, I'm going to suggest going without a tie. However, should you ever need one, or more shirts or a full suit, please come by again and I'll be happy to assist you."

"Thank you, Mr. Bowman."

He rang up the shirt, even gave me a discount for having to deal with Bitsy, and then I was on my way to the next stop. I couldn't remember the last time I'd had a decent haircut, or had my beard professionally trimmed. The last month it had grown a bit wild, and I wasn't the best with a set of clippers or scissors. The barber shop was nearly empty when I went inside, and old Mr. Smithers waved me over to a vacant chair. "I'll be with you in a minute, Saint," he said.

I eased down onto the chair and put my feet on the silver bar across the front. Even though Mr. Smithers had about three other men working for him, he'd been cutting my hair since Torch had brought me here when I was seventeen. He'd never let anyone else help me. When Mr. Smithers made his way over to me, he turned my head one way, then another. "Been a while, boy. You're looking more like a mountain man these days."

I laughed and had to agree.

"Beard trim and haircut?" Mr. Smithers asked.

"Yes, sir. I have a date tonight so I need to look my best."

The man froze and stared at me. "My, my. In all the years you been coming here, not once have you ever had a date. Not sure if I should pray it goes well, or pray that young lady runs the other way."

"Definitely the first one."

He nodded. "Well, let's get you cleaned up and presentable so you don't scare her off."

Mr. Smithers took his time, and when he was finished, I had to admit I looked like a completely different guy. My beard was close-cropped and my hair was neat, the way I usually kept it. I paid the bill, gave him a good tip, and then I was off to the final stop before heading home to shower and get ready for what I hoped would be an amazing date with Sofia. If she agreed to go anywhere with me. By the time I got back to the compound, I found a note from Darian that she'd already stopped by and she wished me luck. At least someone other than Wire was on my side. Isabella had made it sound like everyone was pissed at me for what happened with Sofia.

I locked the front door and went straight to my bathroom. I tossed the sack with my new shirt onto the bed, then stripped out of my clothes. After I had the shower running, the water hot enough, steam filled the bathroom, I stepped under the spray and let the heat seep into my muscles. I was nervous as hell about tonight. If I fucked this up, I could lose Sofia.

I closed my eyes and tipped my head back. Blindly grabbing the soap, I started to wash. I'd always been an Irish Spring kind of guy, and never had any complaints, but I was starting to think I should have bought something special for tonight. There was no guarantee the night would end with Sofia coming home with me, but I could hope. An image of her flashed in my mind, her legs spread as she begged me to fuck her. My dick was so damn hard I ached.

The first stroke of my cock had me groaning. I'd jerked off more times than I could count since the day I'd taken Sofia, and every damn time I was left unsatisfied. Didn't stop me from getting off, but it was nowhere near the same as being inside her. I tightened my grip and tugged on my cock faster and harder. Bending my knees a little, I reached between my legs with my free hand and squeezed my balls. Fuck!

"Sofia." I bit my lip, pictured her on her knees, my cock in her mouth, and I fucking exploded. I opened my eyes and gasped as my cum jetted onto the tiled wall and my heart hammered in my chest.

My dick was still semi-hard, but at least I didn't have a raging hard-on at the moment. Maybe I could control myself enough not to sport wood the second I saw the woman I couldn't get off my mind. I finished my shower, dried off, and tied the towel around my waist. I went through my usual ritual of brushing my teeth, putting on deodorant and a little cologne, then styled my hair. I grabbed the beard butter and worked some into my beard before combing it. Even though there was less of it right now, I still wanted to keep it soft so it wouldn't scratch Sofia.

Chapter Six

Sophia

I didn't know what it meant that Saint had come for me. When my sisters had gone back home with the Hades Abyss, with the men they both loved, I'd thought Saint would come take me home. He hadn't. I'd come to stay with Wire before Violeta and Luciana were even gone, and while I appreciated having a place to live, it didn't feel like home. I felt like an intruder, even though he was very sweet to me. To make things worse, I couldn't stop crying. And when I wasn't crying, I was so damn angry. My emotions were all over the place. Doctor Myron had assured me a great deal of it was pregnancy hormones. It seemed my levels were off the charts, and I could tell he was a bit concerned about me. I'd been told to remain as stress-free as possible, and poor Wire was walking on eggshells to make that happen.

None of it did any good. Without Saint, I was miserable. No, what made me miserable was knowing that he didn't want me. The day we'd shared together had been wonderful, but he'd changed the moment his daughter came home. I'd understood, still did, but that didn't make it hurt any less. He was the only man I'd ever cared about, had ever trusted, and it didn't seem fair my sisters would get a happy-ever-after and I wouldn't. Saint had been up front and told me that he couldn't give me a fairy-tale ending, but I'd still hoped things would be different. Then he'd come here…

I hadn't wanted to push him away. I'd wanted to kiss him, beg him to take me home with him. It had been hard not to turn to him, to hold on tight and not let go when he'd come into my room. Hearing his voice had been both wonderful and awful. I was scared to get close, to believe he really wanted me. Even if that was true, would he feel the same when he discovered I was pregnant? I was still worried about what would happen when he found out. He'd think I'd lied to him, even though I hadn't. I truly hadn't thought I could get pregnant. Torch had pointed out that Saint still should have worn a condom, but I couldn't help but feel responsible. Didn't matter if I was or not, I felt like I'd unintentionally misled him.

But he was here. He'd come for me. The way I'd reacted had forced him to walk away, but I didn't think Saint would give up, not if he truly wanted me. The thought of seeing him again made a part of me giddy with anticipation. The other part, the part that cautioned he would be upset about the baby, made me want to refuse him entrance. I couldn't do that since this wasn't my house, but I *could* lock myself in my room.

Wire knocked on the open door and I motioned for him to enter. He was good about not just walking into the bedroom, even though it was his home. He treated this space as mine, no matter how temporary it would be for me to stay with him. Eventually, I'd have to figure something out. I couldn't live with him forever. With my father out of the picture, I could go anywhere, start my life over, and not have to fear I would be snatched off the streets and taken back to Colombia.

"You doing okay?" he asked.

"I think so."

"Guess I should have asked if you wanted to see him before I sent him in. I just thought maybe if the two of you talked, then you could work things out."

"It's not that simple, Wire, and you know it."

"Maybe it is and maybe it isn't. You'll never know if you don't tell him. He needs to know you're pregnant, Sofia. It's not fair to him or that baby. Or Delia for that matter. Don't you think she'll be excited to find out she's going to be a big sister?"

Now that was a low blow. He knew how much I adored Delia.

"That's hardly fair."

Wire smiled faintly. "Sweetheart, fair doesn't have a damn thing to do with it. You know it's wrong to keep that baby a secret. The entire club is hiding your pregnancy from Saint, and he's going to fucking explode when he finds out. He'll be angry with you for keeping it from him, but he'll be beyond pissed at the rest of us. We're his family, and we're supposed to be on his side. Not yours."

I swallowed hard and looked away. I hadn't thought about the position I'd placed all of them in when I'd asked them to keep my secret. It was wrong of me, and I really didn't want Saint to be mad at them. I was just so damn scared. If he took my baby away, I didn't know what I'd do. Everyone insisted he'd never do something like that, and the Saint I got to know very briefly the day we made love wouldn't. But the Saint I'd seen since that time? I didn't know what the version of him would do.

"Sofia, you know that the club only wants what's best for you. It's just that I believe what's best is Saint. It's obvious you care about him, and the guy who showed up here ready to knock my head off? That guy is crazy about you. I get the feeling he was under the impression I was keeping you. Permanently. He rode up and asked if I'd claimed you. A guy who doesn't care wouldn't act like that."

"What if I tell him and he wants the baby but doesn't want me?" I asked softly.

Wire moved farther into the room and sank onto the edge of the mattress. He reached over and took my hand, causing me to look up and hold his gaze. There was kindness in his eyes, and a bit of understanding.

"He wants you, Sofia. Trust me. The kid was seriously ready to kick my ass over the right to take you home."

"Kid?" I bit my lip to stop the smile that fought to break free. "He's hardly a kid."

"He's twenty-seven. Eleven years younger than me. To me, he's a kid, and so are you."

"Have you ever been in love?" I asked.

His eyebrows arched in surprise. "No. I thought I was when I was a kid. Younger than you are now. I was wrong."

"If you think I'm a kid, and Saint is a kid, it's going to be pretty damn funny if you end up falling for someone a lot younger than you. That seems to be a common theme around here. Torch looks a lot older than Isabella. Darian said Bull was around her dad's age. Flicker is older than Sarge, but he's with Sarge's daughter. Word of advice. If you do find the woman of your dreams, and she's a decade younger than you, or more, don't call her a kid. And if you do, then I hope she gives you a black eye for being stupid."

He chuckled a little. "Good point, but I doubt the right woman is out there for me. I think I'd have met her by now. Besides, there are things about me that you don't know. It wouldn't be safe for a woman to be involved in my life."

"And yet I'm here, in your home."

"Different thing altogether. You're not mine. You're a guest."

I tipped my head to the side and studied him. There were shadows under his eyes, and I realized he looked really damn tired. Not just the sleepy kind, but the type of tired that said he had the weight of the world on his shoulders.

"The thing you're involved in, the reason you don't want a woman in your life, is it really dangerous?"

"Can be. Just depends on whether or not I get caught."

"The type of dangerous that would result in prison time?" I asked.

"No." He smiled a little. "The work I do is for the government, when I'm not juggling things for the club. But Uncle Sam has a tendency to look the other way and deny any knowledge of certain events if they don't turn out accordingly. Someone comes for me and the government will disavow any knowledge of what I've been doing."

"Be careful. You seem like a really nice guy and I'd hate for anything to happen to you. I think the club would be upset too. And not just because of everything you do for them."

He nodded and squeezed my hand.

"Listen, why don't you rest a bit, maybe read one of those naughty books Ridley dropped off. The ones I'm not supposed to know you have, and then you can shower and put on something pretty in time for dinner tonight."

"Dinner?" I asked. We hadn't done any special for dinner in the weeks I'd been here.

"Just trust me. I have a surprise for you."

"Thank you, Wire. And thank you for letting me stay here. I'll think about what you said. Maybe I'll tell Saint the next time I see him. I don't like keeping the baby a secret or asking the club to betray Saint because of it. I'm just scared about what will happen when he finds out."

Wire patted my hand. "It's going to be fine, Sofia. No stress, remember?"

Right. No stress.

Wire left my room and I wandered over to the small bookshelf. Ridley apparently had a thing for romance novels, as did the other Reaper ladies. They'd stuffed all three shelves full of various genres and authors. Everything from historical to shifters, even a few biker romances. I kind of wondered if they planted those in hopes I'd be more open to having Saint in my life again.

Little did they realize there was nothing I wanted more.

I picked one about a wolf pack in Georgia and settled against the pillows on the bed to read. By the time I'd devoured the nearly three-hundred-page story, my stomach was rumbling. I looked at the bedside table clock and saw that I still had a few hours until dinner. Making my way to the kitchen, I paused along the way to see if I heard Wire or anyone else in the house. It was quiet, but that didn't necessarily mean anything. I'd learned that Wire had a special room with all his computers and other gadgets, and it had been soundproofed. I'd decided I didn't want to know why he needed a soundproof room full of computers. After he'd created a valid marriage license and the proper paperwork for me to be a US citizen, I probably didn't want to know what he was doing for the government, or the club for that matter.

I didn't have much of an appetite these days, but I knew I needed to eat. Doctor Myron had insisted that if I couldn't handle large meals that I eat smaller portions more frequently. It had helped me hold my food down. Most of the time. I was still fighting off morning sickness, and it seemed to hit at any point in the day. I dug through the fridge and cabinets, deciding on a grilled cheese sandwich.

I might not be the greatest cook, but I could make simple things. I melted some butter in the skillet, then slathered some of the slices of bread. I toasted the first side of each piece, placed a thick slice of cheddar on top of one, and flipped the other slice on top. After turning it a few times to make sure the cheese melted evenly, I decided to make one for Wire. I didn't see any dishes in the sink, which meant he'd probably forgotten to eat. I'd noticed he did that from time to time.

When I was finished, I slid the skillet to the back burner to cool and put away the extra bread and cheese, as well as the butter. I left my sandwich on the counter, but picked up Wire's and grabbed a cold soda from the fridge. I walked down the hall and knocked on the door to his work room, then waited. And waited. After a moment, the door cracked open and he blinked at me, almost as if he didn't recognize me.

"You okay?" I asked.

"Yeah. Sorry, I was in the zone. I get a little lost in my work sometimes, forget where I am." He chuckled. "Hell, there are times I think I forget *who* I am."

I held up the plate and drink. "I didn't think you'd eaten lunch and I thought you might be hungry."

"Thanks, Sofia. Don't forget to dress nice for dinner."

I nodded and he shut the door, going back to whatever it was he was doing in there. I was on my way to the kitchen when there was a knock at the front door. Hesitating a moment, I decided to go answer it. Wire was obviously in another world and probably wouldn't come out anytime soon. I smiled when I saw Isabella on the other side.

"You won't be smiling when I confess my sin," Isabella said. Then she held up a covered dish. "Cookies. I didn't make them. Darian did."

I cautiously accepted the plate. I knew from experience that Isabella's cookies were something to be feared, but Darian had a knack of forgetting them in the oven too. Especially since she looked like she was about to pop now that she was due any day. It seemed the Reaper ladies tended to get pregnant in pairs, or more. Darian and Pepper were both due any time now.

"She didn't burn them," Isabella assured me.

"I was about to have a sandwich. Want to come in and tell me about this sin you committed? Unless it has to do with your husband or making more babies. You can keep those thoughts to yourself."

She smiled wistfully. "I wish. No, I'm taking longer to heal this time. We tried and it was still a bit painful, so Torch insisted we wait another month. He thinks I don't know about the magazine he has hidden under the bathroom sink. Like I'm going to believe he's running to the bathroom that frequently! My cooking isn't that horrible."

More than I wanted to know.

I led the way to the kitchen and set the plate of cookies down before I got my lunch and a drink for both of us. Isabella sat and sighed as she stretched out her legs.

"Been on my feet all day between chasing the kids, cleaning, and then I ran over to Darian's to help her a bit. I'm wiped out." Isabella stretched again, a slight wince on her face.

"What sin did you commit?" I asked again. If she'd felt it was important enough to come over here, then it had to be something big.

"It's my fault."

"What's your fault?" I asked.

"Saint finding you. He came by and I refused to say anything, but then Torch said that Saint had a right to make amends with you. So I told him where to find you."

Well, I hadn't seen that one coming. I couldn't be angry with her, though. As much as I'd been scared to see Saint, being held by him again had felt wonderful. Even if I did push him away right after.

"It's fine. He came and tried to apologize."

"Tried?" she asked.

"I didn't really give him a chance to stick around. I told him to leave."

Isabella traced a pattern on the table. "When I first came here, Saint was really sweet to me. Torch asked him to guard me, and he did. I think he'd have given his life for me. I've never thought of him as being a bad guy. The opposite, in fact. He got his name because he's the nicest guy out of the bunch, and believes in doing the right thing. He'd give someone the shirt off his back if he thought they needed it. The Saint you told us about, the one who pushed you away and was mean about it doesn't seem like the guy we all know and love."

"So I've heard."

"Did he explain why he did it?" she asked.

"He said he was protecting both me and Delia, and maybe he believes that, but shouldn't I have been included in that decision? Not about Delia, but if he was trying to protect me, I think I had a right to say whether or not I wanted him to do that."

Isabella snorted. "Welcome to the Dixie Reapers. Those men are so alpha they don't stop to ask permission for anything. They do what they want when they want and claim it's for your own good. Good thing they're so loveable. Of course, being sexy doesn't hurt either."

I fake gagged and she laughed.

"No offense. I don't see your husband as sexy, but that's a good thing. I have zero interest in him or anyone else."

"Except Saint."

I sighed. "Yeah, except Saint."

"Eat your lunch and have a cookie. Call me if you need to talk. I need to get home before the kids drive Torch out of the house and we don't see him for hours."

"Does that ever happen?"

"Not really. He's crazy about them, even when they cry all night or throw up on him. Best man I've ever met." She got a dreamy look on her face. "And he's all mine."

Isabella let herself out while I ate my sandwich and tested a cookie. When it didn't seem like it would kill me, I had another, then went back to my bedroom and read another book. As the dinner hour drew closer, I showered and took the time to shave so I could wear a dress without looking like Sasquatch. I'd finished getting ready and was waiting in the living room when I heard a motorcycle pull up. My stomach clenched and I hoped it was just someone passing by. I hadn't seen Wire, but could smell the faint hint of cigarettes, which meant he was on the porch smoking. He seemed to do that rather frequently.

The bike kept going and I breathed out a sigh of relief. Settling on the couch, I decided to wait patiently until Wire was ready. I didn't know where we were going, but I hadn't had a surprise in a while. Not counting the baby in my belly. I only hoped if we were going out to dinner that I'd be able to hold down my meal.

Chapter Seven

Saint

I got dressed, then grabbed my keys. My hand trembled and I realized I was scared as fuck that I'd get to Wire's house and she'd refuse to go anywhere with me. I wouldn't blame her, but I really needed her to give me another chance. I wouldn't fuck it up this time. I'd thought I was doing the right thing, but obviously that hadn't been the case. I should have explained things to her, but I'd known that she would refuse to go if she thought I wanted to keep her. Watching her walk away had been the hardest damn thing I'd ever done. Even harder than bringing a baby home.

Wire was on the porch smoking a cigarette when I pulled up and I frowned as I got out of the SUV.

"Since when do you light up?" I asked.

"Since your woman is stressing me the fuck out. Seriously, Saint. Fix this shit and get her back home with you. All the crying is wearing on my damn nerves, and nothing I say or do seems to make it stop." He dropped the cigarette and stomped it out. "I gave this shit up a long time ago, but I need the nicotine when she's around. And I refuse to smoke in the house. Spent more time on this damn porch since she's been here than I have the rest of the year."

I refrained from flipping him off. It wasn't my fault he was a pansy ass and couldn't handle some tears. Granted, I didn't like it when Sofia cried either, but it wasn't going to make me smoke, or do anything else I normally wouldn't. I still felt like there was something off, something I needed to know about the situation.

"She in her room?" I asked.

"No. Living room. I told her to dress nice, that I had a surprise for her. She doesn't know you're coming so I'm not sure how she'll react."

Shit. I'd left and not said anything else to her, no indication that I'd return for her. I paused in the doorway when her gaze locked with mine. Fucking hell but she looked gorgeous. The dress she had on hugged her breasts, then flared out, stopping above her knees. Maybe it was just my imagination, but she looked a bit bigger on top than before. I'd stared at her breasts often enough that I knew something was different. Before she called me on it, I shifted my gaze to her face. Salivating over her like a damn dog wasn't going to win me any points.

"You look beautiful," I said.

"Why are you here?" she asked, fidgeting with her dress.

"I came to take you on a date."

Her eyes widened a little, and I saw her pulse flutter at the base of her throat. She started shaking her head and acted like she was about to dart past me, but I held up my hands, hoping she'd stay and listen.

"Will you go on a date with me, Sofia? Let me do things the right way. If we'd met under any other circumstances, then I'd have asked you out."

"Would you really?" she asked. Her lips twisted and pain flashed in her eyes. "That doesn't seem to be the biker way from what I've seen around here, and what I've heard from my sisters. The single men seem more interested in sex than relationships."

She had me there.

"I've never dated anyone before," I admitted, "and yes, I've been with my share of women. Not as many as a lot of my brothers, but I've not been a monk. Not until Delia anyway. That's in the past, Sofia.

You're different. You're not like the other women I've been with. They were just a release, a way to blow off steam and sexual frustration. What we shared that day… it was special. You matter. A lot. I care about you and I want to give you everything you deserve, starting with a proper date."

Her lip trembled and she turned away. "I *don't* matter. Not to you. I didn't matter when you said it could only be the one time. I didn't matter when you got cold and distant right after. I didn't matter when you said Delia didn't need me, and implied you didn't either."

"I was an asshole, Sofia, and I'm sorry. I'll get down on my knees right here and now to beg your forgiveness if that will help. Is that what you want?"

"No," she said. "What I want is to rewind the clock and have you hold me afterward, tell me, then that I meant something to you. But I can't go back in time. I can't change the past. I'm not sure anything you say or do now can make up for that."

I moved closer and placed my hands at her waist. Turning her to face me, I tipped her chin up and pressed my lips to hers. She inhaled and stiffened. As I teased her lips with my own, she softened and began pressing closer to me. Soon, she was kissing me back. Regardless of what she said, she still wanted me. I knew I had a lot to make up for, but if she didn't go on this date with me, then I didn't know where else to start.

"Sofia, please go out with me." I ran my hand down her hair. "Let me show you that I'm not the asshole you think I am. I was scared for you and my daughter, and I didn't handle the situation the right way. I'm not perfect, but for you, I'd like to try to be."

"I don't need perfect," she said.

"Then you'll give me another chance?"

She hesitated, then gave me a slight nod. My relief was instantaneous and I gripped her hand, leading her outside to the SUV. Wire was still on the porch, smoking another damn cigarette. In the six weeks Sofia had been under my roof, she'd never been so much of a pain that I'd felt the need to drink or smoke. I had a hard time picturing her driving Wire to pick up a pack of cigarettes. He'd mentioned that she cried a lot, but I figured it had to be more than that.

I helped Sofia into the SUV, buckled her seat belt, then went around to the driver's side. I started the car and drove through the compound to the front gate. Lief was manning the gate and I waved as I pulled through. He hadn't been with us for long, but he seemed like a solid guy, the kind who would have your back when the shit hit the fan.

"Where are we going?" she asked.

"I made a reservation for us earlier. If you see the menu and decide you don't want to eat there, we'll go somewhere else. It's the best place in town, and the lot is always packed. I wanted to make sure we'd have a table."

"You put a lot of thought into this."

"Well, yeah. I don't wear a dress shirt for just anyone, Sofia. I had to go buy one because all I own are T-shirts, but I wanted to look nice when I took you out tonight."

I needed her to know that this was serious, that I was serious about *her*. She wasn't a fling, and I wouldn't tire of her in a few days or weeks. I had a feeling that Sofia was it, the one. Telling her that right this moment might make her turn and run, especially after what I'd put her through.

"You trimmed your beard." She reached over and lightly ran her fingers over my jaw. "I like it."

I grabbed her hand and kissed her fingers. I eased into the parking of The General's Steakhouse and circled the lot at least four times before a parking space opened up. I slid the SUV into the spot, then turned off the car. Sofia was looking around, but I noticed her hands were fidgeting with her dress again.

"What's wrong, sweetheart?"

"So many people. Are you sure you want to be seen with me? We could go somewhere quieter."

What. The. Fuck.

"What the hell do you mean do I want to be seen with you?" I demanded. When she flinched, I realized I'd been a bit too harsh and I reached over to run my fingers down her cheek. "I'm sorry for scaring you. I didn't mean to raise my voice. I just don't understand where that question came from. Why wouldn't I want to be seen with you?"

"I didn't want people to get the wrong idea." She locked her gaze with mine, and I saw resignation, pain, and something fleeting that I didn't quite catch.

"Sofia, I asked you on a date so we can have a new beginning. I'm not going to change my mind, if that's what you think. Hell, I'd have thrown you over my shoulder and carried you back home earlier if I hadn't found you crying in your bed." I rubbed a hand down my face. Christ. I was going to fuck this up. "I want you in my home, Sofia. In my bed. I want to wake up every morning with you in my arms."

The tears trickling down her cheeks nearly sent me into a panic. I'd never done well with crying females, but the fact it was Sofia just made it worse. I was trying to make things better, not worse. I couldn't seem to do a damn thing right with her. She brushed the moisture from her cheeks and sniffled a little.

"We should go eat," she said. "Don't want to waste your reservation."

I swallowed hard and gave her a nod before I got out of the SUV. I opened her door and helped her out, then led her to the front of the restaurant. I gave the hostess my name and she grabbed two menus and asked us to follow her. We wound our way through the restaurant to the side porch. The area had been cleared except for one table with two chairs. Sofia turned curious eyes toward me, but I kept walking. The hostess placed our menus on the table.

"You requested a bottle of Pinot Noir," the hostess said. "I'll notify the bartender that you've arrived and someone will bring it out."

"Wait." Sofia stepped forward a little. "I, um, can't drink the wine."

Fuck. Me. I'd completely forgotten that she wasn't twenty-one yet. I was a fucking idiot.

"We'll pass on the wine," I told the hostess. "I'll take a bottle of pale ale, whatever you've got is fine. Sofia, what would you like?"

"Just water with lemon, please."

The hostess smiled and gave us a brief nod before hurrying off to get our drinks.

"I'm sorry. I didn't think about you not being twenty-one." I rubbed the back of my neck. "Guess that backfired a little."

A strange look crossed her face, but it was gone before I could decipher it.

I pulled out her chair, then claimed the one across from her. Sofia picked up her menu, but I noticed she kept glancing at me over the top. I hadn't eaten here often, but I always got the same thing. Torch and Venom had brought me here when I turned eighteen, and again when I turned twenty-one. I'd been here twice on my own since then. It was pricey, but worth it. I just hated spending that much on food when it was just me eating. It was the type of meal that was better when you have company. Sofia was worth it and so much more. I hoped I could make her see that.

"Get whatever you want. I always order the same thing, but I've been told everything on the menu is amazing."

"You could have taken me to the diner," she said. "You don't need to go to all this trouble."

I took the menu from her, set it aside, and gripped her hand. "Sofia, you're worth all this and more. I wanted to take you somewhere nice, have a special night with you. Let me spoil you a little."

"If you're trying to make up for the last two months, it's not necessary."

Two months. Damn. It really had been that long since we'd been intimate. Longer actually. It had been exactly nine weeks since I'd had her in my bed. Too fucking long. Those were weeks I couldn't get back, time I could have spent with her and yet I'd kept my distance. If I could do things differently, if I'd known that her father would never get anywhere near her... but I couldn't turn back time. Even after her father had been eliminated, I hadn't admitted that I'd fucked up and gone after her. I'd waited like a damn idiot, hoping she'd return to me. All I could do was try to make amends and hope she gave me another chance.

"Maybe I am, but that's because I fucked up. I shouldn't have pushed you away, even if I thought I was protecting the both of you."

She sucked in a breath and her eyes went wide. I paused and noticed the color had leeched from her face and she looked seconds from passing out.

"Sofia, what's wrong? Wire said you hadn't been feeling well, but insisted you weren't sick. What's going on?"

A waiter left our drinks on the table, and Sofia reached for her water with a trembling hand. We ordered our food and after he left, I focused on the woman across from me. Her cheeks were a little pinker than moments before, but I knew something was wrong. She was scared, but I didn't know why.

"Sofia."

Her gaze locked with mine. "We can discuss it later. Let's just enjoy dinner."

I wanted to argue and demand she tell me what was wrong, but I nodded my agreement. As long as she kept talking to me, there would be plenty of time to figure out what was going on.

"Did you enjoy your time with Luciana and Violeta?" I asked.

"Yes, but I didn't get to see Luciana as much. She lost her babies. When she thought her husband was dead, she sank into a terrible depression."

I frowned, remembering Torch receiving a phone call from Spider. Had he never told Luciana that her husband was fine? That didn't sound like him. He'd never let her suffer. The man might have ice in his veins when it came to dealing with assholes, but women turned the guy into mush... at least since marrying Isabella and becoming a daddy. If I remembered, I'd look into that later.

"She's all right now?" I asked.

Sofia nodded. "She was so happy to see him, and I could tell that he loves her. She's lucky. It seems that both my sisters have amazing men watching over them. Rocket hovered over Violeta the entire time they were here. I think she has a bit of hero worship for him, but he wasn't inappropriate with her at any time."

Right. They had amazing guys, and I'd treated her like shit. *Thanks for the reminder*.

"I've been trying not to be angry over what happened between us," she said softly. "It hurt when you pushed me away, and even knowing that you were trying to keep Delia safe didn't make the pain any less. In your place, I'd probably have done the same. Keeping the darkness away from Delia was your top priority, as it should have been."

"Not just her. I remembered what you said about your dad. I thought if he saw that Delia and I cared about you, that he'd use her to get to you. I couldn't do that to you, let him hurt you like that, force you to make that kind of choice. If he managed to get to the compound and saw that you were just there and not part of our family, then you would have fought him. At least, that's what I hoped would happen."

"I'd have gone with him, just to get him away from Delia. It didn't matter if you'd shoved me to the side or not. I'd never let him do anything to hurt her. Not that it matters now. He's dead. Rotting in hell."

Our food arrived and after assuring the waiter we didn't need anything else, the man walked off and left us alone. Though any time our drinks got low, he seemed to come from nowhere and refill them.

Sofia managed to eat half the food on her plate before she pushed it away.

"Not good?" I asked.

"Too full. I haven't had much of an appetite lately, and when I do eat, it's hard to keep anything down." She clamped her lips tight and looked away, as if she'd said something she shouldn't. It made me wonder it had to do with the non-illness Wire had mentioned. Before I could pull my phone from my pocket to discreetly Google her symptoms, the check was placed on the table.

"I'll take care of that whenever you're ready," the waiter said.

I glanced at the amount and dropped enough cash on the table to cover it and a generous tip.

"Keep the change, but could we get a box for the leftovers?"

He nodded and hurried off, only to return a minute later with a clear plastic container. Sofia boxed her food and I carried it to the SUV for her, trying to keep an eye on her for any signs that she might not be feeling well. When we reached the compound, I had a decision to make. Take her back to Wire's, or go to my house. I knew Delia wasn't home, and I wasn't ready to let Sofia go just yet. I went home, hoping she'd not put up a fight when she saw our destination.

"Is Delia here?" she asked as I pulled into the carport.

"No, she's staying with Bull and Darian. I want you to come inside with me, but we don't have to do more than talk. I'm just not ready for the night to be over yet."

"Maybe for a little bit," she agreed and got out of the SUV.

I grasped her hand as we walked up to the front door, and I pushed it open. We stepped inside and I flipped on the entryway light. My heart was hammering in my chest and I was scared as hell that I'd say or do something wrong. I needed Sofia in my life, but I didn't know how to make her see that.

I led her into the living room and sat on the sofa, tugging her down beside me. She pressed against my side and leaned her head on my shoulder. I swallowed hard, feeling like complete shit that we could have had this the last two months but I'd fucked it all to hell. I laced my fingers with hers and lifted her hand so I could kiss the back of it. When my lips brushed against her skin, I heard her quick inhalation and glanced over to see her eyes dark and her lips parted. It seemed I still affected her. That was a good place to start.

"May I kiss you?" I asked.

"Saint, I… I want to say yes, but I'm scared of what it might mean. I know you want to start over, but…"

She couldn't seem to even finish her sentence. I released her and stood up. "I'll take you back to Wire's place."

Her lower lip trembled, and as a tear slipped down her cheek, I found myself kneeling in front of her. She gave a soft sob as she fought not to cry.

"Sofia, if you don't want to be here, I'm not going to make you stay. I want you in my life, but I'm not going to force the issue."

"It's not that. I want you. So much. I just know it's not a good idea. You're going to hate me, and I…" She hiccupped and cried some more.

I reached out and brushed the tears off her cheeks, then slowly leaned toward her. She didn't pull away. My lips met hers and Sofia gave a soft whimper. I ran my hand to the back of her neck and held her to me as I kissed her, soft at first, then more demanding. It felt like forever since I'd kissed her, touched her. My cock was hard and throbbing, and I wanted her more than my next breath. I rested my other hand on her calf and slowly eased it up her leg, pushing her dress up.

Sofia's legs parted and I groaned as my fingers brushed the edge of her panties. I stroked across the cotton material, feeling how drenched she was.

"Sofia," I murmured against her list. "Want you so much. Need you."

"Please," she begged.

I slipped my fingers under the edge of her panties and found her clit, giving it a firm stroke that had her crying out and arching toward me. I rubbed the little bud as my lips devoured hers. When she came, it took every bit of strength I had not to tear her panties off and fuck her right then and there.

"Tie me to your bed," she whispered.

I drew back and stared at her, thinking I'd misheard. Her eyes were bright, but there wasn't a bit of hesitance or uncertainty in their depths. I stood and lifted her into my arms, carrying her to my bedroom. I kicked the door shut and eased her down onto the bed. It only took a moment to get her dress off. The plain bra and panties she had on didn't detract from her beauty. Her nipples were hard and pressing against the material. I reached down and unfastened her bra, tossing it aside, before sliding her panties down her legs.

Taking a step back, I slid my cut from my shoulders and set it aside before working free the buttons on my shirt. Sofia slid from the bed onto her knees and reached for my belt. The breath stalled in my lungs as she stared up at me, her lips swollen from my kisses. I quickly removed the shirt and tossed it aside as she slid my belt free and unfastened my jeans. I pushed the denim and my underwear down over my hips.

Sofia reached up and wrapped her hand around my shaft, giving it a stroke that nearly had my knees buckling. When her tongue lapped at the head, I'd have sworn my eyes rolled back in my head. I gripped her hair, and tugged until she took me into her mouth.

"Remember what I told you before?" I asked.

She nodded.

"If you want me to stop, tell me. If you don't say anything, I'm going to assume you want me to keep going."

She blinked up at me trustingly. With my fingers twisted in the strands of her hair, I dragged her lips up and down my cock, going a little deeper each time. On the next stroke, I didn't stop until she'd taken all of me. She gagged a little and her eyes watered, but I ground myself against her lips before pulling back. Sofia sucked in a lungful of air, and then I started fucking her mouth, taking what I wanted. Her nails bit into my thighs and she moaned, her eyes locking with mine.

"Such a good girl. God, but your mouth feels incredible. I've dreamed of this. Of you on your knees, my dick in your mouth. I'm gonna come and you're going to swallow. Understood?"

She hummed in agreement and I doubled my efforts until jet after jet of cum filled her mouth. She swallowed all of it as I'd demanded, then licked my shaft.

"Damn, sweetheart."

She smiled up at me, then rose to her feet. I'd worried that if I ever did that to her, it would trigger some sort of episode, but she'd surprised the hell out of me. I could see how wet she was and slipped my hand between her legs before plunging two fingers inside her. Sofia tipped her head back, her eyes closing.

So fucking perfect.

"My little angel want to come?" I asked.

"Please, Saint. Please."

"It's just us, Sofia. You can call me Johnny when we're in this room."

"Johnny," she whispered.

Hearing my name on her lips was enough to get my dick hard again. I fucked her pussy with my fingers, driving them into her and stroking her clit with my thumb. Her body trembled and she gave a soft whimper before she came. My hand was soaked, and I was loving every damn second.

"On the bed, sweetheart. Get on your knees and put your hands up by the headboard."

She hurried to obey. I got out the box of toys and used the cuffs to secure her like before. Before I got out anything else, I rubbed the cheeks of her ass before bringing my hand down on each one in two hard swats. She yelped and twisted to look at me, her eyes wide.

"That was for not coming home after your sisters left. I waited, thinking you'd come back."

"I was giving you space."

Smack. Smack. "Did I ask for space? Did I ever use those words?"

"N-no."

Smack. She moaned and I noticed her cheeks were turning as pink as her ass. Interesting. *Smack. Smack.*

"Johnny, please."

"Spread your legs."

She parted her thighs, spreading them wide. Her pussy was soaked and swollen.

"Do you like it when I spank you?" I asked.

She didn't answer right away and I swatted her twice more. She cried out and I watched as her pussy clenched.

"Yes! Yes, I like it when you spank me."

Smack. Smack.

"Are you sorry you didn't come home?"

She didn't answer so I spanked her again.

"Yes! Yes, I'm sorry."

She moaned as I rubbed her ass cheeks, both turning a nice shade of red.

"I tried to keep this part of myself from you," I admitted. "I didn't think you could handle it, that it would scare you."

"I'm not afraid of you." Her voice was soft but I heard her. "I… I like it when you do this to me. Tie me up and spank me. Maybe I shouldn't, but it's not the same as before. You aren't trying to humiliate me or hurt me."

"No, I'm not. If I punish you, it will never be worse than what I've done now. Well, there is one thing worse I could do."

"What?" she asked, her gaze meeting mine over her shoulder.

"I could get you all worked up, then refuse to let you come."

Her eyes went wide and she whimpered. Yeah, that wasn't going to happen tonight, but it seemed that would be an effective punishment in the future. Assuming she still wanted to see me after tonight. Just because she was in my bed right now, it didn't mean everything would be fine.

"You're going to come for me, Sofia. You think you're wet now, just wait. You'll be begging before I fuck you tonight."

I reached for the pink vibrator I'd used on her before and turned it on. I'd barely touched it to her clit when her back arched and she squealed as her body shuddered. I teased the little nub as she came, not stopping until I heard her soft cries. Her body trembled and shook from the force of her release, her pussy so wet her thighs were even soaked. I reached into the bedside table drawer and pulled out the lube before getting out a different toy. I put batteries in the vibrating butt plug, then took my time working it into her ass.

"Johnny, I…" I turned it on and she moaned. "Oh, God. So good."

Placing the pink vibrator against her clit again, I turned it up even higher and smiled as she thrashed and screamed, coming again and again. I gripped her hip with my free hand and thrust hard and deep into her pussy. Sofia sobbed as I pounded into her. I could tell her clit was getting overly sensitive, but I didn't remove the little vibrator until she'd come again. I felt her squeeze my cock as I fucked her. When she begged me, pleaded and said she couldn't come anymore, I shut off the pink toy and tossed it aside.

"I think you can come again." I took her harder and faster, pounding her sweet pussy. "Come for me, Sofia. Show me how much you love this cock."

A loud, keening sound escaped her lips as she came again. She collapsed to the bed, but I gripped her hips and I kept fucking her until I found my release, filling her up with my cum. I grunted as my cock twitched inside her, and I was hesitant to pull out. She felt so fucking incredible, and I worried she'd try to run when I freed her from the cuffs.

I tugged on the vibrator in her ass and she gasped, her pussy squeezing me again. I eased the plug out, then slowly inserted it again. Sofia panted and squirmed.

"More?" I asked.
"Yes. Johnny, please."
"Please what?"

"Fuck my ass."

And that's all it took for me to go from semi-hard to fully erect again. Damn. I pulled the plug out and shut it off, then slipped free of her pussy. I lined up the head of my dick with her tight opening and slowly sank into her, giving her body time to adjust.

"Yes! Saint!" Sofia twisted and I heard the cuffs clink against the headboard. "Don't stop! I need more!"

"Hold on, baby. It's going to be a fast, hard ride."

"Yes! Yes, fuck me!"

I lifted her ass a little higher so I could slide in deeper. Every stroke felt like pure heaven and soon I was driving into her like a man possessed.

"You gonna come for me?" I asked.

"So close."

I reached for the little pink vibrator again and used it to work her clit until she was screaming and thrashing under me, soaking the bedsheets with her release. I grunted as I took her harder, my balls drawing up. I couldn't hold back and came, my hips jerking with every thrust as I drove my dick into her.

After, I was panting and felt like I'd run a damn marathon. Sofia whimpered and murmured under me, her body slick with sweat. I eased out of her and stood on shaky legs, then went to clean myself and the toys. When I returned, I wiped her with a warm, wet rag, but couldn't help smiling as more of my cum slid out of her pussy and her ass.

I tossed the rag into the bathroom and reached for the cuffs, but I froze and covered her body with mine, placing my lips near her ear.

"If I free you, are you going to run?"

"No." Her gaze was drowsy as she looked at me, and there was a soft smile on her lips. "I don't think my legs work anymore."

I kissed her cheek, then her lips before I freed her from the cuffs. I set them aside before stretching out on the bed and pulling her into my arms. It felt right, having her in my bed, getting to hold her. I was hoping she'd decide to stay. I'd been without her long enough, and I was ready for her to come home. This wasn't just my home and Delia's, it was Sofia's too. I just needed to make her realize that.

Chapter Eight

Sofia

Saint was softly snoring, his arms tight around me. He looked so peaceful, and I had to admit that it felt wonderful being in bed with him. Not just the sex, but the cuddling part too. I'd never realized there were men who wouldn't just roll over and go to sleep after, or kick you out altogether. He seemed to like holding me as much as I liked being held.

I started to close my eyes when my stomach knotted and that familiar burning sensation started to creep up my throat. I twisted and turned, breaking free of his embrace, and scrambled to the bathroom. I barely made it before I threw up my dinner. Tears ran down my cheeks and I cried as I slumped on the floor. I was tired of my emotions being all over the place, and tired of not keeping food down. I hoped the doctor was right and the morning sickness would pass after the first trimester, which would mean just another two weeks, but since I seemed to have all-day sickness, I doubted I'd be that lucky.

"Sofia?" Saint called softly as he stepped into the bathroom. He knelt and pushed my hair back from my face. "What's wrong?"

"S-sorry. I'm f-fine."

"No, you aren't. Is this the non-illness Wire mentioned? You never told me what was going on when I brought it up at dinner."

Everything in me went completely still. Wire had told Saint that there was something wrong with me; that's what he meant by "non-illness" earlier. He might not have told Saint that I was pregnant, but he'd planted the idea I was hiding something. I felt sick and started throwing up again. I felt Saint gather my hair, holding it away from my face, and his large hand rubbed up and down my back. When I didn't have anything left to purge, I staggered to my feet and went to the sink. I splashed water on my face and rinsed my mouth. Saint pulled a new toothbrush from a drawer and handed it to me. I brushed my teeth, thankful he'd had a spare, then sagged against the counter. I wasn't ready for this discussion.

"I think I need to go home," I said.

"Home." His jaw tightened. "Wire's house is home now? He said there wasn't anything between you."

I blinked at him, then blinked again. "What?"

"Never mind," he muttered. "I'll get dressed and take you back."

I followed him into the bedroom. Saint was jerking his clothes on, his movements tense and angry. I didn't understand why he was so upset. Had he thought I'd stay all night? What if Delia came home and found us in bed together?

"Saint."

He didn't even look at me.

"Johnny."

He stopped and turned. "What, Sofia? You wanted to go *home* so I'm getting dressed so I can take you back to Wire."

"Is that what you think? That I'm trying to get back to Wire?" I stared at him. "Are you taking drugs? Did you have more than the one beer?"

"Of course not."

"Then stop acting like an idiot." I slapped my hand over my mouth, my eyes going wide. I hadn't spoken back to a man like that... well, not in a very long time. Then again, I had smarted off to Wire earlier. Maybe I was finding myself, finally. I'd learned my lesson the first time I'd talked back to my dad, and I hadn't needed a reminder. I took a hasty step back, my heart hammering in my chest. Oh God. What had I done?

"Sorry. Sorry. I didn't mean…"

The anger melted off his face and he slowly came toward me, his hand outstretched. "Easy, Sofia. It's fine."

I swallowed hard and nodded but didn't stop backing up until I hit the wall and had nowhere else to go. Saint kept coming, not stopping until the heat of his body pressed against me. He gathered me in his arms and just held me.

"You can call me an idiot anytime you want," he said. "Preferably not in front of anyone, but I'd never hurt you for speaking your mind. I'd spank your ass, but I think you enjoyed that."

Just the reminder of his hand on my ass was enough to make me tingle with awareness. He was still mostly naked, and I didn't have anything on at all. My nipples hardened and I glanced up at him, watching as his eyes darkened.

"I wasn't trying to get back to Wire," I said. "But I don't think it's a good idea for me to stay here all night."

"Delia won't be home for a while yet."

"I can't take the chance we'll fall asleep and not wake up until after she's back. I don't want her to find me in your bed and get confused."

He sighed and backed up a step. It wasn't just a physical retreat. I could feel him pulling away emotionally too, and I knew I only had myself to blame. I chewed my lower lip, trying to decide if I should just be brave and tell him about the baby. The worst that could happen was... Well, I didn't really know.

I went to his dresser and took out one of his T-shirts, then pulled it over my head. Before he could finish dressing, I placed my hand on his arm. He paused and looked down at me, but his gaze was shuttered. It made my heart hurt.

"I... I need to tell you something," I said. "But I'm scared."

"Is it about you being sick in the bathroom?"

"Yeah. Can we sit and talk?"

He reached down and took my hand, leading me over to the bed, then he pulled me down onto his lap. His arm went around my waist and he waited patiently. Except, I didn't know where to even start. How did you tell a guy you'd thought didn't like you that you were carrying his kid? I knew differently now, but it was still hard. I was terrified that when he found out, he'd be angry and push me away again.

"Remember when I told you about my time in Colombia? The things they did to me?" I asked.

He nodded but kept quiet.

"They hurt me. Often. I'd always thought the damage done to my body had kept me from getting pregnant, that it would never be a possibility." I swallowed hard and looked away. "But I was wrong."

The silence was nearly deafening, and I worried he'd never speak. When he did, his voice was almost devoid of emotion.

"Are you saying you're pregnant?" he asked.

I forced myself to look at him. "Yes. I honestly didn't think it was possible. I swear I didn't lie to you."

"You're pregnant and it's mine," he said. "And you weren't going to tell me?"

"I thought you'd be angry. You'd made it clear you didn't want me in your home. I didn't know what you'd do if you found out I was pregnant, after telling you it was okay to not use a condom."

"Jesus," he muttered.

His body was tense and he refused to look at me. My throat hurt from holding back my tears as I wriggled free of his grasp. I gathered my clothes and went into the bathroom, then shut the door and locked it. I took a quick shower, washing off the evidence of the previous hours, then dressed. When I stepped out of the bathroom, Saint was gone.

I slipped on my shoes and made my way through the house. When I reached the front door, I noticed it was unlocked. I slipped outside, shutting the door behind me, and started walking to Wire's house. Saint's bike was missing from the carport. The fact he'd left without a word told me plenty. I'd been right to be concerned about his reaction to the pregnancy, and should have just kept my mouth shut.

By the time I got to Wire's, I couldn't hold back the tears anymore. I wasn't entirely sure if they were tears of sadness, fear, anger, or some combination of the three. I let myself in and went straight to my room. After I turned the lock, I stripped out of my clothes and shoved them in the trashcan, never wanting to see the dress ever again, and put on something more comfortable. Unlocking the door, I decided to let Wire know I was home. His bike was outside, which meant he was likely in his work room. I knocked on the door and waited, but he never answered. I'd never ventured into his bedroom, but I knew where it was. Quietly, I crept through the house, pausing to listen for any sounds. If he had company, the last thing I wanted to do was interrupt.

"Wire," I called out. No answer.

I knocked on the bedroom door, but still didn't hear a sound. Feeling braver than usual, I twisted the knob and pushed the door open. The lump in the bed was probably him, and he was likely asleep since it was so late, but I wanted to make sure. When I peered down at him, I noticed he looked younger when he was sleeping. Not wanting to disturb him, I turned to leave when someone else popped up in the bed, her blonde hair in disarray.

"Who the hell are you?" the woman demanded.

"I live here," I said.

Her eyes narrowed and she glared at poor Wire. Without a word, she got up and pulled her dress over her head before grabbing the rest of her things and storming out of the room. I heard the front door slam a moment later and Wire jolted awake.

"Wh-what the hell." He blinked at me, rubbed his eyes, then checked the other side of the bed. "Sofia?"

"I, um, just wanted to let you know I was back, but your girlfriend didn't take it well."

He snorted. "Not my girlfriend. I was just blowing off some steam since I thought you'd be gone all night. Picked her up at a bar."

Nice. Really nice. It seemed men were pigs regardless of how decent they seemed.

"I'll just go to my room. Sorry for bothering you." I started to back away, but he reached out and grabbed my wrist.

"Wait. Why are you home? Did something happen?"

"I told him."

Wire sat up, the blanket falling to his waist. The sight of his bare chest didn't scare me, but it didn't turn me on either. Unfortunately, the only guy I wanted had probably hit the highway and was long gone. He'd have to return for his daughter, but I didn't expect him to come find me anytime soon. Unless it was to sign something regarding the baby I carried in my womb.

"You told him you're pregnant, but you're back here?"

"He didn't take it well," I said. "I'll let you get back to sleep. Sorry again for scaring off your... whatever she is."

I pulled my wrist free and walked out, closing the door behind me. I'd nearly made it to my room when I heard Wire yell "you God damn idiot" and I winced, having no doubt he'd called Saint. Just what I needed.

I washed my face and combed out my hair, then padded into the living room. I was tired, but not enough to actually sleep. Flipping through the channels, I was only half paying attention. The couch sagged and I nearly rolled into Wire as he sat next to me. He put his arm around my shoulders and gave me a quick hug.

"I'm sorry my brother is a moron," he said. "You doing okay?"

"Fine." *Click. Click. Click.*

He reached over and took the remote, put on a movie that I didn't recognize and then turned to face me.

"Look, Saint is a good guy. There's a reason he got that name. He didn't freak over you being pregnant. He got pissed that you, and the rest of us, were keeping it from him. He adores Delia, and his one regret is that he wasn't there from the beginning. Rhianon kept the baby a secret. It was only after she died that Rocket called and told Saint he had a kid."

"I didn't want to do that to him. I was just scared he'd be angry."

Wire nodded. "I get it. We all get it. Except Saint. Give him some time to cool off. He just needs to get his head on straight, and then he'll come for you. I guarantee it."

"You also *guaranteed* that he wouldn't react the way I'd feared. And look where we are now."

"No one likes a smart-ass," he muttered.

"Better than a dumb-ass."

He snorted. "You've been spending time with Ridley, haven't you?"

I shrugged. I didn't really spend much time with any of the Reaper ladies, but they did take turns coming to visit me. I wouldn't exactly say we were friends. Right now, I really missed my sisters. Especially Luciana, but I wasn't going to burden her. She had enough to deal with.

"If you're not going to sleep, I say we pop some popcorn and have a movie marathon," Wire said.

"You don't have to stay up and keep me company. I'm not going to run away or do anything stupid."

"Maybe not, but you look like you could use a friend." He patted my thigh. "I'll get snacks and drinks, then I'll pull up the *Star Wars* collection. I have the digital copy, a Blu-ray for each, and even the old VHS tapes of the original movies."

"Uh, the what?" He wanted me to watch... sci-fi?

He stared. Hard. "You've never seen *Star Wars*?"

I just looked at him. Seen? No. Heard of? Yes. I'd never once been tempted to watch it.

"Not any of them? Ever?"

"No. Is that bad?"

"You're going to get a movie-cation. How the hell can you have gone this long and never watched the greatest series of movies ever?"

Luck? I didn't want to be the bearer of bad news, but I'd never had any interest in science-fiction films. Or books. I was more of a romantic comedy type of person, but if he wanted to spend time with me and watch those silly movies, then I'd humor him. He was being nice so it was the least I could do. But really... swords made of glowing lights and weird-looking aliens? Ridiculous.

Wire returned with a huge bowl of popcorn, two packs of M&Ms, and two sodas. I didn't consume that much sugar and salt usually, but maybe tonight called for it. I accepted the candy and one of the drinks, then Wire sat next to me, holding the bowl of popcorn where I could easily reach it. He selected one of the movies and pressed play. I tried to follow along, but I honestly didn't have a clue what was going on or why. One movie quickly turned into two, then three. The sun had risen and I still couldn't sleep. Neither, it seemed, could Wire since he was still awake as well.

"Can I ask you something?" Wire looked my way and waited.

"If you'd gotten someone pregnant, unexpectedly, but she had the courage to tell you. How would you have reacted?"

"I'd do whatever it took to make her mine, and to protect the baby."

The somber look in his eyes made me wonder if there was a story there. And since I seemed to be the nosy sort when I didn't feel threatened or scared... I couldn't help but ask.

"Do you have a child?"

"No." A sadness entered his eyes. "Not anymore."

Anymore? "But you did?"

"The girl I thought I loved back in high school? I got her pregnant. Found out she'd been using me to make someone else jealous. When she discovered she was pregnant, she had an abortion. I only found out when I overheard one of her friends talking about it." He drew in a breath and let it out. "She didn't want anyone to find out. The guy she really wanted wouldn't have given her a chance if she'd been pregnant with my kid."

"I'm so sorry." I reached over and grabbed his hand. "For what it's worth, I think you'd be a good dad. Maybe you'll get another chance someday."

"Maybe." He smiled a little. "Not sure I want to bring someone into my type of crazy, though. It would take one hell of a woman to handle the club and the other shit I'm mixed up in."

"She's out there," I said. "I'm sure you'll find her when you least expect it."

"You're a sweet girl, Sofia, and I honestly think you're just what Saint needs. Give him some time to pull his head from his ass."

"I can't stay with you forever, and who knows how long it will take Saint to decide if he wants me and this baby? For all I know, he *only* wants the baby. I don't know what I should do."

Wire stared at me a moment. "You really want to know what I think you should do?"

"I'm open to suggestions."

"Go and wait for him. In his bed. Naked. Kid can't stay gone too long. I'll call Bull and make sure he holds onto Delia another few days. Give the two of you time to sort things out."

"*That's* your suggestion? Have sex with him? That's what got me into this mess in the first place!"

Wire grinned. "It's obvious the two of you connect well on a more physical level. Do I really need to tell you how to get a man's attention? Just don't play too easy to get. Give him a taste, but make him work at keeping you by his side and in his bed."

"No. No, you really don't."

"So?"

I sighed and stood up. "Fine. But I think this idea is a horrible one, for the record. When he kicks me out of his bed and tosses me out naked, I'm blaming you. And you'll owe me ice cream. Lots of ice cream!"

"Deal. Now get the hell out of here."

I squared my shoulders and walked out of Wire's house and went straight back to Saint's place. I knew this wasn't going to end well, but it wasn't like I had anything to lose. He'd already walked out on me. What's the worst he could do? And if I was wrong, if he did want me to stay, then I'd have to be strong and not just roll over and give him whatever he wanted. His reaction had hurt me, deeply. I would stand my ground, or at least try. Heaven knew once I saw all those muscles and his pretty blue eyes, my brain tended to stop functioning and reacted on pure instinct… and that instinct said to let him fuck me until my legs stopped working.

Nope, this was definitely not the best decision I'd ever made, but too late to turn back now.

Chapter Nine

Saint

Wire was right. I was a fucking dumb-ass. The one thing I wanted more than anything else was Sofia in my bed, in my life, and the possibility of having kids with her. So what did I do when she told me she was pregnant? I ran. It wasn't the thought of having a kid with her. It was the fact she'd kept it from me, just like Rhianon. Why did the women in my life think I couldn't handle being a dad? I'd thought I was doing a good job with Delia, but maybe Sofia had disagreed.

Running hadn't been the answer. I'd driven all over town, then gone two towns over before hitting the highway. I'd made it nearly four hours outside of town before I'd stopped. I was on Main Street of the quintessential small American town in the South, and the place I just happened to stop in front of? A jewelry store. I considered it fate, or maybe just a big fucking sign to point me in the right direction. Even though it had been early, the shop had been opened and I'd decided to browse a little. I didn't have massive amounts of cash, but I was doing well enough.

The proprietor of the store eyed me, keeping one hand under the counter, no doubt his fingers hovering over the panic button. Couldn't blame him. Guys like me had a bad reputation. I wasn't squeaky clean. No one in the club was, but we didn't go around hurting innocent people either. Trouble was that most people didn't realize that. They just saw a guy wearing colors and automatically assumed we were all asshole murderers and rapists.

"I think you're in the wrong shop," the man said, a slight tremor in his voice.

"I just want to check out your rings. Engagement rings."

The man gave me that up and down look again, probably thinking I wanted to rob the place. I pulled out my wallet and extracted my bank card, holding it up for him to see.

"I honestly just want to buy a ring for the woman I'm hoping to marry."

The man removed his hand from beneath the counter and seemed to relax a fraction.

"What type of ring would you like?" he asked.

"I have no idea. Never bought jewelry for a woman before. I don't think she'd want anything flashy, but I don't want something so small you can't see it either."

The man gestured to the opposite end of the shop. "I may have something you like over here."

In the last case, he pulled out three rows of rings. The first set was typical diamond engagement rings. While none were tiny, the stones weren't too big for Sofia's small hands. None of them really leapt out at me though as the *right* ring for my woman. The second set was diamonds with accent stones in various colors. I had no idea what any of them were called. Some were pretty, but I didn't know that they were quite right either. Glancing at the third tray, one ring in particular caught my eye.

"What's this one?" I asked, pointing to it.

"Interesting choice. The band is white gold with rose gold accents and an Edwardian design."

"I honestly have no idea what that means."

The man smiled. "If she likes antique items, she'll probably like this ring. The stone in the center is tanzanite, and it's just over three carats. It's considered a rare gem despite how popular it is. Most tend to have more of a bluish hue, but this particular stone is more violet. The accent stones are diamond chips."

"And how much is that ring?" I asked, wondering if I had enough in my account. I'd heard of engagement rings costing anywhere from a few hundred to tens of thousands. In this sort of store, I had a feeling everything was on the pricier side. It didn't exactly look like the type of ring you'd get at the jewelry counter at one of the large chain stores that carried everything.

"As my first customer of the day, I'll give you a discount. The ring sells for two thousand three hundred dollars. But I'll let you have it for two thousand even."

That wasn't as horrible a price as I'd feared. And Sofia was definitely worth it. I nodded my agreement and handed my card over to the man. He rang up my purchase, boxed the ring, and gave it to me along with my bank card.

"If the size isn't right, bring her with you and I'll resize it at no charge," the man offered.

"I have no idea what size her finger is, but I'm hoping it fits. Thank you."

The man nodded, then hesitated a moment. "I apologize for my misconception when you entered my store. I thought you were here to rob me."

"I get that a lot, but just so you know, not all clubs are out to hurt everyone."

The man eyed the one-percent patch on my cut, but wisely didn't say anything. I put the ring box in my pocket, put my card back in my wallet, then went out to my bike. It was time to go home and win over my woman. I didn't know how I'd convince her that I wasn't upset about the baby, and that I really did want to spend the rest of my life with her. I'd hoped to have it figured out by the time I got home. But I didn't.

Sam waved me through the gates and I rode through the compound to my house, parking in the carport. I shut off the engine and stretched out the kinks before going inside. The first thing I noticed was a pair of women's shoes in the front entry. I eyed them, knowing they were too large for Delia, and Sofia didn't have anything at my house anymore. Softly closing and locking the door, I pulled the gun from the middle of my back and crept through the house, uncertain what I'd find. Had one of the club whores made herself comfortable? Wouldn't be the first time one of those bitches tried to trap one of us.

I used the toe of my boot to ease the bedroom door open and I froze. Sofia was in my bed, her hair spread across my pillow, and she was sound asleep. The naked shoulders peeking above the blankets told me she likely didn't have anything on, and my dick started to get hard. Why was she here? And naked. The naked part baffled me the most. She'd been upset and locked herself in the bathroom, not that I could blame her. I'd been an asshole. Again. Really needed to work on that. I'd never been that guy before, and I hated that I was starting that shit with the woman I wanted to keep. The *only* woman I'd ever wanted to make mine.

I removed the clip from my gun, emptied the chamber, and locked my weapon in the little safe in my closet. I didn't expect Delia home right now, but I never took any chances with my daughter's safety. I'd checked in with Bull while I was on the road, about the time Wire called and bitched at me. My daughter was safe and having fun. Didn't mean I was going to be careless. Having weapons in the house was just part of club life, but it didn't mean I had to leave the damn things where Delia could get her hands on them. I'd seen too many news reports of kids accidentally killing themselves or someone else because someone left a loaded weapon within their reach. Not happening on my watch. When my kid was old enough, she'd learn how to properly handle a gun just in case, but we weren't there yet.

I pulled off my boots and set my cut on the dresser. As tempted as I was to remove my clothes, I left them on for the moment. If I was reading this the wrong way, that would only cause more problems. Easing down onto the side of the bed, I reached out and ran my fingers through her hair. It felt like silk, and I couldn't help but run my hand through it again. Sofia stirred, mumbled something, then settled back into sleep.

I'd kept her up most of the night, and like me, she probably hadn't slept after she'd left my place. Despite the voice of caution in my head, I stood up and worked my jeans down my legs. I left everything else on, then I slipped under the covers and pulled her into my arms. Sofia burrowed into me, her hands fisting my shirt. And yeah, she was naked. I swallowed hard and tried to think of anything else. I didn't need her waking up to my dick knocking against her, begging for entry.

Breathing in her scent, and just having her in my arms, made my body relax almost instantly. It didn't take long before I felt sleep pulling me under. The last time I'd fallen asleep while holding Sofia, I'd woken to the sound of her puking in the bathroom. The time before that, she'd stared at me in fear. I hoped this time worked out better. Every time I felt my body grow heavy, and my mind started to shut down, Sofia would shift in my arms and I'd jolt awake again. After the third time, I decided to just enjoy holding her and try not to fall asleep.

"Johnny," she said softly, her voice a near whisper.

"I'm here. I won't leave you again."

Her eyes fluttered open and she stared. "You're really here? I'm not dreaming?"

"You're not dreaming." I pressed a kiss to her forehead, then her lips. "I'm sorry I ran. It wasn't because of the baby. Knowing you'd kept it a secret, that my entire club had, hurt a lot. It reminded me of what happened with Rhianon and Delia. But I don't want you to think for a second that I didn't want the baby, or you."

"I wasn't trying to keep it from you because I thought you'd be a bad father. Anyone who sees you with Delia knows you're an amazing dad. I just worried you'd hate me or try to take the baby from me."

"I don't hate you. I could never hate you." I wrapped a strand of her hair around my finger. "I wanted you here with me, in my house, in my bed. I missed you while you were gone. Delia did too."

"You really pushed me away to protect both of us?" she asked.

"Yes. Even though I can admit that it was the wrong thing to do. I never should have made you leave. I can't tell you how sorry I am that I ever made you feel unwanted. You belong here, Sofia, with us." I reached over the side of the bed and grabbed my jeans, pulling the small box from the pocket. "This isn't how I pictured doing this, but…"

I held up the box for her to see and popped the lid open. She gasped and her eyes went wide as she stared at the ring.

"Sofia, I need you in my life, in Delia's life, and I never want you to leave us again. Will you marry me?"

She blinked, then focused on my face. "Marry you?"

"Yeah. So, will you?"

She looked at the ring again, then me. I could see the indecision in her eyes, but I didn't know how to convince her this was truly what I wanted. I closed the box and set it aside, then placed my hand on her belly. She tensed a moment, but didn't move away.

"If you marry me, I promise to be the best dad to this little girl or boy. I promise to be faithful to you, and to stand by your side no matter what comes our way. If you'll give me a chance to prove myself, I'll show you that there's no other woman out there I could ever want, because you're perfect for me." I swallowed hard and felt my heart hammering in my chest. "I love you, Sofia. I've never told a woman that before, so I'm not just saying the words. I mean them."

"You love me?"

"Yes. I know it might take time for you to feel that way about me, but I really hope you'll give us a chance. I know we can be a happy family. Delia already adores you."

She pressed closer to me and put her hand on the back of my neck. Sofia pulled until our lips were touching. Her kiss was soft and tentative. Sweet, like her. I let her set the pace, but I couldn't stop myself from exploring her curves. I cupped her ass and squeezed. Sofia moaned and deepened the kiss, her tongue stroking mine.

I twisted so that she lay under me, bracing my weight so I wouldn't crush her. I felt her hands drift across my chest, down my sides, then she was tugging at my underwear. I helped pull the boxer briefs down until I was able to kick them away. Lying skin to skin with Sofia was my version of heaven. Nothing had ever felt more right. I only wished I hadn't been so stupid. We could have had months of this, of being together.

"This doesn't change things," she said.

I drew back and stared at her. "What the fuck does that mean?"

"I've decided you need to grovel." Sofia smiled a little. "So, for now, no I won't marry you. I will move back in, if only to give Wire some space, but it will be up to you to convince me to stay."

"Grovel?"

She nodded. "You made me feel like I'd done something wrong, like I wasn't worthy of being here with you. I can't just immediately forgive that, Johnny. You hurt me, even if it wasn't your intention."

"Need I remind you that I found you in my bed, naked?"

"A moment of weakness." She trailed her hands down my sides. "Can you blame me? All this is a little hard to resist."

I smirked, accepting the compliment. Yeah, I'd had plenty of women want in my pants, but knowing the woman I couldn't stop thinking about felt the same way was a big turn-on.

"Then I guess I better start groveling." I reached between her legs and stroked her pussy. "Should I start here? Maybe beg forgiveness with my tongue?"

Her breath caught and her eyes darkened. "I think that would be a very good place to start."

I moved down the bed, settling between her thighs. She was already slick with arousal and my dick got harder seeing the evidence of how badly she wanted me. Sofia wasn't just any woman. She was *my* woman, or at least I hoped that's where things were heading. I didn't buy engagement rings for just anyone. I didn't hesitate to taste her, tracing her slit with my tongue. Sofia let out a little sigh and squirmed. Parting her folds, I lapped at her clit, softly at first, then harder. I felt her thighs tense and soon she was squeezing me as I pushed her close to an orgasm, then backed off. I teased the hell out of her, not letting her come.

"Johnny, please," she begged.

"Feel good, sweetheart?"

"So good. More. I want more!"

I sucked the hard little bud unto my mouth, drawing on it until she screamed out her release. Before she could come down from her high, I sent her soaring again. The first two orgasms turned into another, and another. After the fifth, she was babbling nonsensically and my dick felt like it might explode at any second. I refused to get off before I had a chance to feel her wrapped around me.

"I promise I'll do better next time, but I need you."

I covered her body with mine, the head of my cock brushing against her soaked pussy.

"Better?" Her eyes went comically wide. "If you get any better, you'll give me a heart attack. That will be a fun conversation with the emergency responders. Death by orgasm."

I couldn't help but laugh, and it just cemented how much I loved her. Only Sofia could get that reaction out of me when all I wanted was to fuck her long and hard. My gaze locked on hers as I slowly sank into her, her silken walls stretching to accept me. Damn but she felt wonderful. Perfect. Mine. Whatever it took, I'd make her see how much she belonged here.

"I love you, Sofia."

Before she could respond, I set up a fast, steady rhythm, driving into her so hard the headboard banged into the wall. She reached up and gripped the spindles, her lips parted. Her eyes darkened as I pounded into her, and I knew she was already close to coming again.

"That's it, sweetheart. Come for me. Show me how much you love this dick."

"Don't call yourself names."

I faltered a moment, her words surprising a laugh out of me.

"But…" She licked her lips. "I do love you."

My heart swelled, and so did my cock. I took her like a man possessed, not stopping until she was screaming my name and I was filling her with my cum. Marking her as my woman. Knowing we'd created a kid together, that even now there was a baby in her belly that was part her and part me, made me feel a little primal.

"Say it again," I urged.

"I love you." She smiled. "I think I have from the first time you showed me that sex was about pleasure and not pain. You're unlike anyone I've ever met."

"I can't promise that I'll never fuck up again, but you have my word that I'll always make it up to you. However you'd like."

"Might not want to promise that. Your tongue might get sore."

I smiled and kissed her softly. "Baby, tasting you is one my favorite things in this world. I will gladly lick your pussy anytime you want."

"Johnny?"

"Hmm." I nuzzled her neck and nipped at her jaw.

"Put the damn ring on me."

I reached for the box and grabbed the ring, then slid it onto her finger. It was a perfect fit, like it was fate that I'd chosen that one.

"What's Delia going to think of all this?" she asked, worrying at her lip.

"She's going to be over the moon about you being her mom. You're the only one she'll ever remember. No matter how many pictures I keep around of Rhianon, or the stories she hears from Rocket, she'll never truly remember her."

"That's so sad."

"I hope you like braiding hair, baking cookies, and going shopping. She's mentioned more than once the past year or two that she wishes she had a mommy to do those things with her. It wasn't often enough I felt pressured to start dating, but she's noticed that the other girls around here have moms to do shit with them, and all she had was a dad."

Sofia reached up and cupped my cheek. "She has a wonderful dad. The best ever."

I rolled to my side and pulled Sofia into my arms. Now that we'd settled things between us, for the most part, exhaustion was pulling at me again. I no longer worried that I'd lose Sofia. Yawning so wide my jaw cracked, I tightened my hold on her. Sofia snuggled closer and pressed her cheek against me.

"Sleep," she murmured. "We should both sleep."

With a smile on my lips, I closed my eyes and it wasn't long before I was completely out. In hindsight, I really should have locked the bedroom door. Having a four-year-old launch herself onto your bed isn't the best way to tell her she's going to have a mom, and a baby sister or brother. Especially when there's a lack of clothing on the adults' part.

Epilogue

Sofia
Three Months Later

"You're doing it wrong, Daddy." Delia glared at Saint, and I had to bite my lip to stop the laughter.

He glanced at her from where he was adding bedding and stuffed animals to the crib he'd just put together. "How am I doing it wrong?"

"You put green blankets on the bed. I'm going to have a little sister, not a little brother." Delia placed her hands on her hips. "I asked for a sister. You're supposed to give me one."

I had to slap my hand over my mouth because I was seconds from laughing so hard I'd pee myself. Delia had been very clear about where she stood on having a sister instead of a brother. Ever since Hadrian had given Delia an impromptu pee shower during a diaper change, she'd absolutely refused to have a little brother.

"Honey, we've talked about this. It's not like picking out a puppy. There's already a baby in Sofia's tummy. It's either a girl or a boy."

"Why don't you know?" the little girl demanded.

"We'll find out in a few more weeks, remember?" I asked Delia. "Until then, we're picking colors that can be used for a boy or a girl. You like green, don't you? Like your favorite dress?"

She nodded.

"See? If the baby is a girl, the green blanket will be fine. Once we know if you're getting a sister or a brother, we'll buy more stuff. And just like I promised, you can help pick out the clothes and toys."

Delia sighed and wandered down the hall to her room, looking very much like an aggravated adult trying to explain things to a child. I glanced at Saint and saw the bemused expression on his face.

"What's that look for?" I asked.

"Do you think when she finds a boyfriend she's going to just club him over the head and demand he date her?"

I couldn't contain my laugher another moment. "Oh God. You know, I can actually see her doing that. But I thought you weren't letting her date. Ever."

"Well, not until she's at least sixty," he said.

I snorted. Yeah, like that would happen. I rubbed my belly. The sunlight filtering through the window made my ring sparkle. A month after Saint had asked me to marry him, Wire had shown up on our doorstep with a piece of paper in hand. The sneaky bastard had married us with his computer mojo and not said a damn word. As much as I'd have liked a pretty wedding, I had to admit I didn't miss the stress and drama that went along with planning something like that.

"I love you," Saint said as he came toward me.

I wrapped my arms around his waist and leaned up to kiss him. "Not half as much as I love you."

"You know, when Torch said I'd have to let you stay here, I was so damn pissed. I just knew you were going to be a problem. It never occurred to me that you would be exactly what Delia and I needed. I'm glad Casper brought you here. You make my life complete, Sofia."

Tears misted my eyes and I hugged him tight. "Damn pregnancy hormones," I muttered.

"You can only blame the baby for so long."

"I can blame the baby for at least eighteen more years."

Saint laughed, then kissed me until I was breathless. I'd always thought my life was horrible and I'd be better off dead, but I was wrong. I'd endured so that I could find the amazing man I got to call husband, and the sweet little girl I'd claimed as my daughter. Life was perfect, and I had the mysterious Casper VanHorne to thank for it all. I hadn't seen him since the day he dropped me off here, but I hoped that someday I'd get a chance to tell him how grateful I was that he brought me here. He saved me, and my sisters, when no one else had cared. I didn't understand the reason behind it, but I didn't have to. He'd given me a second chance, my *only* chance to find happiness, and I owed him everything.

"Come on, wife. Our daughter is too damn quiet."

"Bet she's contemplating world domination."

Saint snorted. "Or figuring out how to get even with Hadrian without being mean to a baby."

"Our life won't ever be dull, will it?"

"Not a chance." He gave me a wink before tugging me into Delia's room, where we discovered she was plotting ways to get rid of a baby brother.

Definitely not dull. But I wouldn't have it any other way.

Rocket (Hades Abyss MC 2)

Harley Wylde

Violeta -- It's been a year since I was brought to the US and given to Rocket. I'd thought he was like the others and would only cause me pain. I was wrong. Rocket is the kindest, sweetest man I've ever met. I arrived an abused, pregnant teen. Now I'm a more confident woman, and I have Rocket to thank. Falling in love with him was inevitable, but now I need him to see me as a desirable woman and not a girl who needs his protection.

Rocket -- The young girl who came to live with me was more broken than I'd realized. The horrors she faced have made her stronger, but it didn't happen overnight. It's hard not to watch her, to want her. I shouldn't. I'm too damn old for an eighteen-year-old woman. She's not as fragile, physically and emotionally, but I can't shut off the protector inside me that wants to shelter her and keep her safe.

When she's taken, I know that the men responsible will die. I only hope that side of me doesn't scare my sweet Vi, but nothing will stop me from spilling their blood. I just don't know if we can end the war before it starts, or if this will only be the beginning. I'll keep her safe, no matter the cost, because she's mine whether she knows it or not.

Prologue

Violeta

My hands trembled and my stomach felt like it was flipping and knotting up all at the same time. It was no secret my father didn't love me, but I'd never dreamed he'd ship me off to a new country. Even though my sisters had been given away as well, our middle sister, Sofia, wouldn't be with us. She'd been given to a different group of men, and I worried what would happen to her. Our life had been far from easy, but at least we'd always had each other.

I fought not to look at Luciana as I descended the steps of the jet. She couldn't protect me, never could. But as the eldest, she'd always done her best to watch over us, and we'd looked up to her. Nothing could save us from our father or his men, but since we'd lost our mother when we were younger, it had made us all closer. I could hear her coming down the steps of the plane and I hastened closer to the group of men who would now decide my fate.

"You're going to stay with Rocket," an older man said. The writing on his black leather vest said *Spider -- President Hades Abyss MC*. I'd heard that Luciana was to go with this man, and I hoped he'd be kind to her, but there was a resentment in his eyes that didn't bode well for any of us.

My heart hammered in my chest as a tall, blond man lumbered toward me. It took every bit of strength I had not to turn around and run. As his hand closed over my arm, I took a breath to steady my nerves. I could do this. It was just like all the other times. Being in a different country didn't matter. Though his grip was firm, it wasn't overly tight and he wasn't hurting me. Already that was progress over the men I'd known in my past.

"I'll be good to you," I said softly.

The blond man looked confused a moment, shared a look with the man called Spider, then gave my arm a slight tug. I followed him to a motorcycle that was all black and chrome. I didn't know anything about them, nor did I know how to sit on one. He huffed, sounding exasperated, then lifted me and settled me on the seat. His hands pressed against my waist sent a strange feeling through me and my gaze jerked to his face, but he seemed oblivious to whatever I'd just felt.

Rocket climbed on in front of me and when I didn't move, he gave a soft growl before reaching back and gripping my hands, then placed them on the leather of his vest. I let my hands settle there, lightly, not really understanding.

"Hold on or you'll fall off."

I held him loosely, scared that I would offend him and earn myself a punishment right away, but as the bike rumbled to life and shot forward, I squealed and tightened my grip, fisting the material. The wind whipped through my hair, and the bike vibrated under me. Had I not been terrified about what awaited me, I might have enjoyed the ride. There was a certain freedom to being on the back of his bike. By the time Rocket slowed the machine, I found myself wishing we could keep riding.

I didn't know where we were going, didn't really understand what was happening. I only knew the man called Casper VanHorne had brokered some sort of deal between my father and the bikers, and I'd only gleaned that from what little I'd heard discussed between the two men. My father had told us to do as we were told and not anger the men. Each of us knew exactly what that meant. We were to be his perfect little whores or suffer the consequences. A numbness filled me and I knew that I would never escape my fate.

A large gate slid open and Rocket pulled through, taking the bike down the road past homes. I wondered if it was similar to the compound my father had, just a more rustic version. In Colombia, we were protected by high brick walls and lots of armed guards. My father's home was a mansion, easily big enough to house several families. Here I just saw miles of chain-link fencing with that sharp wire on top of it and modest homes.

Rocket came to a stop in the carport next to a small house. It was cute, and under other circumstances, I might have been enchanted by it. Instead, I knew what waited inside for me. The same abuse I'd suffered for years. I got off the bike, my legs unsteady, and I wobbled a moment. Rocket shut off the machine before standing. He gave a slight nod of his head for me to follow him. I tried to calm the rioting swarm of angry wasps in my stomach as I stepped through the front door of my new home.

I didn't know how long I'd remain with Rocket. I'd seen quite a few bikes at the airstrip, and there were even more homes here. How long before he passed me to someone else? My father had made sure I understood none of these men had women in their lives. It was up to me and Luciana to keep them satisfied, no matter what they wanted from us.

The door shutting made me feel as if I were being sealed in a tomb. My fingers trembled as I worked the buttons on my top and then shrugged it off. The atmosphere seemed to change, and I looked over my shoulder to see Rocket frozen in place, his eyes comically wide.

"What are you doing?" he asked.

"I'll be good," I said, shoving my shorts down my legs. "I know my place."

"What? I…"

I reached for the clasp on my bra and as the scrap of cotton fell to the floor, Rocket made a strange noise and bolted from the room. I blinked and stared, not sure what had just happened. I finished undressing and went after him, thinking that maybe I'd messed up and I was supposed to wait until we were in a different room. The door at the end of the hall was closed and when I tried to turn the knob, it wouldn't budge.

"Did I do it wrong? Was I supposed to wait until we were somewhere else?" I asked through the door.

Panic started to well inside me. I'd already messed up. I'd upset him, and now I'd have to pay. A whimper escaped my lips as I sank to the floor, wrapping my arms around my legs. I rocked back and forth, terrified over what I'd be forced to endure to make amends. White noise filled my ears and my vision tunneled until all I could see were scenes from my past. My father's men and the things they'd done to me.

Hands gripped my arms and I screamed, but I'd learned the hard way not to fight. I hung limp, unseeing, and lost in the past. Words were murmured in my ear, but I couldn't make sense of them. My back landed against cool sheets, and then a blanket was drawn over me. A large hand smoothed my hair from my face and I blinked rapidly.

The past faded and I saw Rocket leaning over me, concern etched on his features. "Easy, Violeta. No one will hurt you."

"I'm sorry. I'm sorry." I couldn't stop the words, repeating them over and over, hoping he'd forgive this one transgression.

Rocket backed away and then left the room. I waited, wondering if he would bring something back, one of those prods my father's men used to shock me, or something worse. Instead, he set my clothes on the dresser and stepped into the hall. He pointed at the door and the doorframe.

"This is your space. Yours and only yours. No one is permitted in this room without your permission, including me," he said. "You're safe, Violeta."

Safe? There was no such thing as safe. I was certain he was playing a trick on me, lulling me into a false sense of security so that it would be more traumatic when he showed his true colors. I wouldn't be fooled. Not again.

Rocket stared at me a moment before muttering a curse and stomping off down the hall. I heard the front door open and slam shut, my body tense and waiting for whatever would come next. I waited for what felt like forever, but he didn't return. Eventually, I curled onto my side and let the tears fall. I hadn't cried in so long. Tears had never solved anything. My chest ached and my throat hurt by the time I'd shed my last tear. I didn't know what to make of this strange new life, or the man I now belonged to. Nothing made sense anymore.

Whatever I'd done to upset him, I'd fix it. I had to. It was no longer just me that I had to worry about. I placed a hand over my belly.

"I'll keep you safe," I promised the child growing there. I only hoped I wasn't lying to the both of us.

Chapter One

Violeta
Six Months Later

I peered out the front blinds and couldn't contain my sigh. Rocket was outside washing his bike. Shirtless. It hadn't taken me very long to get over my fear of him. The man had been nothing but kind to me, gentle even, as if he were afraid I'd break. No one had ever treated me better, not a male someone anyway. Even Luciana's husband had frightened me at first. Then I'd seen the way he looked at her, knew that he cared for her, and I'd realized that there were decent men in the world. Spider was one, and so was Rocket. It had taken some time to feel the same about the rest of the Hades Abyss crew, but I now understood that I was completely safe here. None of them would hurt me, or my sister. For the first time in our lives, we were protected.

Once my fear had subsided, the little things Rocket did to take care of me had started to make me feel something. At first, I'd thought maybe I saw him as a friend or older brother, but that hadn't felt right. It wasn't until my sister had given me a knowing look that I'd realized I was falling in love with him. Not that it did me any good. I was seventeen, a child in his eyes. For a little while longer at any rate. I would be eighteen soon, but I didn't know if that would matter. Just because I felt something for him didn't mean he felt the same about me. He never did anything inappropriate or said anything he shouldn't. He was nice, but not in a flirty type of way.

I'd thought I'd heard him in his room one night, my name on his lips and the unmistakable sound of a man jerking off. The next morning, he wouldn't look me in the eye and I'd wondered if he'd been thinking of me while pleasuring himself. To some it might have seemed wrong, but after everything I'd been through, I didn't view life the way most people would. Despite my age, I hadn't been a child in a long while, and back home my father could have easily married me off to someone by now. After the initial awkwardness with Rocket that morning, things had returned to normal between us, which meant he was treating me like a child in need of protection and not a woman. It aggravated me, more than just a little.

"Just a few weeks," Luciana said from where she sat on the sofa.

"What?"

"You're almost eighteen."

I shrugged a shoulder. Rocket was protective, but it didn't go further than that. I didn't think it ever would. He'd already seen me naked that first day. Maybe I wasn't his type. Just because I'd heard him doing *that* and saying my name didn't mean much. Men had needs, and I was the woman he saw day in and day out. It was likely that and nothing more. I'd always thought men didn't really have a type, that any woman would do, but then I'd never met someone like him before. He'd not once brought a woman home. It didn't mean he wasn't seeing someone the times he wasn't at the house, but I tried not to think about that.

"He cares about you," she insisted.

"I know he does, but he doesn't love me. Not the way a man loves a woman." At least, it didn't seem like he did. There were times I thought I caught a certain look in his eyes, but it was gone so fast I'd convinced myself I was imagining things. Wishful thinking on my part.

"I know you think he doesn't see you that way, but you're wrong."

I turned to give her my full attention. "Why? Why am I wrong, Luciana? He barely touches me, and while he's always polite and attentive, it's not in a romantic way. He takes care of me, much like he would a sister or friend."

"He hasn't been with a woman since you came to live with him." She winked. "Spider confided that little tidbit. He thinks Rocket is biding his time and that he'll claim you once you're legal."

Could it be true? Hope started to rise inside me, but I squashed it quickly. There was no point in wishing for something that would possibly never happen.

"No, he won't," I said stubbornly. I'd learned long ago that hoping for things only led to heartache and pain. I wouldn't be tricked down that path again. "Things will remain just as they are now. He'll watch movies with me, make sure I'm fed and protected, and he'll retire to his room at the end of the night. Alone."

And how did I know that? Because after my fear had eased and I'd started to see Rocket in a different light, I'd done my best to get his attention in a non-platonic way. Casual touches, leaning into him, attempting to flirt. All any of it seemed to do was push him further away and put more distance between us. I'd stopped trying after a few weeks. Now I just admired him when he wasn't watching. Like now.

"Maybe he thinks you aren't ready. We all went through something traumatic, Violeta. Spider knows Rocket really well. If he thinks the man is interested in you, then he likely is. Just give it some time."

I placed a hand against my belly. My very flat, no longer pregnant belly. I'd lost my child shortly after coming to live with Rocket. Part of me had been relieved, even though that was a horrible thing to think. I'd worried that a daughter would be stuck living a nightmare and that my son would be raised to become a monster. Even after knowing the Hades Abyss men would never let that happen, it hadn't eased my fears. Human trafficking was a real thing. I'd seen the proof with my own eyes. Just one time of a kid being out of a parent's sight, or even an adult caught unawares, was all the monsters needed.

"We can't change our past," I told her. "I can understand why a man wouldn't want me. I'm damaged. I don't have as many scars on the outside as you, but it doesn't change the fact I was a whore for those men. They used me, did whatever they wanted. What kind of man would ever want to have me in their life?"

Her gaze darted away before coming back to me, but it was enough for me to stiffen. We weren't alone.

"Luciana, could you excuse us, please?" Rocket asked. There was a tense undertone to his voice that told me this wouldn't be a pleasant conversation.

I braced myself, turning to face him. He was still shirtless. Still beautiful. And really damn pissed if the tightness of his jaw and darkness of his eyes was any indication. He didn't like it when I said something bad about myself, even if it was the truth.

My sister got up and walked out of the house, leaving me alone with Rocket. He ran a hand through his hair and looked off for a moment. I took the time to appreciate the hard muscles and overall beauty of the man. His beard had gone a bit wild, but I didn't mind. I'd never been attracted to anyone except him. It hardly seemed fair. I knew he was older than me, by quite a bit, but I didn't care. What did age matter? Luciana and

Spider were happy together, and he was old enough to be her grandfather. Love didn't pay attention to things like age, race, or anything else. The heart wanted what it wanted.

"Is that really what you think?" he asked. "That no one will want you because of your past? You aren't a whore, Violeta. You were abused. There's a difference."

"Same thing. I've been used by more men than you have fingers and toes. Probably twice that amount." I paused a moment and really thought about the last three years of my life. Honestly, it was possibly worse than that. There were times I'd been drugged for days. Who knew what had happened to me during those times?

He growled and his hands clenched and unclenched at his sides.

"Rocket, I appreciate what you've done for me, and that you think I don't see my self-worth or whatever. But I can be realistic too. Men don't want someone like me. Most girls my age have maybe been with one or two guys, if any. I've already been pregnant and lost a baby. I don't even know how many men have used me, much less how many at one time. My life isn't normal, and it never will be. I'm lucky that all my tests came back fine and I'm clean after all that was done to me. I'll count what blessings I have, but I doubt a husband and family will ever be part of my future."

"That's bullshit! Did Spider care about Luciana's past? Hell, he cared, but not in that way. He wanted to beat the shit out of every man who ever hurt her. But the fact she'd been treated like a whore and had been assaulted didn't make him see her as less. If anything, he knew she was strong enough to have survived all that. There's a guy out there who will see that same strength in you, and will love and appreciate you."

"Maybe there is someone for me." I turned to look out the window again. "I don't know that I could do that to someone, though. For all I know, the first time I'm intimate with someone of my choosing, I'll freeze up and everything will go to hell."

"You're seventeen!" he yelled. "Dammit, Violeta! You should be getting an education, dating boys your age, and having fun with friends. Not holed up at the compound avoiding life."

"Is that what you think I'm doing?" I turned to face him. "Avoiding life?"

"You never go anywhere unless it's with me or your sister."

"Maybe I feel safest with you and her. Ever think of that? Just because my father is dead doesn't mean there isn't danger outside the gates, Rocket. The world is a dark and ugly place, and those shadows will forever cling to me." I folded my arms over my chest. "You really want me to go out? Want to get rid of me for a while? Maybe you're tired of not bringing women back here."

His eyes flashed, and it was the only time I'd truly seen him furious, but it was gone as quickly as it was there. He gave me an easy smile that I could tell was completely fake.

"Yeah, maybe I am. Not exactly easy to fuck a woman with a kid down the hall."

I snorted and turned away again. His barb hurt, just as he'd intended. I could tell he didn't mean it, but that didn't matter. Words had the power to hurt, sometimes more than a fist.

"Like parents don't do it all the time. Is that it, Rocket? Are you feeling too much like a father? Should I call you daddy?"

He snarled and I heard his fist slam into the wall. "I'm not your fucking father!"

Well, that seemed extreme for someone who only thought of me as an annoying kid. Which meant... he did care, possibly more than cared, but for whatever reason he didn't want to. Maybe if I pushed him in just the right way, he'd finally admit that I was more than some charity case?

"I'm aware," I said, a rather devious idea starting to form. It could blow up in my face, but if it didn't... then just maybe it would make Rocket admit that he had feelings for me. "I'll do better. I'll make friends and go out. Do... normal... stuff. Whatever the hell that is."

"Jesus fucking Christ."

"Don't worry, Rocket. I'll give you some space. I didn't realize that I was intruding on your life too much."

The words hurt to say, but what else could I do? Even though I was very much a grown-ass woman after all I'd survived, I was still legally a child where I lived now. And I knew that Rocket was far too honorable to ever make a move as long as I was underage. As I'd told Luciana, even when I turned eighteen, I doubted he'd claim me. In his mind, I needed to experience the life of a teenage girl. I had no interest in giggling over manicures or the latest Hollywood gossip, or whatever girls here did. It all seemed so pointless.

I didn't understand why he was being so difficult. Both of my sisters had found amazing men. Even though Saint had pushed Sofia away, I could understand his reasoning. He had a kid to think about, and he'd thought he was protecting both his daughter and my sister. It had been the wrong thing to do, which he'd learned the hard way.

"You're not --" Before he could finish, I turned from the window and walked off, brushing past him. He could deny it all he wanted, but he was pushing me away. If that was how he wanted things to be between us, then I'd give him what he wanted. I'd treat him like a big brother, or a friend. I'd go out with people my age and have fun. And if I was lucky, it would be just what Rocket needed to come to his senses. I loved the idiot and I was willing to wait him out. But if this didn't work, I didn't know what else to do.

I stepped out on the front porch and saw Teller heading down the road. I waved my hand at him, hoping he'd stop. He pulled into Rocket's driveway and cut the engine on his bike before swinging his leg over the seat and approaching.

"Everything all right, Violeta?"

Teller was safe. I'd been terrified of him at first, but after I'd gotten to know him better, and saw the way he watched over Luciana, I knew I could trust him. We were close to the same age, and he was a nice-looking guy. Just not the one I wanted, but Rocket didn't know that. He wanted me to go have fun? Then that's what I'd do.

"Are you busy?" I asked.

He glanced around, his gaze locking on Rocket's newly washed bike.

"Shouldn't you ask Rocket if you need something?"

I snorted, unable to hold it back. No, I most definitely didn't need to ask Rocket. He'd made that perfectly clear. He wanted me out and about? That's what I'd give him. On the back of Teller's bike.

"It's been pointed out to me that I never have fun. I need to change that."

"Fun?" He stared at me, as if my words were completely foreign to him.

I remembered that Spider had told Luciana the Prospect had a tragic past. I wondered if maybe we had more in common than I'd thought. Maybe Rocket had been right when he said I needed more friends, and Teller could be my first one.

"Yeah, you know go to movies or whatever people our age are supposed to do."

He smiled faintly. "Yeah, I hear the movies are a must for a Friday night. Or the nearest party, but you don't seem like the partying type."

"Neither do you."

He shoved his hands into his pockets. "Are you asking me to take you to a movie?"

"I've never been."

Teller rocked back on his heels and then nodded. "All right. But it's not a date."

He glanced at the house and I knew he was thinking about Rocket. I needed to tread carefully. I wanted Rocket to take notice, to admit that he wanted me maybe even needed me, but not at the expense of Teller getting hurt.

"Just friends," I said.

He nodded again.

"Can we go now?"

His gaze scanned me from head to toe. "You aren't really dressed to ride a bike."

"I can change my clothes." I glanced down at what I was wearing and realized he was right. Shorts and the tank I'd been wearing around the house weren't appropriate for being on the back of a motorcycle. Spider had drummed it into Luciana's head that she was never getting on his unless she had on jeans and boots, and the property cut he'd had made for her. After all the scarring she'd had placed on her body from assholes, he'd left it up to her if she wanted to be inked, but my sister had wanted to go all in and had *Property of Spider* in a small block print on the inside her right wrist.

"You're not taking her on your bike," Rocket said from behind me.

"I've ridden on yours," I pointed out, even though I'd seldom been allowed the privilege.

"I'm safe. Teller hasn't been riding as long as me."

I turned and glowered at him. "You wanted me to hang out with people my age. I'm trying to do that."

Rocket just stared at me, but after looking evil in the eye every day for three years, he didn't intimidate me. Not once I knew how sweet he was. Besides, he was doing that overprotective thing again. I found it endearing, if a bit annoying.

"If you insist on hanging out with Teller, he can use one of the SUVs," Rocket said.

"I'll go get one," Teller said, practically jumping onto his bike and peeling out of the driveway.

I sighed and tipped my head back, closing my eyes. Great. My first chance at making what Rocket considered an age-appropriate friend and he was scaring him off. I had no romantic interest in Teller at all, but I didn't want the guy running off every time he saw me either, out of fear Rocket might hit him. If the stubborn man would just…

"I'm trying to do what you asked," I said.

"Yeah, well... I thought you'd go into town and meet some girls your age. Teller is trouble."

"He's good enough to Prospect for the club and help guard Luciana."

It wasn't like Spider would take in just anyone. I wasn't stupid. The club didn't exactly walk on the right side of the law. He needed to trust the men he called family. And I knew he damn sure wouldn't leave my sister in just anyone's care.

Rocket stalked closer. "He touches you, kisses you, or does anything else you don't want, I will rip his spine out."

Well. That cleared a few things up. If I wasn't mistaken, it almost sounded as if Rocket was a little... jealous. I bit my lip so I wouldn't smile, then reached up and patted his cheek.

"I'll be fine, but thank you for being so concerned."

I walked past him and into the house, going straight to my room. I shut the door and pulled out a pair of jeans and a plain shirt, then quickly changed. Even though I wasn't going to be on the back of Teller's bike, I still didn't want to parade around town in what I'd been wearing at home. After living through the last horrific three years, I wasn't about to try to tempt anyone. Even a harmless flirtation might send me into a panic attack. The more layers I had on, the more skin I had covered, the safer I felt.

Except Rocket. I wanted to tempt him more than anything.

Besides, I didn't want to make Teller uncomfortable. It was clear he had wanted to ensure I knew he didn't want me as a girlfriend, which was fine. He seemed nice, but I didn't want to date him either. I'd only intended to use him to make Rocket have some sort of reaction, preferably one that brought us closer together, but now I really did want to make friends with the guy. Maybe we could help each other heal, even though I didn't know anything about his past. It was obvious he hadn't had the *Leave it to Beaver* type of upbringing. The first time I'd watched some of the old fifties and sixties TV shows with Rocket, I'd snorted and told him life wasn't like that.

By the time I'd changed, pulled my hair up in a ponytail, and grabbed my small purse, Teller was in the driveway with Rocket glaring at him. I felt a little bad for the guy. He was giving Rocket a wary look and didn't seem too eager to get out of the SUV. I shoved past Rocket, making him growl, and opened the passenger door before jumping inside. I closed the door a little too hard, but no one seemed to notice.

"So…" Teller glanced at me. "What time do I need to bring you home to avoid being chopped up and buried in various locations?"

I snickered, then glanced at Rocket and realized Teller might not be too far off on that. I rolled down the window and stuck my head out.

"We're going to a movie, then getting something to eat."

Rocket pulled his wallet out and came closer, shoving two twenties at me.

"I fully expect Teller to pay for your date, all of it, but just in case." He glowered at Teller, who seemed to be shrinking back in his seat. Poor guy. I really had put him in a bad situation. "Call me if you need a ride home."

"Rocket."

His gaze locked on me.

"I'll be fine," I assured him. "Now stop scaring Teller. You wanted me to make friends so that's what I'm trying to do."

I reached up and ran my fingers along the beard on his jaw. There was a flicker in his eyes, then he backed away. Teller put the SUV in reverse and drove off, not even glancing once in Rocket's direction.

"Maybe you should start by telling me exactly what I'm getting myself into," Teller said. "Because I really don't want to end up dead, and everyone knows how protective Rocket is over you."

"Rocket is being difficult."

"Difficult?"

"I think he likes me, as more than his annoying houseguest, but he won't do or say anything to show he's interested. He told me today that I needed to make friends my age and go do teen girl stuff."

"And that's the last thing you want or need," Teller said. He drummed his fingers on the steering wheel as he drove through the compound.

"Right."

"Just don't get me killed, or kicked out of Hades Abyss. These guys are the only family I have." He shot me a quick look. "I don't mind helping you, but I don't want to lose my place here either."

"Don't worry. I won't let things go too far. I'm just making a point." I smiled a little. "Besides, maybe I do need a friend, and I think you could use one too."

"Maybe." He drove out the front gates and headed toward town. "I don't have to express my feelings and all that shit, do I?"

"No. But if you ever do need to talk, I'm here. I think that's what friends are for. Never really had one before."

"Me neither."

I looked over at him and we grinned at each other. Yes, picking Teller had been the right choice. Now I just had to somehow make Rocket jealous enough to tell me how he felt without getting my new friend killed.

Chapter Two

Rocket
One Month Later

I was hiding. Even I could admit it. To myself, anyway. The clubhouse was off limits for Violeta and Spider's wife, Luciana, which meant it was the only place where I had any peace. The day I'd brought Violeta home, a horror had filled me when she'd stripped off her clothes and offered herself to me, as if that was what would be expected of her. After hearing what Casper VanHorne had to say about the girls, I could understand better. And I'd been fucking furious.

I picked at the label on my bottle of beer, barely acknowledging my brothers, much less the club whores parading around in very little or nothing at all. At one time, I'd have picked one and had a bit of fun. Since Violeta had come to live with me, that had all changed. I'd been told to expect a seventeen-year-old girl. What I'd brought home was… a very broken woman. Didn't matter the number of her age. She'd ceased being a girl the day those monsters had put their hands on her. The baby she'd carried had been lost, though I had to wonder if that wasn't some sort of blessing. I knew she would have loved the kid regardless of how it was conceived because that's just the type of person she was, but at seventeen, to me it seemed she'd been too young to carry a baby when she was still a child herself. She'd mourned when she'd lost it, and I'd realized in that moment that Violeta was definitely a fully grown woman. If not by age, then because she'd been through pure hell and had somehow made it out alive.

"Are you here to party or to hide?"

I turned to face Fox and just stared. The fucker smirked, knowing damn well why I was here. Not only was there a now very desirable woman living in my house, but I'd never been so attracted to someone in my damn life. To make matters worse, she'd gotten really close with Teller the last few weeks. It was my own fucking fault. I'd pushed her to make friends and go out. Never occurred to me she might want to date someone. If I'd told her how I felt, then maybe things would be different. I'd been a coward. I was still a fucking coward when it came to Violeta.

"Right. Hiding it is," Fox said. "When are you just going to tell her how you feel?"

"She's spending time with Teller," I muttered.

Fox snorted.

"What's that supposed to mean?" I demanded.

"Are you really that damn stupid?"

Apparently I was, because I still didn't know what the fuck he was talking about.

"Jesus, Rocket. She's not dating Teller, dumbass. She's friends with him, and from what I've seen, I think she's been trying to make you jealous. They only stand close or hold hands when you're around. The second you leave, they move apart. She likes you. The girl has been over the moon for you since before that shit went down with her daddy. Everyone knows it except you, it seems."

Violeta was interested in me? I didn't see how. I was about to turn thirty-six and she was... Eighteen. I'd know that, but it hadn't hit me until just now exactly what that meant. Shit! Shit, shit, shit. I was such a fucking asshole.

"Violeta's birthday was today," I said.

Fox choked on his beer. "Are you fucking with me?"

"No. She's eighteen as of today." I ran a hand down my face. "Fuck. I knew she was eighteen now, but it didn't really click in my damn head that it was her birthday."

I glanced at the clock. It was nearly six at night, and I didn't have a present for her, or anything planned. Hell, I didn't think anyone had acknowledged her birthday. Luciana and Spider were off on some getaway while Teller watched their adopted daughter. Which meant my woman was alone, at home, on a day that was supposed to be special. I was a fucking moron.

I pulled my keys from my pocket and leapt off the stool. "Can you do me a favor?"

"Have your head surgically removed from your ass?" Fox asked.

I flipped him off. "Go make sure Violeta isn't going anywhere. I need to run make a few arrangements. Hell, tell her that there's a surprise planned and she needs to shower and dress pretty."

"And just what surprise do you have planned?"

"Nothing. Yet. But I'm about to."

Without waiting to see if he'd do as I'd asked, because even I wasn't stupid enough to make demands of my VP, I raced outside to my bike and took off. Poor Marcus was guarding the gate and barely got it open before I shot through it. I hit the town and went into the nearest jewelry store to buy a present for Violeta, along with a little something extra I hoped she would accept, then stopped to get something decent for me to wear and booked a room at the nicest hotel in the area. Before I returned home, I made a reservation at the local Italian place, taking a moment to explain the importance of tonight and leaving something behind as a surprise during the course of our dinner. I knew she liked pasta and hoped it was the right choice. My heart was pounding the entire time, and I felt like I was in a race against time. How the hell could I have not prepared something special for her birthday? Had Spider known he was taking Luciana away on a day her sister might need her? I doubted it, but I'd have to make sure they brought something back for her. With everything they'd been through, I didn't know if Luciana had even remembered her sister's birthday.

By the time I got home, I could hear Violeta getting ready in her room. After shooting off a quick text to Philip to leave an SUV at my house and another to Spider to remind him what today was, I shut my bedroom door, and stripped off my clothes. I took the world's fastest shower, making sure to scrub quickly but thoroughly. My beard was longer than I preferred, and I contemplated shaving it off. I'd had the beard since Violeta came to live here, but I wanted to make tonight special for her. After another moment of staring at my reflection, I grabbed my beard kit and trimmed it down, then used the clippers until it was tight along my jaw. I washed my face, fixed my hair, and put on some cologne before throwing on my clothes.

Violeta was waiting in the living room, a white floral dress hugging her curves and heels on her feet. She stole the breath from my lungs with how stunning she looked, but then I had the same reaction every damn time I saw her. She'd left her hair down and it hung in waves down her back nearly to her waist. I'd never seen her wear make-up, but her eyes seemed to stand out more and her lips were glossy. I didn't know what she'd done, but I liked it.

"You look beautiful," I said.

Her gaze scanned me from head to toe. I still wore my cut, but I'd bought a pair of black jeans and a gray button-down shirt. It wasn't anything fancy, but it was a step up from my usual worn-out jeans and T-shirts. I hoped she appreciated the effort I'd put in, even if it had been last minute.

"We're going somewhere?" she asked.

"Yes. I made a reservation for dinner. To celebrate your birthday."

Her eyes lit up. "You remembered?"

"Of course I did." I would never admit that I'd forgotten all damn day and had nearly missed it because I'd been wallowing in self-pity. The last thing I wanted to do was hurt her more than I already had. If what Fox said was true, then the way I'd been treating her had to have at least hurt her feelings.

"I had one of the SUVs brought over. I didn't think you'd want to ride on my bike while you were dressed up."

She smiled, her lips curving in a way that my dick twitch. I held out my hand and she came toward me, her fingers sliding along mine. Her hands were soft, something I'd noticed other times, but the glide of her silky skin against my rougher palm made me want things I shouldn't. She seemed so small and delicate next to me, even though she'd filled out some since being here. Instead of looking like a waif, she had curves that I itched to touch. I led her outside to the SUV and helped her inside, then buckled her seatbelt. Whatever scent she was wearing teased my nose and made me want to breathe her in deep.

My gaze caught hers and I couldn't help but get lost a moment. Pulling away, I shut the door and made my way around to the driver's side. The Prospect had left the keys in the ignition and I started the engine. As

I drove through the compound, I tried not to think about what could happen tonight. If I laid all my cards on the table, told Violeta how I felt and that I wanted her to be mine, then we could be going home as a couple. Assuming she accepted my claim. I'd never wanted a steady woman in my life. Not until her. But after everything she'd been through, if she didn't want me, I wouldn't push the issue.

I noticed her hands twisted in her lap. Tightening my grip on the steering wheel was all that kept me from reaching for her. I didn't know why she was anxious, but I couldn't be certain that touching her wouldn't make it worse. Just because Fox said that Violeta was interested in me, didn't mean he was right. Tonight could end up being a colossal disaster, or it could be the beginning of something truly great.

I pulled into the parking lot outside the restaurant and heard a slight gasp. Turning off the SUV, I faced Violeta and fought back a smile at the look of wonder on her face. For a woman who had been raised in a mansion, it was hard to believe something as simple as an Italian restaurant could bring her such pleasure.

"I made reservations for us," I told her.

"I've been dying to eat here. I've heard it's expensive." She cast me a worried glance. "Rocket, it's too much."

"Nonsense. You only turn eighteen once. We're celebrating, Violeta."

I got out of the car and walked around to help her. After locking the vehicle, I looped her arm through mine and escorted her inside. The hostess eyed me up and down before smiling at Violeta. She was different from the lady who had helped me earlier when I'd made the reservation. This one didn't seem too impressed with my cut.

"Reservation for Rocket," I said as we walked closer.

"Of course. Your table is ready. If you'll please follow me." She picked up two menus and started walking across the restaurant.

Violeta gripped my arm tight as we maneuvered past the other diners. The table we were shown was small with only two chairs, which was all we needed. Soft candlelight flickered at the center of the table next to a vase with a single red rose. I pulled out a chair for Violeta and after she sat, I claimed the one across from her. The hostess placed the menus on the table.

"Your server will be with you in a moment."

With a look of disdain cast my direction, she rushed off.

"I don't think she liked you much," Violeta said.

"Some people around here are more accepting of the club than others. It seems a lot of the women in town fear that we're a bunch of murderers and rapists." I snorted. I'd never hurt a woman, not like that. Although there was evil in all shapes and sizes. If there was ever a woman who had that darkness inside, I wouldn't hesitate to rid the world of her presence. But the average, non-killer type of woman was safe from me.

"How could they ever think such a thing of you?" Violeta asked, her brow furrowed and her lips turned down at the corners. "Nothing could be further from the truth. You and the Hades Abyss have kept me safe. It was nicely dressed, charismatic men in suits like my father who caused me pain."

"It's all about appearance. Your father probably would look like a well-to-do businessman, someone of great financial worth. That would be enough to make most people ignore the ice-cold look he'd had in his eyes. They see what they want to see. With me, they see a biker who doesn't walk the straight and narrow, and that's fine. As long as they treat you with respect, that's all that matters to me."

She reached across the table and grasped my hand. "You're so sweet to me, Rocket."

Not always. I looked down at our joined hands. I'd been a bit cold and distant with her, thinking I knew what was best for her, but now I had to wonder if I'd been wrong. Maybe what had been best for her all along was me.

I extracted my hand and stood. "I'll be right back."

She nodded, though her gaze shuttered. I hated that I'd possibly made her second-guess herself. I quickly walked to the back of the restaurant and tapped on the door to the kitchen. The woman I'd spoken to earlier popped her head out, a wide smile on her face.

"Did you bring it?" she asked.

I pulled out the small jewelry box and offered it to her.

"I'll make sure your birthday surprise is the best she's ever had," the woman assured me before disappearing into the back again.

I went back to the table, where Violeta was perusing the menu. A waiter came over and took our drink order. I noticed there was a slight tremor in her hand and I reached over, pulling the menu from her grasp, and taking her hand in mine.

"Violeta, I wasn't pulling away from you. I just needed to take care of part of your surprise."

"It's fine." She pressed her lips into a tight line.

My gaze narrowed as I studied her. She was paler than she'd been earlier, and the outer rims of her irises were darker. I'd noticed that happened when she was upset or stressed. What the hell? She hadn't looked like this when I walked away. Had my leaving the table bothered her that much?

"Talk to me," I said. "What's going on?"

"It's nothing." She forced a smile to her lips, and it was far from the easy genuine smile I'd seen so often since she came to stay with me.

"I call bullshit. Now tell me the truth."

For a moment, I thought she'd balk, but I watched as her shoulders seemed to slump and her head bowed a little before she held my gaze.

"The woman who seated us came back. She had a few words to say to me. It's fine, Rocket."

"What kind of words?" I asked, trying not to gnash my teeth together in annoyance. This was supposed to be a good night. A night she'd always remember. I wasn't about to let someone ruin it.

"She said only whores would be with men like you," she said softly, her gaze now locked on the table.

Whores. That bitch had called my woman a whore? I stood so fast my chair fell over and I stormed off to the kitchen door. This time, I didn't gently knock. I slammed my fist into the damn thing so hard I nearly knocked it off its hinges. The woman who had helped me set up this night stared at me, her lips parted, her eyes wide. A man in a suit simply lifted his eyebrows as he approached.

"Is there an issue?" he asked, his tones clipped and crisp.

"Yeah, there's a fucking problem. Your hostess just called my woman a whore."

The man blinked once. Then twice. He turned to face the lady who now looked even more shocked, her face having gone nearly as pale as Violeta's, her eyes so wide she looked like a damn owl. The man gave a nod of his head and turned to face me again.

"I'll handle it, and I apologize for her behavior. We don't tolerate such nonsense in this establishment. Please allow me to cover your meal, including our best dessert and perhaps a bottle of wine?"

"My date doesn't drink."

"Of course. Then please permit me to give you a complimentary meal at any day or time of your choice in the future. I'll go handle the issue immediately."

The man brushed past me and headed to the front of the restaurant. I watched from the kitchen doorway as he pulled the hostess aside and spoke with her. The woman's cheeks turned red, and her mouth and jaw tensed. She cast a furious look in my direction, pointed, and then started ranting at the man in the suit.

"Well, that just sealed her fate," said the other lady.

"Pardon?" I glanced at her.

"Mr. Richards is not only the manager of this location, but he's also a co-owner. Not many people know about the ownership part, only that he's the manager. She not only won't get a good reference, but I can assure you that Mr. Richards will have her blackballed at every restaurant in town, even the fast food places."

"I don't understand. I'm just a biker, and now that he's comping my meal, I'm not even a paying customer."

She smiled softly. "Perhaps I should properly introduce myself. I'm Carrie Richards. His niece. I told my uncle of your plans for the young lady you brought with you, and he's a romantic at heart. There's also been gossip in town since all those men were shot out at the airfield. Someone managed to snap a few pictures, not only of your President standing up against the mobsters, but also of one of your men ensuring the safety of a woman."

"Luciana," I murmured. "She's married to my President. Her father was the mobster, and he's also Violeta's sperm donor. There's no love lost between them."

It wasn't my place to tell Ms. Richards the horrors that Violeta had been through, and yet I wanted her to understand exactly how bad it was the other woman had called Violeta a whore. I hesitated, not wanting to break my woman's confidence, and yet wondering if doing so might garner her more protection and understanding. If the community had a hint of what had happened to her, then when they saw her out somewhere they might be more inclined to keep an eye on her. Small southern towns had to be good for something other than gossip.

"Violeta was badly abused by her father and his men. The fact your hostess called her a whore was..." I bit my lip. "It's not far off from what they forced her to do. Do you understand?"

She gasped softly. "Oh, no. That poor girl."

She reached out and squeezed my arm and then rushed to her uncle's side, whispering in his ear before turning and hurrying to where I'd left Violeta. I went to join them and saw her hunkered down next to Violeta's chair.

Ms. Richards held my gaze as I righted my chair and retook my seat.

"I was just apologizing to her for what happened and letting her know we don't tolerate workers like that one."

"I told her an apology wasn't necessary," Violeta said, but her accent had grown thick, which meant the altercation had bothered her far more than she was letting on. It was only during times of high emotion that happened.

"Sweetheart, they damn sure did need to apologize. I brought you here to celebrate your birthday, and to give your present to you. I wanted tonight to be special and that bitch ruined it."

"No!" She reached out and grabbed my hand. "No, Rocket. It's still a special night. She didn't ruin it."

"Did the two of you get a chance to order?" Ms. Richards asked.

"Not yet," I replied.

"Would you permit me to surprise you both with our best dishes?" Ms. Richards asked. "Unless either of you have food allergies?"

"I don't," I said.

"I don't either," said Violeta.

"Very well. I'll bring you the best we have to offer. If you'll give me a moment, I'll start you off with our Caesar salad, the best rolls you've ever had with our homemade raspberry butter, and a bowl of cheddar potato soup."

"Sounds wonderful," said Violeta with a soft smile.

Ms. Richards hurried off, leaving us alone. I hoped that Violeta was right and the spiteful words of that hostess hadn't ruined her evening. The last thing I ever wanted was for someone to hurt her, even with words. She was too precious, too sweet. Too mine.

The food arrived and I had to admit it was the biggest and prettiest salad I'd ever seen, with tons of shredded parmesan on top, and the perfect amount of croutons. Violeta smiled widely as she picked up a fork and dug in. A platter of steaming rolls was set down in the center of the table, with the special butter which had a slight pink tinge to it. Then the bowls of soup, which were also piled high with shredded cheese and green onions.

"Everything looks wonderful," I assured Ms. Richards, who had delivered the food herself.

"I'll be sure to let my uncle know. Enjoy! If you need anything, please let me know. Your main course will be ready shortly, and we have something decadent for dessert."

Silence reigned at the table for several minutes before Violeta finally spoke up.

"Why did you decide to do all this for me?" she asked.

"It's your birthday."

"Yes," she said slowly, letting the word draw out. "But you've hardly spoken to me the last few weeks. When you left earlier, I figured you'd be gone most of the night."

I cleared my throat and knew it was time to come clean. She'd either be thankful that I'd finally pulled my head out of my ass, or she'd tell me that Fox was dead wrong and she really did have a thing going with Teller, which would gut me, but I'd respect her decision. It would be hard not to stomp him into a mudhole, but I'd refrain. He was a decent guy, worked hard, and if that's who could make Violeta happy, then who was I to stand in the way?

"Fox mentioned that things with you and Teller might not be as they seemed." I toyed with my fork, twirling it between my fingers. I suddenly felt like I was in junior high and couldn't find my words. "I didn't want to be in the way of your finding happiness."

"But…"

I held up my hand. "When Fox told me that you and Teller were only friends, and then asked if I was ready to pull my head out of my ass, I realized that I was done waiting. I want you to be mine, Violeta. The way Luciana belongs to Spider."

"You want to ink me?" she asked.

"Not exactly."

A throat cleared and I saw Mr. Richards standing just behind me, one of the presents I'd brought clutched in his hand. He handed the long thin box to me before disappearing.

I slid the box across the table toward Violeta. "Happy birthday, sweetheart. I hope you'll accept this, and what it means."

Her hand hesitated a moment before she picked up the box, removing the silk ribbon, then she pulled out the dainty bracelet. But it wasn't just any bracelet. The delicate silver links held a rectangular silver plate with filigree edging, and the words *Property of Rocket* etched across the center.

She stared at it a moment before holding it out to me. My heart nearly stalled, thinking she was refusing my gift, until I saw the soft smile on her lips.

"Put it on me?" she asked.

I got up and walked around to her side, taking the bracelet and kneeling next to her. I grasped her hand, kissed the back of it, before fastening the bracelet. I reached up and threaded my fingers into her hair, then pulled her closer, my lips brushing against hers. I kept the kiss brief, but it was the hardest damn thing I'd ever done. I'd never allowed myself to kiss her before, not a true kiss, and now I hungered for more.

"Rocket," she said softly.

"Jesse. When it's just us, call me Jesse."

She smiled again. "Jesse. Are you sure this is what you want?"

"Yes. You. You're what I want, Violeta. And I'm probably going to hell because I've wanted you for over a month now. From the beginning I was attracted to you, even when I shouldn't have been. Once you started to heal emotionally and began to trust me, the protective feelings I had for you turned into something else."

She leaned forward again, kissing me once more, then I stood before I was tempted to do far more. I reclaimed my seat and admired her beauty in the glow of the candlelight. The rest of our meal went well, and I had to admit that Ms. Richards had outdone herself. The food was the best I'd ever had, and Violeta could barely contain her moans of pure bliss. When dessert arrived, there was another box nestled next to the plate.

Violeta eyed me before picking it up. I rubbed my hands up and down my denim-clad thighs, unsure how she'd take this particular gesture. The bracelet had gone over well, but this was entirely different. It was a huge step, and I hoped I hadn't made a big mistake. It was one thing to claim her verbally, and another to...

She lifted the lid and picked up the hotel keycard, lifting her gaze to hold mine.

I cleared my throat. "There's something else in there."

She checked the box again and pulled out an engagement ring.

"Violeta, I know that for someone who dragged their feet all this time that I'm suddenly moving very fast. Possibly too fast, but I wanted you to know that I don't just want you as my woman. I want you as my wife." I licked my lips. "I thought, if you accepted my proposal, that perhaps we could go to the hotel for our first time being intimate together. I wanted it to be memorable for you. Something better than just being at home."

"You want to marry me?" she asked, gazing at the ring.

"Yes. If you'll have me?"

I realized I was still sitting in my chair like an idiot and quickly got up and moved to her side. It was bad enough I'd done this at a restaurant, the most clichéd of all proposals, but I was fucking it up too. Taking the ring from her, I knelt and reached for her left hand. I slid the ring partway up her finger, then paused.

"Violeta, will you do me the honor of becoming my wife? Will you let me love and cherish you for the rest of my life? Protect you and support you in whatever way you need?"

I waited, as she stared at the ring, her expression unreadable in that moment. My heart was hammering in my chest and I was more terrified than I'd ever been before. If she said no… I wouldn't force the issue. She'd accepted my name on her wrist, and that would be enough if that was all she could give me. I should have given her more time. I'd gone from keeping my distance to asking her to spend the rest of her life with me, and I knew her head had to be spinning right now.

I started to get up, to slide the ring back off her finger, thinking I'd royally fucked up. Then glanced at her face and froze.

Her lips trembled as she smiled. "Yes. Yes, Jesse. I would love to be your wife."

The ring easily slid the rest of the way onto her finger, then she flung her arms around my neck and hugged me tight. My heart was pounding, as the fear she'd refuse slowly ebbed.

"You're not just saying yes because you think you have to, right?" I asked as I drew back.

"Of course not."

I kissed her again, then reclaimed my seat. We finished dessert and I left a hefty tip, then I hurried Violeta out of there. I was anxious to get her alone. Even though we'd had plenty of time at the house when it was just the two of us, tonight would be different. This time, I was making her mine in every way possible.

The ride to the hotel was uneventful, and since I'd already checked in and had the keycard, we went straight up to the room. I only hoped I didn't fuck things up. She might not be a virgin, but as far as I was concerned, this would be her first time. This was the night she should have had when she lost her virginity, and I wanted it to be a night she'd remember forever, with happiness and not pain.

No pressure, Jesse. None at all.

Chapter Three

Violeta

Maybe I should have been nervous, but I wasn't. Rocket asking me to be his had been huge, and I'd never felt happier… until he'd asked me to marry him, too. Seeing that ring, knowing what it meant, had filled me with a warmth I hadn't known in so very long, if ever. I didn't know why he was suddenly acting like he couldn't live without me. Had whatever Fox said really had that big of an impact on him?

The hotel room he'd rented for the night wasn't as elegant as some of the places I'd seen, but it was special because he'd gotten for us. I ran my fingers over the bedspread and a shiver of anticipation went through me. There was still a bit of fear that I would freak out, or disappear into the void, whenever we were intimate, but this was Rocket and I knew he would be patient and understanding.

"I bought you one more thing," he said, picking up a box from the top of the dresser. He handed it to me, a pretty pink ribbon tied around it.

I took the package and sat on the edge of the bed, tugging the bow. When I removed the lid and folded back the tissue paper, a beautiful nightgown lay inside. I couldn't help but rub the silky material before removing the garment. The box tumbled to the floor as I held up the gown, admiring the simplicity and elegance of it.

"You don't have to wear it," he said. "I just didn't know if you'd feel more comfortable if you had something available to wear to bed."

"Is that your way of asking if I'll be scared if you see me naked? I believe I already undressed for you once."

His cheeks flushed and he cleared his throat as he glanced away. "That was different."

"Yes." I held the gown to my chest and moved closer to him, placing my hand on his arm. "You didn't hurt me then, and I know you won't hurt me now. I'm not a child, Jesse. I haven't been one for a long time. Even though I was broken when I came here, you've helped me heal and I'm stronger than I was before."

"You were always strong," he said, gazing down at me. "You survived when others might not have. No matter what they did to you, you refused to give them the satisfaction of completely breaking you."

"I don't really see myself that way."

"I do," he said softly. Leaning down, his lips brushed mine. "You're strong, beautiful, and amazing, Violeta. And mine. I'm only sorry it took me so long to act on my feelings."

My lips twitched as I fought not to smile. He'd mentioned his conversation with Fox, and I could see the Hades Abyss VP telling him to pull his head out of his ass and saying those exact words. Even though Fox had terrified me at first, I'd learned that he was funny, sweet, and a good guy. All the men of the club were. They'd treated me and Luciana like we were made of spun glass, afraid we'd shatter if a harsh word was spoken in our presence.

I set the nightgown aside and reached up, sliding his cut from his shoulders, then carefully placing it on the dresser. Within a week of being at the Hades Abyss compound, I'd learned the significance of what I'd been calling a leather vest and knew that it was to be treated with respect. Next, I began unbuttoning his shirt, my gaze locked on his. Passion blazed in his eyes, but he didn't rush me, didn't even reach out for me. Rocket stood still, letting me lead the way. Maybe he thought that was what I needed or wanted. Honestly, I'd just worried if I didn't make the first move, he might talk himself out of it.

His shirt fell to the floor and when I reached for his belt, he placed a hand over mine, a smile curving his lips.

"We have all night, Vi. No need to rush things."

Rush? I'd been waiting for him to notice me as a woman for over a month! Several months if I was being completely honest. I'd flirted, tried to make him jealous, and I'd started to think it was hopeless. Now I had him here, all to myself, completely mine, and I was tired of waiting. I kicked off my shoes and unzipped my dress, letting it pool at my feet. The bra and panties I had on matched even if they weren't a set, but they weren't pretty or sexy. One was plain white cotton, and the other was white cotton with small blue polka dots. The look in his eyes said he didn't care.

"Nothing you haven't seen before," I told him.

"I was too busy running last time to appreciate the beauty before me." He smiled faintly. "This time I plan to savor every second."

I reached behind me and popped the clasp on my bra, letting it drop to the floor. He sucked in a breath, his eyes going dark as he stared at my breasts. Shimmying out of my panties, I stood still and let him look his fill. For the first time in my life, being naked in front of a man made me feel desirable, and a bit powerful. I could see the need etched on his features, and the proof of his arousal tenting his pants. Rocket didn't take me, didn't force me to my knees. He just stared, his nostrils flaring and his jaw tight as if he was having difficulty holding back. It didn't scare me. With another man, it would have, but not with Rocket.

"You can touch me," I said softly. "I want you to."

He groaned and quickly removed his boots and the rest of his clothes, then stalked toward me. I didn't feel like prey, though. No, I felt more like a lioness being approached by an alpha male lion. My heart was thrumming hard in my chest and my clit pulsed with need. Slowly, he reached for me. Pulling me close, Rocket cupped my breast and stroked across the nipple.

I hissed in a breath at the contact, and everything in me went tight. Not in fear, but with this burning need I'd never felt before. He froze, his gaze locking with mine, but I gave him a nod, letting him know I was fine. More than fine. I ached, but in the best of ways.

"Please, Rocket. Don't stop."

He pinched my nipple, making me gasp.

"Jesse. Call me Jesse."

I bit my lip and he growled.

"Say my name, Vi, or so help me…"

"You'll what?" I asked.

"Punish you," he said, his words a near whisper. "I'll get you so hot and ready, take you to the edge again and again, but never let you come. Make you beg for my cock."

I whimpered and my body trembled at his words.

"I think you like that idea," he murmured, his hands skimming down my sides, then back up to palm my breasts. He rubbed his thumbs over my nipples before giving them a little twist. "I wanted to be gentle. To go slow."

"I don't need gentle and slow, Jesse. I just need you. Don't hold back because you're afraid to hurt me."

"You've seen enough darkness in your life, Vi. I won't be the one to trigger a memory or send you tumbling down into the abyss."

I reached up and cupped his cheek, my heart aching from how sweet and caring he was. People looked at Jesse and saw a rough biker. A guy most people feared, especially the ladies around town, but I saw my savior. An angel who had helped me heal, cared for me, protected me. He was my hero in every sense of the word, and I wasn't about to put the burden of my past on his shoulders, to have him fear that he could ever send me back to that place emotionally or mentally by being himself.

"Jesse, I love you. I know that you would never hurt me on purpose, that I'm safe with you. If you become a bit… exuberant when we're intimate, it's not going to scare me. I'll know it's you with me and not the monsters from my past." I leaned up and pressed my lips to his. "Don't hide who you are. I want you, Jesse. All of you."

"I can be a bit demanding in bed, Vi. I don't think you're ready for that. Not this first time. Let me show you how it's supposed to be. When you lost your virginity, it should have been exceptional, the best night of your life. I want to make tonight special. Vi, I need to do this. For both of us."

I nodded, understanding why he wanted slow and tender this time. I didn't care, as long as I got to be with him, that was all that mattered. I loved that he wanted to make tonight memorable, but he'd already given the greatest gift in the world. Himself.

He lifted me into his arms and carried me to the side of the bed, then eased me down onto the mattress. I shivered as his fingers trailed up my leg, then teased the inside of my thigh. Parting my legs, I waited impatiently for him to touch me where I wanted it most, but he didn't. He stroked back down my leg before caressing the other one.

"So beautiful," he said. "No matter how many times I look at you, I'm always in awe of your quiet beauty and your grace."

"I'm far from beautiful," I argued.

"To me, you're stunning. And I'm the only one that counts, right?" he asked with a smile and a wink.

I reached over and took his hand, lacing our fingers together. "You make me feel beautiful, and special. Make love to me, Jesse. Please. I need you so much. I don't care how fast or slow it is, or how hard or soft. All that matters is that you're the one here with me."

He audibly swallowed, then joined me on the bed, pulling me tight against his body.

"It amazes me," he said.

"What does?"

"That a tiny little woman like you can turn me into a sappy guy with a romantic side. I'm supposed to be a big, tough, badass biker."

"You are those things." I ran my fingers along his jaw, feeling the rasp of his whiskers. "But you can still be those things and be sweet too. I kind of like that only I get to see this side of you, that it's all for me and no one else."

His lips kicked up on one corner before he pressed his mouth to mine. The kiss was soft and slow, but a flick of my tongue against his lip had him growling and taking what he wanted. The passion of his kiss left me dizzy, and I felt like I couldn't get close enough to him. I lifted my leg over his thigh and scooted closer, feeling the brush of his very hard cock against me. Feeling more brazen than I'd have ever imagined possible, I reached down and grasped his silky-smooth shaft, positioned him at my entrance.

"Now, Jesse," I begged. "Make me yours."

He thrust hard and deep, making me cry out in ecstasy.

"You've been mine since the moment you got on the back of my bike at that airstrip. I felt things I didn't want to feel, shouldn't have felt because of your age. You had my stomach all knotted up because I wanted you, then felt like a sick, twisted bastard for wondering what it would feel like to kiss you."

"I haven't been a girl in a long time," I said.

He kissed me hard as he drew his hips back, then surged forward again. He filled me over and over, his movements almost frantic. Every slam of his cock inside me made his pelvic bone brush my clit, sending sparks of pleasure through me. I clung to him, my nails biting into his back as I pleaded for more.

"Yes! Please, Jesse! Don't stop!"

"Need you to come, Vi." *Thrust. Thrust.* "Pinch those pretty nipples. Tug on them for me."

I released him and wiggled until both my hands were free. I cupped my breasts and did as he'd commanded, pinching and tugging the hard tips. He took me harder, faster, and soon a tidal wave swept over me, dragging me under as pure bliss filled me. It felt like I was flying, and I never wanted it to end. He rammed into me a few more times, grunting as his cum started to fill me up. When he stilled, I felt his cock twitching and my inner muscles clamped down on him.

"Christ, Vi! You're going to make me…" He sucked in a breath as I squeezed his cock again. With a slight growl, he thrust a few more times and I felt a bit more cum spurt out of him. "Damn, sweetheart. No one's ever done that to me before."

I kissed him, threading my fingers in the longer strands of hair on top of his head. I ground my hips against his, and pulled back, my eyes going wide when I felt him start to get harder.

He pulled from my body and slapped my ass before lifting me onto my hands and knees. Leaning over me, he gripped my wrists, crossed them and demanded that I keep them there. I widened my thighs and cried out as he entered me hard and fast. I felt his hands grip my hips as my eyes slid shut, and I was helpless to do anything but feel. The slide of his cock, the tightness of his hold, the pounding of his hips against me. He snarled as he slammed into me again and again, taking me like a man possessed. Rocket released one of my hips and his hand slid around my belly, then between my legs. He parted the lips of my pussy, then pinched my clit hard enough I saw stars and came screaming out his name. Rubbing the little bud firmly between his fingers, he made my orgasm last and last.

The world was spinning and I could barely breathe as the headboard rammed against the wall with every stroke of his cock. He shifted and seemed to go even deeper, while his fingers played with my pussy, drawing another release from me. By the time he came, I was nearly sobbing from the pleasure he'd given me. I'd never felt anything so intense, and my body ached, my clit pulsing and throbbing. When he eased out of me, I whimpered, wanting to pull him back inside.

He covered my body with his, caging me between his arms and he kissed my upper back and my shoulders.

"I should let you shower, but I don't want to."

"Why not?" I asked, prying my eyes open to look at him.

"Because I like seeing my cum all over your pretty pussy. I like seeing you swollen from being thoroughly fucked, knowing it was my dick that did that, brought you so much pleasure that you screamed for me."

"Jesse," I whispered.

"Too much of a caveman thing to do?" he asked.

"No. I like being covered in your scent."

He kissed my shoulder, then rolled to his side and pulled me into his arms. Within minutes, he was snoring softly, but I was wide awake. I hadn't freaked out liked I'd worried I would, but only because it had been Jesse. My sweet, protective Rocket. Time seemed to pass slowly and still sleep wouldn't come. I managed to pull myself from his embrace and slipped on the silk nightgown he'd bought for me, then pulled on a hotel robe over it.

My throat was dry and a little sore from all the noises I'd made, and the little fridge was empty. I pulled Rocket's wallet from his pants and drew a few ones from inside, then crept to the door. Glancing at him, I couldn't help but smile at how young he looked when he slept. I quietly left the room, positioning the safety lock so that I could get back in without waking him, then went to find the soda machine we'd passed when we got off the elevator.

I'd just fed a bill into the machine when a hand clamped down on my shoulder, and I was spun to face a group of men. The cold, hard look in their eyes was enough to tell me I was in a world of trouble, with no one having any idea where I'd gone.

"Looks like his little whore ventured out without us having to go after her," one of them said, a leer on his face.

"I'm not a whore," I said, my accent growing thicker with my unease.

"Maybe. Maybe not. But you're here with that Hades Abyss guy, which makes you my new toy." His hand stroked down the sleeve of my robe and I shuddered, trying to pull away. "Be nice to me, and maybe I won't break you."

"If you take me, he's going to kill you," I said.

One of them gripped my left hand and lifted it, studying the engagement ring Rocket had given me just hours ago.

"Looks like this one might be more important than we'd thought. I think we need to send a message."

The others laughed and I struggled. One of them tied a gag around my head, keeping me from screaming for help, as they jerked me down the hall back toward the room I was sharing with Rocket. My robe was nearly torn from my body and dumped on the ground in front of the door. One of the men unzipped his pants and I quickly looked away. Closing my eyes might have blocked the sight, but I could still hear him jerking off. The zip of his pants wasn't any more reassuring. If he wasn't a kidnapper and who knew what else, I'd feel sorry for the women in his life. That hadn't even taken a full minute.

"I think that will get the point across," said the cruel man still holding me in his grip. "Come on, boys. Let's get our little prize back home."

He lifted me and tossed me over his shoulder. My hair fell in a curtain, hiding my face, but I was able to peer through and read the cut of the closest man. *Chaos Killers MC*. A memory was just out of reach. I'd heard that name before, but I didn't remember where. I had a feeling that I might be in more trouble than I'd thought. I'd survived my father and the mob, and I'd survive this too. My heart broke when I realized that Rocket would blame himself for anything that happened to me.

I was tossed into the back of an SUV, like I was nothing more than cargo, before the door was slammed shut. The tires squealed as they pulled away. I didn't know how they'd gotten me out of the hotel unseen, or if they'd paid someone off. Either way, I hoped that Hades Abyss would rain down hell on them when Rocket found out who had taken me.

Hurry, Jesse! I need you!

My hands and feet were bound, but they had removed the gag. Not that it did me any good now. If I screamed, I doubted anyone would notice. The parking area seemed empty except for darkened cars.

"He'll come for me," I said. "And then he'll kill you. All of you."

"Bitch talks too much. Shut her up, Skeeter."

I saw the fist coming and couldn't dodge fast enough. Pain exploded in my temple before everything went dark.

Chapter Four

Rocket

I bolted upright, a sense of dread filling me. I scanned the bedroom, noticing a faint light coming from the door. I tossed the covers aside and pulled on my pants. Placing my hand on my back pocket, I realized my wallet wasn't there. A quick glance was all it took to find it on the dresser. Violeta was gone and it seemed she'd needed cash. But for what? And how long ago had she left?

I walked to the door and pulled it open, then nearly tripped over a pile of white terrycloth on the floor. No. A hotel robe. My brow furrowed as I hunkered down, then ice flowed through my veins when the smell of semen reached my nose and I saw the garment was splattered in it. I stepped over it and searched the hall, checking near the elevators and the vending machines. Some one-dollar bills were on the ground near the soda machine, and my heart started pounding so hard it was thundering in my ears.

Snatching up the money, I hurried back to my room and grabbed my phone. My hand trembled as I dialed Fox, and I tried to hold it together, but I was seriously close to losing my shit. Someone had snatched Vi, jacked off on the robe outside our door, and I had no fucking clue who had her or why, much less how to get her back. If they hurt her, I'd kill every last motherfucker who dared to touch her.

"Aren't you supposed to be celebrating?" Fox asked, sounding groggy. "What the fuck time is it?"

"Late. Early. I don't fucking know. Someone snatched Vi."

I heard the rustle of sheets and a woman in the background. It seemed Fox had found someone to spend the night with him, and I didn't give a shit if I was interrupting or not.

"What? What do you mean by snatched?" he asked.

"I got us a room at the Clearmont, trying to make our first night together special. Woke up to Violeta missing, and there's a robe outside the door with cum all over it. I think she got money from my wallet and went to get a drink. There was some money on the ground in the vending machine area and my wallet wasn't where I'd left it."

"Anything else? A ransom note? Something that might tell us who took her?" Fox asked, and I heard him pulling on clothes.

"Nothing. Who the fuck would take her, Fox? I just fucking made her mine and now she's gone." I swallowed hard. "After everything she's been through… I don't know if she'll survive with her mind intact this time if they touch her. She'd finally healed and now…"

I wanted to beat the shit out of something, or someone. Wanted to scream at the injustice of finally making Vi my woman, and I'd already let someone take her from me. I never should have kept her outside the compound overnight. Even though the danger her father presented was gone, it seemed we had someone else after the club. Unless taking Vi had merely been an opportunity someone couldn't pass up? But if that was the case, why leave the robe like that? It was like they wanted me to know she was gone and would be hurt. No, this seemed personal.

"What enemies do we have right now?" I asked Fox.

I heard Fox's bike start up. "I'll be there in ten minutes, Rocket. Don't do anything stupid."

"Like what? Call the cops? Notify hotel security? Burn the city to the fucking ground?"

"Right. Don't do any of that shit. Let me see what's up, figure this out, then we'll decide what steps to take next. Take a picture of the robe, then drag it into the room so no one else sees it." He paused. "And, Rocket? Keep your shit together. We'll find her, and then we'll bury whoever took her."

I hung up the phone and shoved it into my pocket, then did as Fox had said. Just seeing that robe was keeping the fury flowing in my veins. I scanned the room again and noticed the silky gown I'd bought her was missing, so at least she wasn't naked. That I knew of. I went back out into the hall and scoured the area, looking for other signs that might tell me what happened. I noticed a discreet camera in the corner of the hall near the stairway, and another in the corner of the little room that contained the vending machines.

Snatching my phone from my pocket, I quickly called Surge.

"Fox already put out the word," he said when he picked up. "A few of the guys are heading your way, and I'm already hacking into the hotel systems. I'll pull a list of all the guests from the past twenty-four hours."

"There's a few cameras on this floor." I gave him the room number where we'd been staying. "I didn't notice one by the room, but that doesn't mean it's not well-hidden."

"I'm on it. We'll find her, Rocket."

I hoped like hell he was right. I finished dressing while I waited for Fox. The club hadn't had any trouble in the last few weeks. Not since Violeta's father had been killed, along with any men he'd brought with him, but that hadn't been the club's doing. Specter had taken care of that little issue. That didn't mean someone wasn't still after Vi and Luciana, but I didn't think that was the case. As far as I knew, all of the men who had abused them were still in Colombia. With Mateo Gomez out of the way, I didn't think any of them would come after his daughters.

Then again... Tugging my phone from my pocket again, I scrolled through my contacts and hit the green call button when I found Venom's name. Even I wasn't brave enough to call the Dixie Reapers' President at this time of day, but his VP would do.

"What the fuck? It's too damn early for this shit," the man grumbled.

"Sofia is safe, right?"

"What kind of question is that? Of course, she is."

"Good. Keep it that way."

Venom growled. "Watch your tone, boy."

"Someone snatched Violeta. Don't tell Sofia. It would only worry her."

"Wait. Violeta is gone? What about Luciana?" Venom asked.

"She's off somewhere with Spider."

"If you need help finding Violeta, let me know. We'll get some men to you."

"Thanks, Venom. Sorry for waking you up so damn early."

"Just get her back. I'll keep this quiet as long as I can."

By the time I'd hung up with him, there was a fist pounding on my hotel door. I pulled it open and Fox stormed inside, then stopped to stare at the robe on the floor. He snarled and the glare he leveled at me would have scared a lesser man.

"Those fuckers are going to pay," he said, his voice more of a growl.

"I called Surge."

"I know. He's already pulled the video feed for this floor. Chaos Killers have her, the same bastards who put two bullets in our Pres. We're not going to stand for this shit."

"So you think they took Vi on purpose and it wasn't just a random snatch and grab?"

"I think they've been watching us and waiting for a moment to strike. They probably saw you enter the hotel with her, then just bided their time in hopes of getting her alone."

"Fox, if they hurt her..."

"I know. She has so much as a scratch on her, and none of us will stand in your way. Just remember that Violeta hasn't seen that side of you and she might be scared. But there isn't a single man in the club who would deny you revenge on the assholes who took your woman." He narrowed his gaze. "She is officially yours, right? Because I know Spider gave you the okay a while ago."

"She's mine. I didn't think she'd want to be inked, so I gave her a bracelet that said *Property of Rocket*... and I asked her to marry me. She said yes."

Fox clapped me on the shoulder. "Then let's work on getting your wife-to-be back where she belongs."

Another knock sounded on the door and Fox opened it, letting in Bear, Shooter, Fangs, and Dread. I glanced at the doctor turned biker and hoped we didn't need his medical services, but I knew it was smart to have him here just in case. Before Fox could close the door, Jack, Philip, Yankee, Slider, and Gunner entered the room.

"Teller wanted to come, but he's watching Marianna," Jack said. "I volunteered to come in his place."

"Thanks. The fact you and Philip are here won't go unnoticed by Spider when it comes to patch in new members," Fox said. "And I'm sure Marcus would be here too if we didn't need someone on duty at the gate."

"Does Spider know?" I asked.

"He does, and as much as he'd like to be here to take these fuckers out, I suggested he might want to keep Luciana busy a bit longer. I can only imagine her reaction if she finds out her sister has been taken by the men who shot her husband."

"Anyone know where these bastards have been holed up?" I asked.

"Surge is working his magic, with the help of Wire and Shade. Between the three of them, we should have some answers soon. In the meantime, I need to bag up this robe and you need to check out and act like everything is fine. Surge is going to wipe the section of footage showing Vi's abduction. If the hotel security sees it, they'll notify the authorities, and that's the last thing we want," Fox said. "We're handling this shit our way, and putting an end to those dickheads once and for all."

"I thought Spider already sent them a message, loud and clear," I said.

"Apparently they saw it as a challenge." Bear snorted. "Dumbasses. They're a bunch of snot-nosed kids. No offense to you youngsters."

Fox rolled his eyes and flipped off the Sergeant-at-Arms. Bear was nearly fifty-two and acted like he had one foot in the damn grave. The club pussy would say different since they couldn't seem to keep their hands off the guy. He was welcome to them. All I wanted or needed was my Violeta.

"They shot at our Pres and took my woman. They may be lacking in intelligence, but they aren't complete idiots or they couldn't have pulled this off," I pointed out.

Bear held up his hands. "Not my fault you haven't learned to cuff your woman to the bed."

My mouth opened and snapped shut. Nope, there were just some things I didn't need to know about the club's Sergeant-at-Arms. Judging the looks on the other's faces, they felt the same. Except Slider. And I really didn't want to delve into the look on *his* face since I knew he didn't much care about the sexual orientation of his partners. And now I needed brain bleach to remove the image of Slider cuffed to Bear's bed.

"I need a drink," I muttered.

"I think I need something stronger," said Fox.

"Pussies," Bear muttered. "Like I haven't seen both of you banging the club whores out in the open. The thought of me cuffing a woman to the bed scares you that much."

Fox shook his head and pointed at Slider, and I knew he'd seen the same thing I had. Our brother just grinned unrepentantly.

Bear growled. "That shit isn't happening."

Slider winked at him. "Not my fault you're a sexy beast."

"Maybe when Surge finishes with this, he can work on creating a device for a memory wipe," Yankee said. "I'm first in line."

Everyone laughed and the tension eased a moment, until my gaze landed on the robe again. I grabbed a plastic laundry bag I'd noticed on the dresser and shoved the robe inside, careful not to touch the semen. I gathered Violeta's clothes from the night before and handed them to Fox, then made my way downstairs to checkout while my brothers went out to their bikes.

The kid behind the counter paled about four shades when he saw me walk up. He eyed my cut and audibly swallowed. I was used to the reaction, but the way his eyes kept shifting told me this was more than just fear because I was a biker. It was something else. I studied him, leaning onto the counter, my gaze locked on his face. When I had his attention, I could see a bead of sweat running down his forehead and my gut told me this little shit knew something about Vi disappearing.

"I think we need to have a chat," I said, my voice low and hard.

"I'm sorry. So sorry. I didn't have a choice," the kid babbled.

"Everyone has a choice. You made the wrong one."

"They have my mom!" he blurted. "They said I'd get her back if I helped them. I didn't know what they'd planned until I saw them carry that girl out the back of the hotel. I was hiding in the dark, taking a smoke break."

"You're officially off the clock, kid, and you're going to tell us every damn thing you know. Not only about Vi's kidnapping, but about the Chaos Killers. Understood? Because if you don't, it won't matter if your mom comes home because you won't be there. You'll be buried in a place no one will ever find you."

He whimpered and nodded, then rushed around the counter. I gripped his arm and hauled him out of the hotel, not even caring if I had to pay for the room another day or two. All that I cared about was finding out everything this little shit knew.

When I got outside, Fox stared at me with raised eyebrows and I shoved the kid toward the SUV the Prospects had driven. I didn't know why they hadn't brought their bikes, but right now I didn't care. We drove back to the compound and went straight to the clubhouse. Fox had the kid by the collar, forcing him to the back and into Church. We didn't typically allow outsiders in this room, and personally, I'd have taken him somewhere to torture the hell out of him. Until I noticed the piss spot on his pants. Maybe just a few harsh words would suffice this time.

"Start talking," I said.

The kid babbled non-stop, not making much sense most of the time. From what little I could understand, the Chaos Killers had been snatching up women under the age of fifty within four counties. The kidnappings had been spaced out far enough the local police hadn't noticed a trend. They'd grabbed the kid's mom and another woman from his neighborhood. The Chaos Killers had said he could have his mother back if he helped them tonight. While I hated that his mom could be suffering at the hands of those men, I was too fucking furious that he'd helped them take Vi.

"You don't know where they're keeping the women?" I asked.

"N-no. They said they'd take my mom home if I helped." Tears streamed down the kid's face and the wet spot on his pants had grown larger. "Are you going to kill me?"

"Guess that depends on what they've done to my fiancée." I lowered my face to his and narrowed my eyes. "For your sake, you'd better hope she's safe and sound. One scratch, and I'm going to kick your ass."

"Anything happens to Violeta, and Rocket will be the least of your worries. Her sister is married to our Pres. What do you think Spider will do to you when he comes home if we don't get Violeta back in one piece?" Fox asked. "Matter of fact, we're all pretty fond of that woman. The entire club might decide to take out their anger and frustration on you."

"F-five miles d-down the h-highway," the kid stammered.

"What's five miles down the highway?" I asked.

"Th-their hideout." He whimpered. "There's rumors around town. People are saying the Chaos Killers have a place down the highway the past week or two, off the road down a dirt path. Some of my friends got drugs from them."

"Which way?" Fox asked.

"S-southeast." The kid audibly swallowed. "Please, if they find out I told you, they'll kill me."

I pulled the knife I kept in my boot and pressed the blade to his throat. "They hurt my woman, and you won't be breathing much longer anyway. I will personally gut you if they've violated her."

"Oh, God." The stench of urine filled the air as the kid pissed himself again.

I wrinkled my nose and glanced at Fox, who snapped his fingers at Philip. "Clean up this mess and tie the little prick to a chair out back. If he's going to piss and shit himself, I'd rather it not be in the clubhouse."

"What's the plan?" Slider asked.

Surge rushed into the room, slamming down a handful of papers and pictures. I picked up the images and realized they came from the hotel cameras. I flipped through, seeing Vi gagged. Another image showed her over the shoulder of one of the assholes who would die soon. A growl erupted from me as I scanned each one, then started skimming the papers.

"What. The Fuck." I lifted my gaze to Surge. "Are you fucking kidding me right now?"

"Sorry, Rocket. I wish I had better news."

Fox snatched the paper from my hand and started cussing. It was passed to my brothers, and I was trying damn hard to hold it together.

"What is this?" Yankee asked.

"It's a price list," Surge said quietly. "They're going to do a live feed. People will be permitted to bid. The items with the highest amounts are what will happen to Violeta."

Gunner scanned the list, then promptly threw up. I wasn't far behind him, but the rage building inside me was overshadowing my need to purge the contents of my stomach. If they thought for one second I would permit this to happen... I locked my gaze with Surge again.

"Take it down. If they can't go live, then maybe we can stop them before any of this can happen to her."

Surge looked away before meeting my gaze again, tears gathering in his eyes. I'd never seen the damn man cry in all the time I'd known him. "Rocket... the bidding already started."

My heart hammered in my chest as he set his laptop on the table and opened it, showing us an image of Vi strapped to a chair, stripped naked, and gagged. If that wasn't terrifying enough, I could tell that she wasn't really there. She'd escaped into her mind in an attempt to rise above what was happening. I knew it was how she'd survived before, and my precious girl was trying to hold on until I could get there.

"Screw the fucking plan," I said. "I'm not waiting. I can't."

Fox squeezed my shoulder.

"I failed her," I said, my voice nearly a whisper. "I can't let those monsters hurt her more than they have. Do whatever you deem necessary. I'm going after Vi."

"I'll come with you," Yankee said.

Brazil and Patch stepped forward. "Count us in too."

I gave them a nod and headed out, not caring if Spider chewed my ass out later. I wasn't going to sit on my ass while they hurt Vi. If Surge learned anything new, anything that would help me save her, I knew he'd send me an update. As I pulled up to the gate, the roar of Harleys made me turn to look. It wasn't just Yankee, Brazil, and Patch with me. Marauder, Shooter, Fangs, and Dread were coming too. Even if I didn't know what we'd find when we got there, it didn't matter. Knowing they had my back, that they had Vi's back, was enough.

Marcus opened the gate and we pulled out onto the street and hit the highway within minutes. I counted the miles and as we neared the five-mile mark, I watched for the dirt road the little shit had mentioned. It was more of a path than a road, but I pulled down it anyway. A clearing was ahead and I pulled over, cutting the engine on my bike. The others followed suit and we stood to survey the area. There didn't seem to be any guards outside, which made my gut clench and I had to wonder if maybe the kid had lied, or if Vi was being held somewhere else.

Yankee signaled that he was going to search the area and Gunner went the other direction. My phone buzzed not long after with a message from Yankee.

Bikes and three guards at the back.

When it buzzed again, I saw Gunner's name.

Two in the trees. They're down and won't be getting back up.

Before we went any further, I knew I needed to ask one more thing of Surge.

Cut the feed when we find Violeta. I don't plan to leave witnesses.

And if he'd found two, there were likely others lurking. I showed the message to the others, then motioned for Shooter and Fangs to head in the same direction as Gunner. I sent Brazil and Patch the other way. Marauder and Dread followed me straight to the front door. No point in knocking. I pulled my foot back and kicked in the door. Cobwebs hung from the rafters and the windows were covered in grime. It looked like no one had used the place in years. As we made our way farther into the crumbling structure, I spotted one of the Chaos Killers guarding a door. His gaze swung our way, but I'd put a bullet between his eyes before he had a chance to even react.

"One down, a lot more to go," I muttered.

Yankee, Gunner, and the others came through the back.

"All clear," Yankee said.

I twisted the knob on the now unguarded door, and made my way down the flight of stairs, gun in my hand and ready to fire if necessary. The lighting was dim, but I could see clearly where I was going and how many people were in the room. My sweet Vi had blood dripping off the chair, her hands and feet tied to it. The things they'd done to her made my stomach nearly revolt, but I knew I had to stay strong for her. Without warning or thought, I started shooting, and the first man I took down was the one beside my woman. My brothers fired alongside me and soon the room was bathed in blood. When my clip was empty, I dropped it and loaded another. I wasn't stopping until every fucker in the room was breathing their last.

When the gunfire stopped, my chest was heaving and I surveyed the destruction. My sweet Vi sat in the center, surrounded by dead bodies, but the moment she saw me, a smile tipped the corner of her lips.

"I knew you'd come," she said, her words a little garbled.

I holstered my gun and rushed to her side, quickly untying her from the chair. I removed my cut and handed it off to Patch. Then I unbuttoned my shirt and helped Violeta into it. My brothers had already seen far more of her than I liked.

"Got one still alive," Yankee said.

I turned to see who and snarled. It was the man who had carried Vi from the hotel. Dread made his way over to me and reached out for Violeta, giving me a nod to handle business while he got her out of here. I didn't want her to see this, to know what I was capable of, but I also wouldn't let this man get away with dying an easy death. I only wished I could bring back some of the others and spend a little quality time with them and the tools they'd used to hurt my woman.

"Your turn," I said, hauling the man up by his collar. I shoved him onto the chair and used my knife to slice the clothes from his body, then strapped him down like he'd done to my woman. "Everything you did to her, I'm going to do to you. Does that sound like fun?"

He spat blood at me and grinned. "Can't hurt me, fucker. I'm already dying."

"Guess I better hurry, then."

His gaze wavered a moment, uncertainty entering his eyes as I reached for the blowtorch on the crude table nearby. The man began screaming and thrashing, but nothing would save him from my wrath. Every wound they'd inflicted on Violeta, I gave back. I tortured the asshole until he passed out, then revived him to do a little more damage.

"You looked at her. Touched her. Spoke to her." I reached for the paring knife. "Seems only fitting I send you to hell without your eyes, fingers, or tongue."

The man died before I'd even finished with him, and if I could have brought him back and started all over, I would have. How many others had there been? How many had suffered the way Violeta had? Or possibly worse? I wanted to know every move they'd made, every woman they'd taken and tortured, raped, killed, or sold. Any who were still living would be found, no matter what it took. I owed that to Violeta and Luciana. I wouldn't allow anyone to go through the same hell they'd endured in Colombia, or what had been done today to Violeta.

"You need to clean up before you see Violeta," Yankee said softly. "You'll scare her if she sees you like this."

I looked down and the blood and gore covering me and had to agree.

"There's a bathroom in the corner," Gunner said. "Not the cleanest, but maybe the water works and you can rinse off."

I went into the small room that contained a tiny shower, sink, and toilet. I stripped out of my boots, jeans, and underwear, handing everything over to Gunner so I wouldn't have to set it down on the filthy surfaces. The shower sputtered a moment, then ran ice cold. Stepping under the spray, I washed away the evidence of the carnage my fury had brought about, then got out and quickly dressed again, putting my cut on over my bare chest.

"Dread already called the clubhouse. Someone is bringing an SUV to transport Violeta back home. Fox was updated on what happened and he said a cleanup crew would arrive within the hour," Patch said.

Shit. I'd been so focused on getting to her, I hadn't given much thought to how I'd get her back home.

"Vi." I looked at the staircase and hurried that way, stepping over the bodies on the floor, then rushing upstairs. Dread had taken her outside, for which I was grateful. I hoped she hadn't heard the man's screams, didn't know what I'd done.

"She's going to need better care when we get home," Dread said. "I treated her best I could with what I had in my saddlebags, but it's not enough."

A blue truck came tearing down the path and I reached for my gun, then stopped when I realized who was behind the wheel, and the damn truck was too familiar. One I'd seen often enough before its owner had joined the Navy, leaving behind his cut and his bike.

"When the fuck did Cotton come back?" I asked no one in particular. I knew his ass hadn't been at the compound when we'd left. No way anyone could have kept that quiet. The fucker had been gone for too damn long.

"I'm guessing now," Dread said with a smile. "Good timing too."

The truck slid to a stop and Cotton leapt out. The smile on his face fell when he saw Violeta. His gaze held mine and I gave him a nod. Yeah, I'd dealt with the fuckers responsible. They wouldn't be hurting anyone else, ever again. Didn't mean there weren't other Chaos Killers we'd need to handle, but for now, we could hopefully take some time to come up with a plan. Between shooting our Pres and what they'd done to my woman, I wanted every one of those fuckers in the ground. The only good Chaos Killer was a dead one.

"Cotton, this is my old lady and fiancée, Violeta." I looked at my woman and knew I needed to make a decision. As much as I loved my bike and loathed the idea of anyone else riding it, I knew Vi needed me. "Take my bike back to the compound and I'll drive Violeta in the truck. No way she can ride on back of the Harley right now."

I'd been a fucking idiot not to think about the need for something other than a bunch of damn motorcycles, but I hadn't exactly been right in the head when I'd left. All I'd thought about was reaching Vi in time to save her. Nothing else had mattered at that moment.

Cotton blinked a few times, probably surprised as hell that I'd let him touch my bike, then he held out his hand. I dropped the keys onto his palm before helping Vi over to the passenger door of the truck. Once I had her buckled in, I hurried to the other side and slammed the door shut. I eased along the bumpy path, wincing with every soft sound of pain that slipped past her lips. I knew she was fighting to be silent. My brave girl.

Reaching over to take her hand, I gave it a gentle squeeze. "You make as much noise as you need to, baby. Scream if it will make you feel better. I won't judge you for it."

"Hurts so much, Jesse," she whispered.

There was a burning need to know just how badly they had hurt her, but I didn't want to make her answer. My love for her wouldn't fade even the slightest bit if they'd... I couldn't even think it. Not because I'd feel differently about her, but because the thought of them hurting her that way made me sick to my stomach.

"Love you, Vi. So fucking much."

"I love you too, Jesse. I knew you'd come for me. Warned them that they'd all die when you found me."

My lips twitched as I fought a smile. "Yeah, honey. I made sure they weren't coming for you again."

I glanced her way before focusing on the road again. I didn't know how she felt about that, knowing I had their blood on my hands. Her father had been a violent man, and I didn't like thinking that she might lump me in with her sperm donor. I'd never hurt anyone who didn't deserve it, and those assholes should have suffered a lot more. Except the one who'd lingered long enough for me to make him pay. I didn't even feel like he'd felt enough pain for all that he'd put her through. If I could have kept him alive longer, I would have.

"Good." She gave my hand a squeeze. "There were others. Before me. Other women, and young girls. A lot of them."

"How do you know that?" I asked.

"They bragged about it, talked about how some of the men bidding were repeat customers. Jesse, they've been doing this to women for years, not just here but other places. They abduct them from various states, hoping no one catches on." She licked her lips. "I don't think this was their usual spot. It seemed... unused."

I translated that into too dirty and not enough blood staining the floor, which made me grimace. I wanted to wipe the memory of today from her mind, but I didn't know how to even attempt to lessen her pain. Not the physical pain, because I knew that would fade over the upcoming days or weeks, but the emotional and mental anguish she'd suffered could last her a lifetime.

"If Surge discovered what they were doing to you, I'd imagine he can find a trail that will tell us how many times they've done this, maybe even find images of the women or names. If they're alive, they deserve to be found and taken home."

"And if they aren't?" she asked.

"Then their families should know so they can have closure."

She took a shaky breath and I thought I heard rattling in her lungs, making me wonder if she had a broken rib that could have punctured a lung. Or maybe she just had too much blood in her mouth and nose. I glanced over at her again and noticed she'd pressed a hand to her ribs. They'd been bruised and now I had to wonder if far more damage than that been done. I worried she'd punctured a lung, which meant I needed to get us home faster. Once the truck tires gripped pavement, I floored it, eating up the miles between the hell we'd left behind and the safety of home.

"You're a good man, Jesse. I don't care what you've done outside the law. You have a big heart, and that's what counts."

I didn't feel like a good man, nor did I feel like I deserved a woman like Violeta, but she was mine and I wasn't letting her go. I'd never loved anyone before, not the romantic kind of love. She was special, and I hoped like hell I didn't fuck this up. Without her, I'd fall apart. Life wouldn't be worth living anymore, and I'd just go through the motions.

But for her… I'd be a better man. Or at least I'd try.

Chapter Five

Violeta

I dreaded having to tell anyone exactly what had happened to me. They hadn't raped me. They'd threatened to, and had done their best to scare me, to break me. I didn't want Rocket in the room when I talked to Dread. I'd held the doctor off as long as I could, but I knew once he had his medical bag at the compound and was ready to check me over more thoroughly that he'd have questions, and he'd likely demand answers.

"Jesse, I need you to leave while he patches me up," I said.

I saw him glare at me and I winced at having used his real name in front of someone else. Not to mention it was his house, and I'd just told him what to do. "Sorry. I meant Rocket. Please. I don't want you to remember me like this. Give Dread some time to clean my wounds and bandage them. Let me wash and put on some clothes."

He growled but leaned down and pressed his lips to my forehead. "I'm not pissed you called me Jesse. I'm angry that you want me to leave, but I won't stay if that's really what you want."

"Just for a bit." I reached up and ran my fingers along his beard. "Promise I'll have Dread let you back in when he's done."

Rocket and Dread shared a look before my sexy biker walked out, closing the door behind him a little harder than usual. My gaze locked with Dread's. His eyes were dark and anguished, no doubt thinking he knew what I needed to tell him, or what he'd discover during his exam.

I slowly unbutton the shirt Rocket had put on me and undressed. Dread catalogued my wounds, but I could tell he was completely professional and not the least bit turned on by my naked body. If he weren't an actual medical doctor, then I likely wouldn't have exposed myself so willingly. Rocket trusted him, as did Spider, so I knew I could as well.

"As I clean, tell me what happened in each instance. Don't leave out the details to spare me. I don't think you should keep shit from Rocket, but I won't go blabbing to him. Right now, I'm just your doctor and you're my patient."

He touched a spot on my shoulder where there were a series of cuts. I told him about the knife. As he worked down my arm and reached the burns on my hip, I shared that part of the story as well, watching as his jaw tightened and his face paled. When I had to explain they'd used things to torture me in other ways, he got up and put his first through the wall, breathing heavily, before he could continue treating my wounds. When he'd placed the last bandage, Dread helped me into the bathroom where I washed my face and hair in the sink, then he got a hot, wet rag and helped clean the rest of me so Rocket wouldn't have to see the evidence of what they'd done. I didn't want him to think of me battered and bloody.

I let the first of the tears fall, the ones I'd held back during my torture. Gripping the counter tight, I tried to breathe, but it hurt so damn bad. Not just because Dread feared I might have a cracked rib, but because I'd barely held it together until now. I didn't want Rocket to see me like this, to watch me fall apart. Dread helped me into one of Rocket's soft T-shirts, and then tucked me into bed before retrieving my fiancé. Except Rocket didn't enter right away and I heard the murmur of voices in the hall, which meant he might not be telling Rocket everything, but Dread was most likely telling him about my recovery time and how to help me heal.

"She can't have sex for at least a week, but two would be better," I heard Dread telling him. My heart sank because I knew my sweet man would automatically think the worst.

The roar that Rocket released shook the windows and I heard his fist pounding into the wall again and again. Despite the pain, I made myself get out of bed and pull the door completely open. He'd fallen to his knees, his shoulders shaking with silent sobs. Going to him, I knelt at his side and placed my hand on his arm.

The tortured gaze that locked with mine nearly tore my heart in two. "I failed you. I was supposed to protect you, and I led you right to them, took you out of the safety of the compound overnight," he said, his voice cracking at the end.

"Jesse, it's not your fault. It's no one's fault but theirs. The Chaos Killers did this. Not you, not me. None of us could have known what would happen." I smoothed my hand up and down his bicep, and he wrapped his arms around me, but didn't squeeze too tightly. "Come lie down with me?"

He nodded and slowly rose to his feet. I clutched his hand as we entered the bedroom. Dread followed, but stayed on the other side, then pulled the door shut with a soft *click*. The sheets were still mussed from me lying down moments ago and I crawled back under them. Jesse stood next to the bed, just staring at the mattress, unmoving.

"Take off your boots and jeans. I need you to hold me." Although, truth be told, I had a feeling he needed *me* to hold *him* just as much. Today hadn't broken me, but I feared that it had damaged some part of my sweet Rocket, the man who had saved me, cared for me. It was one thing to hear about what I'd been through after the wounds had healed, and another to see the brutality of it in person.

"I'm sorry. So fucking sorry," he said, tears thickening his voice. "So sorry." He kept repeating himself, and I felt tears soaking my hair. I leaned back and pressed my lips to his, soft kisses until he started to respond.

"We can't, Vi. Dread said..." He audibly swallowed. "Fuck."

"Jesse, they only hurt me with objects. They didn't... didn't... They didn't rape me. I have some cuts down there from them threatening me and trying to break me." I knew to him it didn't make a difference. Whether they'd fucked me or not, I'd been tortured and my big teddy bear of a biker wasn't handling it well. "You told me I'm strong. Do you remember?"

"Of course," he said. "Strongest woman I know."

"I survived years with my father's men. A short time with the Chaos Killers is barely a bump in the road. I'll heal, Jesse. The wounds will go away, and even if they leave scars, what happened today won't define me. I won't let it."

He took a shuddering breath and nodded, pressing a kiss to the top of my head. "I know, baby. Like I said, strongest woman I know. Love you so fucking much, Vi. If I could have traded places with you, I would have in a heartbeat. I never want someone to hurt you ever again."

"They need to be stopped, Jesse. They can't keep kidnapping women. I don't think they expected me to live, or be in a position to cause them trouble. They talked, even bragged a bit about the harm they'd caused and the fun they'd had doing it. The women who live are sold. Sometimes to private buyers, and sometimes to brothels worldwide. Someone has to do something," I said.

"I'll talk to Spider, and we'll see what Surge can find."

I ran my hand up his chest and around the back of his neck. "You're not invincible. None of you are, but your club is bigger than just Hades Abyss. Your family has a wider reach. This club has a tie to the Dixie Reapers, and they have ties to other clubs, don't they?" I asked.

"Yes."

"Then use that. Call in every connection any of you have, reach as far and wide as you can, and then strike out against the Chaos Killers and take them down. Even if it means working with the government."

He blinked at me. "Government?"

"Isn't it illegal to kidnap women and children? To sell them to buyers in other countries or even here in the US?" I asked.

"Yeah, it sure the fuck is."

I thought for a moment. When I'd arrived here, I'd believed Casper VanHorne was every bit as evil as my father, and I'd been wrong. If the man had helped take down Mateo Gomez, then would he be willing to help with this too? I didn't know anything about him, but he'd saved me and my sisters.

"Would Mr. VanHorne help?" I asked.

Jesse faintly smiled, the first one I'd seen since he realized what had been done to me. "Yeah, I believe he just might, and if he's willing to help, then I bet Specter would too. They're two of the most badass men in the world. If anyone could help take down those assholes, it would be Casper and Specter."

I tried to keep a straight face. I'd met Casper, but his name paired with Specter struck me as humorous.

"Casper? And Specter? Seriously?"

Jesse shrugged. "Far as I know, Casper is the man's real name. Specter, however, is a different story. I don't think anyone knows that man's real name, and that's exactly how he likes it. Casper, on the other hand, pretty much just says a big fuck-you to anyone who would dare come after him."

I ran my fingers along his beard and scraped my nails along his scalp. Jesse shut his eyes and took a deep breath.

"I'll call Spider after we've rested a bit," he said. "Nothing will happen until he comes home anyway. Just be prepared for your sister to lose her shit when she sees you. He's tried to keep her from finding out you were missing, but there's no way we can hide what they did to you."

I hardened my jaw and thinned my lips. "Some of it can be kept secret. Don't you dare tell her everything, Jesse. She doesn't need that burden. No one does. I'll keep as much of me covered as I can so she only sees the bruises on my face and my split lip."

"I will gladly carry all your burdens, Vi. From now until forever."

I knew he would, but it didn't mean I wanted him to. I'd handled things well enough so far. Just knowing that he was there for me was enough. When I'd been snatched from the hotel, it hadn't occurred to me that Rocket would blame himself. The blame definitely didn't lie at his feet. It was the Chaos Killers, and only them. If they couldn't be stopped, I didn't know that I would ever feel safe leaving the compound. And even if they were dealt with, it didn't mean there weren't others out there who were every bit as bad, if not worse. The world was full of evil, which I'd learned firsthand. I knew there was good in it too, like the man holding me, but sometimes the bad seemed to outweigh the rest.

There was a knock at the door and Rocket growled.

"What?" he asked, his tone biting.

Dread pushed the door open and came in with a glass of water and a bottle of pills. "She needs to take something for the pain. I've called in some antibiotics and pain relievers, but if she takes this now, she can't have more pain meds for at least eight hours."

"It's fine. I'll take the pills now," I said, trying to sit up and wincing. I remembered someone mentioning that Dread still practiced medicine, and not just when the club needed to be patched up. Right now, I was grateful he could give me medication without me needing to go to a clinic.

I took the medication from Dread and swallowed it with the water he'd brought. Then I handed the glass back and Rocket helped me lie down again. Everything hurt, but I was used to pain. Or at least, I'd been used to it before coming here. I didn't remember hurting this much before.

Dread went to the door, then hesitated. "I know the two of you were together before Violeta was taken, and since I wasn't sure how careful you were, I've made sure everything she's taking wouldn't hurt a baby. Just in case."

I closed my eyes and tried not to groan. Wonderful. Now Rocket would be freaking out that I was injured like this and carrying his kid. And I'd thought he was protective before. *Thanks, Dread.* I tried to glare at the man, but didn't have the energy to pull it off. Instead, I curled against Rocket's side and closed my eyes. I was safe, back home where I belonged. That's all that mattered right now. I'd deal with everything else later. Much later. I felt like I could sleep for a year.

I heard the bedroom door shut and Rocket shifted, holding me a little closer. Breathing in his scent, I felt a calm wash over me. It wasn't the house that was home, but the man in bed with me. Wherever Rocket was, that's where I wanted to be. It still seemed unreal that I was lying here with him, that he actually wanted me as much as I wanted him. Loved me, for that matter. My hand clenched and my heart broke a little.

"They took my ring," I said. "And my bracelet."

"They're just objects, Vi. The only thing that matters is that I have you back. I can replace the ring and bracelet, but I can't find another Violeta." He kissed my forehead. "Right now, you need to focus on healing and resting. Don't worry about anything else."

I nodded and the tension slowly eased from my body. Rocket ran his hand lightly up and down my back, the one part of me that was barely injured. I had a few marks on my upper back, but that was all. The chair had protected me from just beneath my shoulders to my hips, not that I doubted for a second they'd have untied me if they wanted to hurt me elsewhere. Thankfully, they hadn't had time to get that far. It sickened me that people had bid on ways to hurt me. How could someone become so dark and twisted? It really made me wonder if some people were born without souls. I didn't understand how anyone with an ounce of humanity could do that to another person.

"Do you want another bracelet?" Rocket asked after several minutes of silence.

I bit my lip, then whimpered, having forgotten about my injured mouth for a moment. Did I want a bracelet? Yes and no. I'd been thrilled when he'd given it to me, but those men had easily taken it away. If I'd been marked like Luciana, they couldn't have taken his name from me. Then again, they could have burned it off.

"I think I'd like a tattoo," I said. "But I don't know that I just want a plain one like Luciana has. I'd like something pretty, if that's all right."

Rocket kissed me gently, careful not to hurt me. "You can have whatever you want, after you're better. No way I'm having someone ink you while you're injured. In the meantime, I'll have a property cut made for you, and I'll find some time to get you another engagement ring."

"The ring couldn't have been cheap, Jesse. I don't need another one."

His jaw tightened. "Whether you think you need one or not, you're getting one. And don't worry about the cost. Don't you know that I'd do anything for you? Give you anything, even the last cent in my bank account?"

"Doesn't mean I want the last cent in your account," I said dryly. "I'd rather you have money for stuff like food, the bills, and things you need than a ring. I know I'm yours and don't need a piece of jewelry to tell me that."

"Maybe not, but the other fuckers out there might need proof you're taken. Consider the ring my peace of mind if you go outside the gates without me."

He was such a caveman, but I had to admit I liked it. After the way I'd been treated previously, an alpha guy like Rocket should have scared me off, but I knew he loved me, wanted to protect me, and that made all the difference. Yes, he could be overbearing at times, but I knew that it was because he was scared to lose me, and after today I could hardly blame him. I'd wear his ring, a property cut, and anything else he asked of me, not because I was weak or letting him walk all over me but because I loved him just as much. I was proud to be his, and for other men to know that I was taken by the sexy biker lying in bed with me. I'd gladly scream it from the rooftops.

Although, I had a feeling he wouldn't be far from my side after today. I doubted that I'd need clothing or jewelry to tell men I was taken. The teddy bear I'd known since coming here had grown fangs and would likely rip out the throat of any man who looked at me wrong.

Was it wrong that I not only liked it, but was turned-on by how possessive Jesse was?

Chapter Six

Rocket

I'd talked Spider into keeping Luciana busy for another two weeks while Violeta recovered. I didn't know how he managed it, and I wasn't going to ask, but I was grateful for the time. My woman looked much better. Her bruises had faded and were mostly gone, except for a few along her ribs that were now a yellowish color. The burn marks had healed, but were scarring, and same for the cuts. I hated that she'd have visible reminders of what happened, but she wasn't letting it keep her down.

"Luciana, I'm fine," she insisted. "All you're doing is giving me a headache."

My Pres's woman folded her arms over her chest and glared at her little sister. "I can worry. I'm allowed."

Vi sighed. "Yes, you can worry, but as you can see I'm healing well. If you'd been here, you wouldn't have been able to stop it from happening, you couldn't have made me better any faster. Stop blaming yourself and just give me some breathing room."

Luciana sagged, looking a bit defeated for all of two seconds, then her eyes were flashing again. "Fine. You don't want me to worry? You don't need me here? Then I'll go home. You can come find me when you're ready to be reasonable."

I could have sworn I saw Spider roll his eyes as he herded her from the house. They'd only been home a few hours, but nearly every second of that time had been here with me and Violeta. While I could understand her concern, it was also apparent to anyone with eyes and ears that Luciana was annoying her little sister, who didn't want to dwell on what she'd been through.

The front door softly clicked shut and Vi slumped on the couch. There were still dark circles under her eyes. She didn't think I was awake all the times she screamed out in her sleep, but I'd been there for every single nightmare, holding her and trying to snap her out of it. I felt like a complete failure and an utter shit for letting her get taken to begin with, even if she didn't blame me.

Now that Spider was home, hopefully we could come up with a plan to ensure the Chaos Killers wouldn't be a problem anymore. It didn't mean that my woman would be safe. There would always be someone out there putting a target on the club, but at least this particular threat would be gone, and from what Surge had found, the world would be a better place. I only hoped that if we went after them, I wouldn't be asked to leave Vi. After seeing her tied to that chair, witnessing what they'd done to her in such a short amount of time, I didn't want to let her out of my sight if it could be helped. Eventually I'd have to loosen my grip or drive her away, but for now, I just needed the reassurance that she was safe.

"Need anything?" I asked, as I studied her. She really did look exhausted, more so than before Luciana's visit. I could understand her sister needing to see her, but it had been hard on Vi.

"I think I'll just curl up on the couch and watch a movie," she murmured.

I pushed away from where I'd been leaning against the wall and walked over to her. Kneeling down, I ran my fingers through her hair before kissing her forehead. It still amazed me that in the short time Violeta had been in my home, she'd become the most important person to me. She was my entire world. My club had always come first, but if she asked me to walk away, I might very well do it. It wasn't something she'd ever do, though. Despite the way she'd feared everyone at first, I knew that she now accepted my brothers and felt safe around them. She liked living at the compound, or she had so far.

"Teller came by again this morning," I told her.

She closed her eyes and sighed, then buried her face in the couch a moment. When she looked at me, her eyes held a great deal of pain, but I didn't think it was the physical kind.

"I can't handle any more visitors right now," she said. "I know he's worried. They all are, but it's too much. I can't get past it if everyone is constantly reminding me of what happened. Looking in the mirror is enough of a reminder."

"What do you want to do, Vi? You can't hide in the house forever. I'll hold them off as much as I can, but everyone here is worried about you."

"I know they are. I appreciate the concern, and I love that they want me to feel like I'm part of the family, but… it's too much. I just need some space." She reached out and ran her fingers along my beard. "Except from you. I don't want you to leave me."

"I'm not going anyway, sweetheart. Not if I can help it. You know if Spider gives me orders, I have to follow them."

My phone chimed and when I saw the message I winced. *Speak of the devil.*

Church in ten.

Great. The man was back in town for a few hours and it looked like the fun would start already. I wasn't about to leave Vi alone, so whether she liked it or not, a

Prospect was going to come sit with her. If she didn't want to see Teller, then I'd ask someone else.

"Baby, I have to go to the clubhouse for a bit. I need someone to stay here with you, but if you don't want Teller here…"

She groaned. "Fine. Send Teller, but if he does that puppy-dog eye thing, I may kick his ass. I'm tired of sympathy. I'm not a pathetic, weak woman who's going to break."

I bit my lip so I wouldn't smile, then kissed her softly. No, my woman wasn't weak or pathetic by any means. I'd never met anyone stronger in my life. She hadn't cried much the last two weeks, unless she thought no one was watching. Even the nightmares were something she'd thought no one knew about. Even though I soothed her when they happened, I knew she wouldn't like me seeing her that way, so I always feigned sleep when she snapped out of it. The last thing my sweet Vi wanted was anyone to view her as less than a fearless, capable woman. She was the perfect old lady. While I'd refused to let her get a tattoo just yet, the property cut I'd requested was finished and now hung on her side of the closet. She'd had it a week, but there hadn't been a chance for her to wear it yet.

"Love you, Vi."

"Love you too," she said softly, then smiled.

She tugged on my beard until my lips pressed against hers once more, then I pulled back before I was tempted to take things further. Technically, her recovery time was up as far as sex was concerned, but I didn't know that she was quite ready… or me for that matter. Even if I wanted her more than air, I also didn't want to risk hurting her.

I shot off a quick message to Teller to get his ass over here immediately, then I went to the bedroom to get my cut and put on my boots. By the time I was ready to leave, Teller was in the living room and my woman looked ready to murder him. I almost felt sorry for him, until I thought about the weeks I'd suffered believing there was more between them. That alone was enough for me to let him suffer Vi's wrath a bit longer.

"Vi." She lifted her gaze to mine. "Be good. Don't kill him, or Spider might get upset."

She snorted and rolled her eyes, then picked up the remote and ignored Teller while she channel surfed. As for the Prospect, he was frowning at her and seemed to be at a loss. The Violeta who had emerged the last few weeks had a bit more bite than she'd had previously. She wasn't afraid to get snarky with anyone, or let them know exactly what she thought or how she felt. If anything, her ordeal seemed to have released her inner warrior.

I pulled my keys from my pocket and went out to my bike. It didn't take long to reach the clubhouse and I went straight to the back and pushed open the doors to Church. Looked like everyone was already present, which explained Spider's glare as I took my seat.

"Sorry," I said. "Had to make sure Teller was there to keep an eye on Vi."

His features softened a fraction and he nodded. The Pres was still a hard-ass and wouldn't hesitate to gut some asshole who deserved it, but he'd also developed a soft spot for Luciana and Violeta. It was the most human any of us had ever seen him. Even his son, Diablo, had commented on the changes in his dad during one of his visits.

"Surge gave me everything he had on the Chaos Killers," Spider said, flipping open a file folder in front of him. "Human trafficking is just a small portion of what they do. As we learned the hard way, they're also into torture for profit. They run a site that permits people to bid on what happens to the women they kidnap. Those who survive are sold, usually to low-level brothels that don't care about looks. The women die a few months later from disease."

My stomach knotted, realizing Vi could have suffered that fate if we hadn't been able to find her. How many women had been put through that? As much as I wished I could have kept her from facing that nightmare, if she hadn't, we might have never discovered what the Chaos Killers were doing and more people would have suffered.

"They're also snatching kids from larger cities. Rocket was able to trace a few who were sold to private collectors," Spider said.

"I'm sorry but what?" Marauder asked. "What the fuck is a private collector when it comes to a damn kid?"

Spider looked like he'd sucked on a rotten egg. "Pedophiles who are extremely wealthy and think they can do whatever the fuck they want. They buy the kids, groom them, and then when they're too old they sell them to the highest bidder."

"That's fucking disgusting," Fox said. "I'm surprised the universe hasn't decided enough is enough and wiped out the entire fucking planet. It seems like no matter how many assholes like that are taken down, fifty more crop up in their place. Anyone else sick of this shit?"

"The world is a truly fucked-up place," Bear said. "And it ain't getting any better. Even if taking out the

Chaos Killers doesn't fix everything, it will at least save some lives. I've done a lot of bad shit in my life, but I don't condone hurting women and kids."

"I think we can all agree on that one," Knox said.

"I spoke with Casper VanHorne, but he's dealing with a personal issue right now. He had Specter contact me and the man agreed to help, but on his own terms. Honestly, we can't afford to say no," Spider said. "Every club I reached out to this morning is on board. Our new Chapter in Mississippi has been having some problems with Chaos Killers as well, so they were eager to join the fight. I spoke with their Pres, Titan, and he's ready to kick some ass."

"What about DCA?" Shooter asked. "If we could get them on board, along with Specter, then I bet this shit would handled within days."

With everyone throwing out ideas and possible ways to end the murderous Chaos Killers, all I could think about was whether or not any of those plans would leave Vi vulnerable to another attack. The rest of the Chaos crew had to know that Hades Abyss was responsible for the bloodshed in that cabin. And if anyone had passed along my name since Vi had been wearing her *Property of Rocket* bracelet, then it could put an even bigger target on me, and by association, on her as well.

"What about Luciana and Violeta?" I asked. "How will all this affect them? Are they going to be safe here? Is there any place that will be safe for that matter? Or have we painted such a big fucking target on ourselves at this point our women are in danger?"

"Don't you mean haven't *you* put a big fucking target on us?" Spider asked. "I heard what you did when you rescued Violeta, and while I can't blame you, your actions have consequences, Rocket. You didn't just put a bullet in everyone. You tortured the fuck out of one of them in the name of revenge."

"Would you have done anything different if it were Luciana?" I asked, my voice harsher than I'd intended and I got looks of warning from the Pres and VP. "I didn't mean anything by it, but seriously. If Luciana had been taken and tortured the way Vi was, would you have just put a bullet in them and walked away?"

Spider stared me down, silent. After a few minutes, he sighed and shook his head. "No, I wouldn't have walked away."

"I need to stay with Vi. No matter what the club plans, I need to be here with her. The thought of not knowing if she's safe makes me a bit batshit crazy right now. If you'd seen her…" I swallowed hard, thinking of my first glimpse of her in that damn cellar. "They burned her. Cut her. Bruised her from head to toe. Cracked her ribs. She's going to have scars from what they did not just on her skin but emotional ones too. She's acting all tough and shit, but she's having nightmares."

"The Prospects will remain here," Spider said.

"I don't give a shit if they're staying." My jaw tightened and I knew I was treading on thin ice, probably half a second from the Pres beating my ass, but I didn't care. "I'm not leaving her. I can't."

Fox studied me and I noticed that Spider's cheeks were flushing, his eyes were narrowed, and it looked like his teeth would break if he ground them any tighter together. Yeah, I was possibly getting my ass kicked today.

"I'm not trying to buck your authority," I said. "I didn't know where the fuck she was or who had her. Then I had to see her bloody and broken. She's my everything, Spider. If that makes me a pussy, then so be it, but my life isn't worth living without Vi."

"Let Rocket stay behind if we have to go after the Chaos Killers," Bear said. "We should leave a few patched members to hold down the fort anyway. Since I have no doubt that you and Fox will both go, and as Sergeant-at-Arms I'm sure as fuck going, these bastards could very well wipe out all the officers."

"Yeah, because my ass isn't staying home either," said Knox, the club Treasurer.

Spider shook his head. "All right. Then I guess it's time to add a few more officers and leave their asses here to watch over the compound. Congratulations, Brazil, you're our new Road Captain. Slider, you're the Secretary for the club. Should have filled those roles long ago, but we were doing fine without them after the last two retired."

Dread snorted. "Retired. Good one."

"I'll have patches made for both of you," Spider said.

"Seeing as how the other ones are six feet under," muttered Marauder.

Fox snorted. "No vote, Pres? Your word is law and all that shit?"

"Do I look like I give a fuck if those assholes want the jobs or if the rest of you fuckers are happy with my decision?" Spider asked, his tone biting. "Motherfucking pansy ass --"

"Think you can find another way to squeeze fuck in that sentence one more time?" Bear asked.

Spider narrowed his eyes.

"You don't scare me, old man," Fox said, and I watched the vein in Spider's head pulse.

Without warning, Spider launched a punch right for his VP's face. Fox worked his jaw back and forth, then had the audacity to smirk at Spider. Some days I swore the dickhead had a death wish. Bad enough I was pissing off the Pres, but with Fox winding him up too, we were all going to get our asses beat before Church was over.

"Rocket, Slider, Brazil, and Cotton. The four of you will remain behind with the Prospects to keep an eye on things. If shit goes south, Brazil will be in charge," Spider said. "The four of you can get the fuck out of here. The rest of you stay behind so we can work on a plan to take down the Chaos Killers once and for all. I'm tired of their shit. I'm tired of everyone's shit, including you pains in my ass. I'll make sure the four of you receive an update once we have everything ironed out."

I didn't need any further urging to get the hell out of here. My chair scraped across the floor as I hastily stood and started for the door. I felt the others at my back as I stepped out into the main part of the clubhouse, and the doors of Church hadn't even swung shut before I heard Spider bellowing at Fox to "stop being a fucking asshole." It seemed that being married to Luciana had only mellowed him for a short while. The Pres was back to his usual self, around the club anyway.

My bike kicked up dust as I sped down the streets through the compound. I parked in front of the house and couldn't help but smile a little. Since Vi had come to live with me, the place had changed. She'd once commented on the flowers Luciana had planted at Spider's place, so I'd created a flower bed and brought home a bunch of plants. Vi had transformed the place. The wind chimes she'd hung off the front porch tinkled in the slight breeze. Even though she'd been broken and abused when she'd first gotten here, she'd made my house into a home. Our home.

I got off the bike and went inside, quickly finding Teller and Violeta in the living room. She'd fallen asleep watching TV with her feet now in Teller's lap. I'd have yelled at him to keep his hands off my woman, except he seemed to be napping too. It pissed me the fuck off. What was the point in him staying here with her, if they were both asleep?

I stomped over to the TV and shut it off, then turned to face them, ready to give the Prospect a tongue-lashing. Then everything in me went still. There was a dart sticking out of Teller's neck, and another in Vi's hip. What. The. Fuck? Snatching my phone from my pocket, I called Dread, not giving a shit if Church was still in session or not.

It took four times of me calling back to back before Dread picked up.

"Spider is pissed as fuck. What do you want?" Dread asked.

"Get to my house now, and bring backup. Teller and Vi were shot with darts and both are unconscious. I have no fucking clue how someone managed to get them both, unless maybe Vi was already asleep. She likes to take naps."

"Did you check the house?" Dread asked.

"No. I'm not leaving this fucking room. If I leave her…"

"Understood. We're on our way," Dread said.

The line went dead, and not even two minutes later it sounded like every brother I had was outside my house, the pipes on their bikes loud enough to rattle the windows. Dread, Spider, and Fox came through the front door, guns drawn. Three more brothers followed them and started checking the house, and I heard more coming in the back. Dread came straight to the couch, where Vi and Teller still hadn't woken.

I'd left her. She'd been out of my sight only long enough to attend Church, and some fucker had gotten to her again. I couldn't keep her safe. The love of my life, the woman I couldn't live without, and I'd failed her yet again. Bringing her back here with me, keeping her in my house had been a mistake. She needed someone better than me, stronger, a man who could keep her safe. That obviously wasn't me.

Dread gently removed the dart from Vi first. He studied it, turning it around, then sniffing it. When Dread set it aside and reached for the medical bag I'd just noticed, I hoped that meant he could help her. And once he'd managed to wake her, ensured that she was all right, then I'd find a safe place for her to stay because it obviously wasn't here with me.

"Chaos Killers aren't this fucking smart," Dread said. "This is more like something ex-military would use, or one of those groups of assassins."

"So you think the club has another enemy?" Spider asked.

"Maybe." Dread pulled out a vial and a syringe from his bag, withdrew some of the serum inside, then injected it into Violeta. When he was finished, he turned to Teller and did the same thing using a clean needle. "If I'm right, they should wake up soon."

"If you're right? *If*? Are you fucking kidding me right now?" I demanded. "What the fuck do you mean by if?"

"I couldn't exactly test the damn darts at your house, now could I? No. I don't have a full-service lab handy, Rocket. I'm about ninety-nine percent sure what they were dosed with, and I treated them the best I could."

"Jesse?" Vi called softly.

I spun to face her, falling to my knees next to the couch. She reached for me and I pulled her into my arms, breathing in her scent as she clung to me. Even though I'd put her in danger by leaving, she still came to me. It made my heart ache. She was so fucking trusting, and while I'd earned that trust, I no longer felt like I deserved it.

"Teller's waking up," Dread said.

"Can you get him and ask everyone to leave?" I asked quietly. "I need a minute with Vi."

Spider placed a hand on my shoulder. "Don't do anything stupid. Your thoughts are written all over your face, boy, and you're wrong. This isn't your fault."

"He's right," Fox said. "It's not your fault, and it's not the Chaos Killers. Found a note. Marcus did this as a distraction."

"Distraction from what?" Spider asked.

"He's gone. The reason the Chaos Killers knew where to find Violeta didn't have anything to do with them watching us, not in the way you think. Marcus was planted here," Fox said. "The fucker has been spying on us and reporting back to the Chaos Killers since before the girls even came to stay with us."

"That motherfucker," Teller muttered as he staggered to his feet. "It's my fault, Pres. I vouched for him, said you could trust him."

"He fooled all of us," Spider said. "Every last one of us. And that little shit is going to pay when I get my hands on him."

Chapter Seven

Violeta

Marcus had betrayed the club? I didn't understand why. Even though he'd scared me at first, everyone with Hades Abyss had terrified me back then. After I'd learned to trust them, I'd been comfortable around Marcus. Not once had he ever made me feel that he would hurt me. If what Rocket said was true, then Marcus was to blame for the Chaos Killers abducting me from the hotel. Why would he do something like that? He had to have known what they planned. Was he just as evil as my father and his men? I didn't understand how I hadn't seen it, how none of us had seen it.

"Did anyone else know Marcus had a sister?" Spider asked.

Teller shook his head, then winced and pressed his fingers to his temple. "No. I've known the guy for years and he never once mentioned a sister. Met his mom once when we were younger, but his dad has been MIA pretty much all his life from what he'd told me."

"I'll get Surge to do some digging. I need to know how that little shit slipped through the cracks and got in with us deep enough to pull this crap, and then I need to find him," Spider said. "He'll pay for what happened to Violeta."

"Could…" I stopped and licked my lips. "Could he have a good reason? You mentioned a sister. Is she the reason he did it?"

"The note says he didn't have a choice, that the Chaos Killers had his sister," Fox said. "But he could have come to us with that shit and we'd have helped him get her back. If he'd trusted us, we could have found a way to bring her back safe without you ever being placed in danger."

"If they have his sister, then I can understand why he did it," I said. "What they put me through is nothing compared to what others have suffered at their hands. If they still have her, there's a chance she's either held captive at one of their hideouts, or she's been shoved into a brothel somewhere."

Spider tapped on his phone a moment, then it started to ring, on speaker.

"What's up, Pres?" Surge asked when he picked up.

"I need you to find everything you can on Marcus Brosier's sister. Supposedly, the Chaos Killers MC has her. I need to know if she really exists, where she is, and I need to find a way to extract her and Marcus from those assholes," Spider said.

"He was behind everything," Fox said. "He's the reason Violeta was taken. She seems to be willing to give him a chance to explain. I'd rather pound on him a little first."

Rocket took my hand and gave it a slight squeeze. "If she's willing to listen to him, then so am I, but no promises I won't beat the shit out of him when he's finished speaking. They could have killed her, and it would have been his fault."

"I'll see what I can find and get back to you," Surge said. "When he asked to Prospect, I did see that his father dropped off the map when Marcus was a toddler and his mom was his sole caregiver as he was growing up. I didn't see a damn thing about a sister, though, so it's news to me too."

"Maybe she's not his biological sister?" I asked. "Could it be someone he was raised with, or maybe just a close friend he considers a sister?"

"I guess that's possible, but I don't think she's just a friend," Teller said. "There was a girl who was always hanging around a few years ago. She's about the same age as Marcus and she's mixed race like him. I never thought about them being related since he didn't mention it, but she could very well be a half-sibling or something. One way to find out for sure."

"What's that?" Fox asked.

"Go ask his mom. If she has another kid, one who has been snatched, then she may be willing to talk if we promise to bring the girl back home," Teller said. "I think the girl's name was Addie or something."

"Will the mom come with you?" Spider asked. "Does she know you well enough to let you bring her to the compound?"

"Yeah. She'll come with me, but I'll need one of the SUVs or trucks to get her here," Teller said.

"Do it. I don't want the clubhouse to freak her out so bring her to my house. Rocket, I want you and Violeta to be there too. If the woman understands exactly what her son did, she might be more inclined to help," Spider said.

"I'll have her here within a half hour," Teller said.

"Do I have time for a shower before we leave?" I asked. "I feel… I just don't like how I feel after being knocked out like that."

Rocket kissed my cheek. "Soon as they leave, I'll start the shower for you."

I glanced at him and wondered if he knew I was going to do my best to drag him in there with me. He hadn't touched me intimately while I'd been healing, but according to Dread it was safe for us to have sex again. Being held by Rocket was wonderful, I loved the gentle kisses he'd given me the last two weeks, but I wanted more.

It seemed like I'd waited forever for Rocket to see me as a woman, then we finally had a nice night together at the hotel and it had gone to hell. I was more than ready to feel his hands on my body, to have him kiss me with the same fire I'd felt that night, but he was treating me like I'd break at any moment. It was starting to piss me off. I wasn't some fragile flower. I'd survived far worse than what the Chaos Killers MC had done to me, and if life knocked me on my ass again, I'd survive that too.

After everyone left, I followed Rocket to the bedroom and started stripping off my clothes while he got the shower going. When I walked into the bathroom naked, his eyes widened slightly before he took a hasty step back. It would have been funny if it didn't make me so damn angry. I left the shower door open as I stepped inside and let the water soak into my hair. My gaze locked on Rocket and I noticed the way he watched the water running down my body.

"I can't reach my back. Would you get in and help me wash?" I asked, trying to sound as innocent as possible.

He hesitated only a moment before he removed his cut and the rest of his clothes. Rocket pulled the shower door closed behind him as he stepped inside, but he didn't immediately reach for me. I moved in closer, placing my hands on his chest and I felt his heart racing. It was galloping as fast as a racehorse, and I fought not to smile. At least I knew he was still affected by being this close to my naked body. I'd started to worry that he didn't think of me like that anymore.

"Jesse," I said softly. "It's been two weeks."

"Uh-huh," he said, his eyes burning bright, but he still didn't reach for me.

All right, he wanted to play it that way? I'd get a reaction out of him. Before he could stop me, I dropped to my knees and licked his shaft. He hissed in a breath and his hands went to my hair. With a slight tug, he tried to pull me away, but I wasn't about to let him. I reached up and cupped his balls, rolling them as I sucked the head of his cock into my mouth.

"Goddammit, Vi. You're not playing fair." His grip on my hair tightened, but this time he dragged my lips down his shaft until I'd taken all of him. Using my hair, he guided me in slow strokes as I flicked the underside of his cock with my tongue. "I don't want to hurt you."

I sucked harder and swirled my tongue over the slit in the head, making his cock jerk as he growled. I glanced up with just my eyes and saw that he was glaring down at me, but his cheeks were flushed with arousal. I knew I'd won this round.

He tipped my head back more. "Relax your throat, baby. I'm going to fuck your mouth."

I placed my hands on his thighs, letting my nails bite into him as he drove into my mouth again and again. His pre-cum was coating my tongue and I could tell that he was getting close to his release. At the last second, he pulled out and let me go, taking a step back as his chest heaved as if he'd run a marathon.

"Fuck, Vi."

I slowly stood and went to him, wrapping my arms around his waist. "I need you, Jesse. Don't push me away. If you see me differently after what happened, then --"

I didn't get to finish my statement before his lips were crashing against mine. His tongue worked its way into my mouth and soon I was lost to him. His kiss dominated me, bent me to his will, and made my knees go weak. My nipples scraped against his chest and my pussy ached, needing to be filled by him. I felt his hand slide down my body, stopping at my hip. He gave it a squeeze and I rubbed against him, wanting more.

"Jesse, please," I begged.

"What do you need, Vi?"

"I need you to touch me."

He grinned. "I am. See?"

His hand moved up and down my side again, but he knew damn well that wasn't what I meant. I gripped his hand and shoved it between my legs, making him chuckle softly. His fingers stroked the lips of my pussy and I shuddered before widening my stance. The first swipe against my clit and I was trembling and really close to coming. It had been too long since he'd shown me how wonderful sex could be, and now I craved it. Craved *him*.

He placed his lips against my ear, the scruff of his beard tickling me. "Does my sweet Vi need to be fucked?"

"Yes! Yes, Jesse."

He thrust a finger inside, stroking in and out, then added a second one, stretching my pussy. I clung to him, murmuring incoherently as he pushed me closer to orgasm. When he started fucking me with his fingers and rubbing my clit, I shattered, screaming out his name as my body tensed and pleasure washed over me. He kept going, not stopping until he'd made me come twice more, then he licked his fingers clean.

Jesse turned me to face the tiled wall, then caged me in with his body. "I thought you were too young to have a baby, but I think I've changed my mind. You could be pregnant now. We didn't use protection at the hotel."

My breath caught.

"I'm going to fuck you bare, Vi. Fill you up with my cum, and I'll keep fucking you bare until I stop breathing. You're going to carry my kid, and you'll be the sexiest momma ever."

Oh, God. I couldn't handle him saying stuff like that. It turned me into a whimpering, needy mess. I wanted that. Wanted his kids. I had no doubt that he'd be an amazing father.

"You want my cum, Vi? Want me to fill you up?" he asked, his voice low and raspy.

"Yes, Jesse. Yes! I want that. Want you!"

He slid his hand around to my stomach and pressed until I pushed my ass back, then he nudged my feet farther apart, and rubbed his cock along my slit. Every bump against my clit made me feel like sparks were shooting along my nerve endings. When he entered me, slowly stretching and filling me, it was beyond incredible. How could I have missed something so much that I'd only had that one night? It felt like forever since he'd been inside me, and if we didn't have people waiting for us, I'd beg him to stay in bed with me all day.

It only took two strokes before he was driving into me, fucking me hard and deep, and I was loving every second of it. My toes curled against the shower floor and I pressed back against him.

"Need you to come for me, baby," he said.

I was close. So close. I reached between my legs, feeling the slide of his cock against my fingers before I started playing with my clit. It wasn't long before I was coming. The second my pussy squeezed him, Jesse growled and lost his rhythm, slamming into me until I felt the spurts of his cum. When he stilled, I could feel his cock twitching inside me.

"Fucking hell," he muttered. "I took you like a damn animal."

I looked at him over my shoulder. "Did you hear one word of complaint?"

"No. Doesn't mean you didn't deserve better than that."

He pulled free and I turned to face him, reaching up to cup his cheek.

"What I deserved was for the man I love, the man I'm going to marry, to make me scream his name. And I got that. I don't need slow and sweet. I just need you, Jesse. I love that you lose control with me. It means that you're every bit as hot for me as I am for you, and I hope we have that forever."

"We will, Vi. I will want you until I breathe my last. I'm sorry if you felt like I didn't want you anymore. I've been trying so damn hard to control myself. After what happened, I didn't want to hurt you, but I just ended up bruising your feelings instead of your body. It wasn't my intention."

I pressed my lips to his. "Let's clean up and go to Spider's house. I want to meet Marcus's mom and see what she knows."

He helped me wash and I did the same for him, then we dried off and dressed. By the time we reached Spider's house, everyone else had already arrived and gave us disgruntled looks for having to wait. I smoothed my hair behind my ear and felt my cheeks warm as I thought about exactly why we were late.

Rocket led me over to a seat in the corner, then he sat and tugged me down onto his lap. The woman seated near the window slightly resembled her son, mostly his lips and the shape of his eyes. Her skin was a few shades darker, and I wondered if his lighter coloring came from his father, along with his eye color and other features. It always amazed me how two people could come together and create a miniature version of themselves. Would a child between me and Rocket have his fair hair and blue eyes, or take after me?

"Miss Tremaine has agreed to speak with us," Spider said. "Now that everyone is here, we can begin. Miss Tremaine, as Teller explained, your son claims his sister has been taken by the Chaos Killers MC. He nearly got one of our women killed by sharing the information of her location when she was outside the gates."

Marcus' mother winced, then her gaze met mine. "Was it you?"

I nodded. "Yes, ma'am. They kidnapped me the night Rocket asked me to marry him, and they... they tortured me. I also heard what they'd done to the women before me, and what they intended to do to me as well."

Tears gathered in her eyes and she gave a slight nod. "My Marcus isn't a bad boy. His half-sister, Addie, was taken by the Chaos Killers MC nearly a year ago. She was only seventeen when she disappeared. Several months ago, one of them came to Marcus and said there was a way he could get his sister back."

"By infiltrating our club, then betraying us?" Spider asked.

"He was to give them information about any deals you had, and about any women. I didn't like it and tried to talk him out of agreeing, but he adores Addie. I know my baby won't be the same if I get her back, and that's if they haven't lied and she's even alive." Miss Tremaine dashed away the tears slipping down her cheeks. "I don't know much. He meets with them at a place two towns over. Some bar that's on the rough side. No one asks questions there."

Surge cleared his throat. "Miss Tremaine, your daughter is alive. Addie has been moved to a, um…"

"I know what the Chaos Killers do," she said. "She's in a whorehouse, isn't she?"

Surge nodded. "I'm sorry, but yes. She's in the Florida panhandle, and we're reaching out to a club nearby to see if they can help extract her. We're also putting things into motion to take down the Chaos Killers permanently."

"My baby… I'll welcome her home, no matter what she's faced, but I don't know she'll want to come to me. Can you make sure she's safe?" Miss Tremaine asked. "That's all I want -- for her to be safe and happy. What she's been through… it's going to damage her. I'll never see her differently, but I know she'll be changed from what happened."

"She'll have a home here if she wants, or with any of the clubs we call allies. Someone will take her in and help her heal," Spider promised. "I know a lot of people around town are scared of us, but we'd never hurt a woman or child. Well, not a woman who isn't a backstabbing bitch at any rate. Someone hurts my family, I don't care what gender they claim."

Miss Tremaine nodded. "I appreciate your help saving my baby girl. Now what are you going to do about my boy? He thought he was doing what he had to do. He's not a bad kid, never has been. Not really."

"Marcus betrayed the club, and nearly got Rocket's old lady killed. She'll have scars for the rest of her life from the ordeal," Spider said. "I'll listen to Marcus when we find him, but I don't know if I can trust him again. I need to know that if shit happens, I can count on the men in this club to have my back."

"If I hear from Marcus, I'll let you know," Miss Tremaine said. "For now, I think I'd like to go home."

"I'll take her," Teller offered.

After they left and the front door closed, Spider sighed and ran a hand down his face. I knew he was frustrated to say the least. The glances Luciana kept casting his way were enough to tell me that Spider was troubled over the latest development. She couldn't conceal the worry in her eyes as she watched her husband.

"Where's Marianna?" I asked.

"Sleeping," Luciana said.

"Where do we really stand on taking down the Chaos Killers?" Rocket asked.

"Specter said he'd handle the problem," Spider said. "But extracting Addie isn't his top priority. I'll ask Cinder to send a crew after her. Maybe the Reapers can step in and help them."

"I'll get her location to you, along with any security measures they have in place," said Surge. "I'll also contact Shade and get him anything I have that might help."

"So, none of you are going after them?" I asked. "Everyone will be here?"

Spider nodded. "I was asked to stand down, and as much as I'd like revenge on those fuckers, I have no doubt that whatever Specter has planned will be worse than anything I could do to them. He has the contacts to pull off a massive strike that could hit every Chapter those fuckers have all at the same time."

"Then Rocket and I can go home?" I asked.

Spider smiled faintly. "Yeah, y'all can go home. I'll make sure you're undisturbed the next twelve hours or so, unless an emergency comes up."

I glanced at Rocket and when his heated gaze met mine, I felt my cheeks warm. Twelve uninterrupted hours sounded pretty good, especially now that he knew I wouldn't break. Having him fuck me in the shower had only made me want him more. He growled softly, then stood, lifting me into his arms as he rose from the chair. With brisk strides, he carried me from the house. I heard Spider chuckle behind us, but I didn't care. All that mattered was the man I loved had me in his arms, and I hoped he was about to take me to bed, and preferably keep me there for a while.

Chapter Eight

Rocket

I probably shouldn't have hauled her out of Spider's house the way I did, but knowing that Violeta was healed enough for me to do more than hold her was all it took to make my blood heat and keep my cock hard. I wanted her, needed her, and I was damn sure going to have her. Multiple times. I might be in my thirties, but with Vi I felt like a damn teenager again. It had been a long-ass time since I'd been in a constant state of arousal, until I met her.

The second the door shut behind us at our home, I paused only long enough to lock it, then carried Vi to the bedroom. She giggled and cuddled against me as I walked at a brisk pace. Even though I'd turned the bolt on the front door, I shut and locked the bedroom door too, not wanting to chance anyone barging in. The second I set Vi down on her feet, she started removing her clothes, the light in her eyes telling me she was every bit as eager as me.

"Looks like we'll get that day in bed after all, or at least half a day," I said. "Prepare to be sore, baby, but you're going to be thoroughly fucked before the day is over."

She smiled softly. "I have no problem with that at all."

"Do you know how fucking hard I've been? It's been torture to hold you and not be able to do anything else. I understood, and I damn sure didn't want to do anything that would cause you pain, but I've wanted you, Vi, so damn much."

"I've wanted you too, Jesse. I worried that you'd never make a move. It's why I asked you to join me in the shower."

I reached for her, sliding my fingers into her hair. "Not a damn thing has scared me in my entire life, except the thought of losing you or being the one to cause you pain. I just needed a little nudge. Now that I know you can handle some lovin', you won't be able to keep me away. I'll be pulling your clothes off every chance I get."

"Promise?" she asked.

"Oh, yeah."

"No holding back?" she asked.

I hesitated for a moment, and she narrowed her eyes. It wasn't that I didn't think she could handle a little roughness in the bedroom, but I still worried it might trigger a bad memory. I'd love to tie her up, spank her ass, and maybe even have some toys delivered to the house. It was concern over whether or not she could handle that side of me that made me treat her differently. There was a darker side of me I didn't want her to see, not after everything she'd been through.

"I won't break," she said.

Physically she might not, but emotionally? Mentally? I didn't feel comfortable testing that theory. While she'd healed since she'd come here, it didn't mean she was ready for more than we'd done already. An intimate relationship was still new for us. I'd hoped to have some time with her before I let out any of those tendencies in the bedroom.

"You're the most important thing in my life," I told her, dragging her closer to me. "Maybe I don't want to show you that side of me right now. I like the way you look at me, all trusting and like I'm sort of damn hero. I'm no one's hero, Vi, but you make me want to be yours."

"You already are." She reached up and cupped my cheek. "I trust you completely, Jesse."

"I'm not the man you think I am."

Violeta pressed her lips to mine, then traced my bottom lip with her tongue. I refused to be so easily distracted and fisted her hair, tugging her back. The heat in her eyes hadn't diminished. If anything, it burned even brighter.

"Do you know what I want?" she asked.

"What?"

She licked her lips and ran her hands up and down my chest, over the clothes I had yet to remove. Gently touching my cut, she traced the stitching. When her gaze locked with mine again, there was a spark I hadn't seen before.

"I want you to use me," she said.

I balked and took a step back, but she clutched at me and was still every bit as close as she'd been before. Maybe even closer.

"Vi, I…"

"Jesse, I want you to keep your clothes on and fuck me like you would any other woman. Take what you want, what you need. Show me that I'm yours, that you're in charge."

I stared down at her, my heart hammering as I wondered if she'd lost her damn mind. My cock was fully on board with her idea, but my brain wasn't too sure it was a good idea.

"You want to erase the bad memories?" she asked.

I nodded.

"Then replace them. Force me to bend over, put me on my knees. Do whatever you want to me, Jesse. I'll know it's you, if that's what concerns you. Release whatever part of you that you're trying to lock away in order to protect me."

"Vi, why would you even ask that of me? You're asking me to… to treat you like a damn whore. You're not a whore, baby. You're my woman, my fiancée, the woman I love."

She leaned in closer, her lips nearly touching mine again. "Maybe I want to be your whore. Yours and only yours. I love you, Jesse, and that means every part of you. I don't want you holding back because you're worried I can't handle it. Show me what's so big, bad, and scary about you. If it's too much, then I'll let you know."

I fisted her hair, gripping it tight and tilted her head back so I could stare into her eyes. What I saw was enough to make my resolve crumble. The broken girl who had moved in with me wasn't here anymore. The strong, vibrant woman challenging me? She was completely different, and she was all mine.

"On your knees, Vi." My voice was harsher than I'd intended, rough from arousal. She sank down in front of me, waiting patiently for my next order. "Unfasten my belt and pants, then take my cock out."

Her hands were completely steady as she obeyed. The pink tinging her cheeks made me think maybe it would be okay, maybe she really could handle it. The rasp of my zipper was fucking loud in the otherwise quiet room. The moment her fingers wrapped around my dick, I had to close my eyes and fight for control. I'd never been so gone for a woman before. One lick of her lips, seeing her bend over -- hell, just a touch anywhere on my body and I was hard as fuck.

"Lick it," I demanded, opening my eyes to watch her.

Her tongue ran the length of my shaft, then the little tease flicked the head, making me hiss in a breath. I narrowed my eyes and reached out, pulling my dick away from her. She blinked up at me innocently, but I didn't believe that look for a moment. She'd done it on purpose, probably hoping to get a reaction out of me. And she had. Dammit.

"Open."

Her jaw dropped and I reached for her with my free hand, grabbing a handful of hair and dragging her toward my dick, using my other hand to guide myself into her mouth. I didn't stop until she'd taken every inch, then I ground myself against her. Vi didn't gag. She reached up and clutched at my thighs, holding onto me as if she was afraid I'd move away.

I pulled back, then drove deep again. I fucked her mouth with long, deep strokes, pre-cum coating her tongue with every stroke. My balls were high and tight, and I knew it wouldn't take much more for me to blow. When I was knew I was too fucking close, I pulled free of her mouth and took a step back.

"Get up," I said.

She rose to her feet, her lips plump from sucking my cock, and her body flushed. Her pretty nipples were hard and just begging for attention. I reached out and pinched one, giving it a tug. Her eyes went dark with desire and I repeated the motion with the other side.

"Does my sweet Vi need a good, hard fucking?" I asked.

"Yes, Jesse. I need you so much."

"Show me," I commanded.

Vi turned and bent over the side of the bed, her ass in the air, then spread her legs. Her pussy glistened with how fucking wet she was, and other than pulling on her nipples, I hadn't touched her. Fuck me.

"Is that all it takes?" I asked. "Put my dick in your mouth and tug your nipples and you're ready for me?"

She looked at me over her shoulder. "No. All you had to do was say we were going to the bedroom for sex and I was wet and ready. But in all honesty, I just have to be near you and I want you. If I hear your voice, it's enough to make me crave your touch."

"Get on the bed, up by the headboard, and kneel."

She crawled up the bed, gripped the headboard, and waited. I retrieved a pair of handcuffs from the bedside table, then moved up behind her, my weight making the mattress dip. Pressing against her body, I reached for her hands and fastened them to the bed. She didn't resist, and if the tremor that raked her body was any indication, she was enjoying this as much as I was.

I placed my lips near her ear and slid my hands around her waist, then up to cup her breasts. I traced the shell of her ear with my tongue as I gave her perky breasts a squeeze. It was enough to make her moan and press her ass back against me. As hard as I was, I wouldn't take her just yet. I nipped her ear the same time I pulled on her nipples and she gave a soft cry. Taking my time, I played with her breasts and rubbed my beard against the soft skin along her neck and shoulder.

"Jesse, please," she begged.

"Please, what?"

"Please. Fuck me. I need you."

I gave her nipples a slight twist. "Think you can come just from this? Can you come for me, Vi? Show me just had badly you need my dick inside you?"

"Y-yes. I-I can do that."

"Prove it," I said, my voice little more than a growl I was so fucking turned-on.

I kept palming her breasts and playing with her nipples. The next time I squeezed the hard little nubs, she shuddered and called out my name. I slid a hand down her belly, down between her legs, and groaned at how slick she was.

"Fucking hell. That's the sexiest damn thing ever," I said.

I teased her clit in small circles, my touch light as I lined my cock up with her pussy, then pushed inside. The first few strokes were slow, but the second her inner walls squeezed me, my control snapped. I started pounding into her, taking her hard and deep. The headboard slammed into the wall with every stroke, even though she was clinging to the damn thing. Shifting my angle, I must have hit just the right spot because seconds later Vi was coming, her body tight as she threw her head back and said my name over and over. I didn't stop until I unloaded every drop of cum from my balls, filling her up.

Panting for breath and my heart racing, I stayed buried inside her. I splayed my hand across her belly, holding her against me, and hoping that maybe we'd made a baby. It was the one thing I wanted most. A kid with Vi. Maybe a daughter with her pretty eyes and dark hair. As my dick twitched inside her, I amended that thought. No, not a daughter. Then some fucker would want to do this to her one day, and I'd have to shoot the little asshole.

I rubbed my beard against her neck again before kissing her there softly.

"Love you so fucking much, baby."

"I love you too, Jesse." She tugged on the cuffs. "But do you think you can unlock these?"

I smiled and slowly withdrew from her body. Watching my cum trickle down her thigh was hot as fuck, but I had the crazy urge to shove it back inside her. Reaching into the bedside table drawer, I removed the key, then unlocked the cuffs, setting her free. She rubbed her wrists, then leaned back against me.

"No bad memories?" I asked as I ran my hand down her arm.

"No. I knew it was you, and that made all the difference. Now if someone had blindfolded me and I hadn't seen who was locking me to the bed, then I probably would have completely freaked out."

I tossed the cuffs aside and stretched out on the bed, pulling Violeta down beside me. She curled against my side, her head on my shoulder and her hand splayed across my chest. I'd been with my fair share of women in my life, but all their faces had blurred since meeting Vi. She outshined them all, and while part of me wished I hadn't been quite as much of a man-whore over the years, I was grateful for the experience so that I would know exactly how to please her.

Trailing my fingers up and down her arm, I had to admit that I couldn't remember ever being this damn happy. My life had gone to shit after my sister died and left behind her daughter. Then I'd called the baby's father, who hadn't even known she existed, and he'd taken her back home to the Dixie Reapers. Being alone had sucked big-ass donkey balls, and I'd tried to drown my sorrows in alcohol and pussy. It hadn't really worked, but at least I'd not felt quite so alone. Then Violeta came into my life and turned it upside down.

"I know I'm not the best man for you, but I'm so fucking glad you're part of my life, Violeta. I was lost before you came along, just drifting and existing from day to day." I pressed a kiss to the top of her head. "I know you feel like the club saved you, but it was *you* who saved *me*."

"There's no one I'd rather be with than you, Jesse. I'm really glad that Casper VanHorne and Spider said I should stay with you. If I had been given to anyone else, I don't know that I would have recovered, and I certainly wouldn't have fallen in love."

She tightened her hold on me and I toyed with her hair as I stared up at the ceiling. I didn't like that she'd been in danger twice in the last few weeks, and it didn't sit well that the club wasn't handling the problem. It wasn't that I didn't trust Specter to handle it, or the Devil's Boneyard for that matter, but this wasn't their fight. Some part of me knew that the Chaos Killers were a threat to everyone and not just my woman and club. This shit felt personal. They'd come after my woman, planted someone in our midst. It was hard for me to believe Spider was really just going to sit back and let someone else take care of the problem.

"Can I ask you something?" Violeta asked.

"Anything. The only time I won't answer is if it's club business."

"I know I'm not the first woman you've been with, but have you ever wanted to get married before now?"

I turned so that we were facing one another and stared into her eyes, hoping she'd see the truth. No one had ever made me want forever with them until her.

"I've never been in love with a woman before you, never asked someone to marry me, and I damn sure never wanted a kid with anyone else."

"I guess I just don't see what's so special about me."

I cupped her cheek, then kissed her softly. "You're special because you're you. I've never met anyone sweeter, stronger, or sexier than you, Vi. You've been through hell, but you still came out on the other side and were willing to take a chance on a life with me."

"It's not exactly a hardship to be with you," she said, her lips curving up a little. "With this beard." She tugged on it. "These rock-hard abs." Her fingers trailed down my abdomen. "And the cut you wear that declares you're a badass, I'm sure women fall at your feet. You know you're sexy, so don't be stupid, Jesse."

"Don't really give a fuck what any woman thinks about my looks but you. The others were just a diversion, a way to blow off steam. Maybe that makes me an asshole, but I never made them promises. The club whores should know better, even though there are some who are hoping one of us will claim them. Didn't really have a need to pick up a woman anywhere else, not when there were plenty right here willing to do whatever I wanted." I winced. "Guess I shouldn't have confessed quite so much. But I don't want to hide who I am, not from you."

She toyed with my beard, ran her hands down my chest, then smiled at me.

"I know you think you're some horrible man for being with those women, or rather that I'll think you're terrible. But you aren't, Jesse. I don't know too many men who would turn down a willing woman. That's the key part of everything you've said. Willing. You've never forced yourself on a woman, and I know you never would. Despite what you think, you're an honorable man. Do you break the law? Maybe. And maybe some of those laws need to be broken."

I arched an eyebrow. "So you think all drugs should be legal and we should just throw the gun laws out the window? Because that would actually be really bad for business."

"No, but I know you hurt the men who took me. And I'm okay with that. I don't want them to be able to harm another woman or child ever again. If that means you put a bullet in them, I'm all right with that."

I blinked at her, thinking I was either a really lucky bastard to have such an understanding, if slightly bloodthirsty, woman. Or she was only telling me what she thought I wanted to hear.

"Jesse, did you forget that I grew up in the mafia? All the things your club does isn't new to me. The difference is that you try not to hurt innocent people, and my father and his men thrived on destroying defenseless people. You're not a monster."

My throat was a little tight, but I refused to acknowledge that she damn near made me cry with how accepting she was of my way of life, or that she thought I was a good, honorable man. No one had called me that. I'd always been the bad boy moms warned their daughters to avoid. Even in my younger years, the good girls wanted me but not for anything more than bragging rights. Then there was my sweet Vi, who looked at me like I could take on the world and win, like I was her hero.

She made me want to be a better man. Whatever it took, I vowed I'd keep her safe, and any kids we had. Anyone who came after my family would die a painful death, and I'd use them as a warning to anyone else who thought to come for my woman.

Chapter Nine

Violeta

Rocket hadn't lied. I was sore, but in the best of ways. I couldn't help but smile as I thought about the last twelve hours or so. I honestly didn't even know what time it was, only that he'd spent all of yesterday and through the night making me scream his name. If someone had told me a year or two ago that I would be this happy, I'd have called them a liar. And I'd have been wrong.

Rocket had rolled out of bed this morning, muttered something about food, then quickly dressed and grabbed his keys. I'd assumed he was going to get something and bring it back, but he'd been gone for a while. Since I didn't know when he'd return, I took a shower, taking the time to wash and condition my hair, then shaved my legs and underarms. By the time I got out and dressed, he still hadn't come back, which was making me worry.

I made some coffee and sipped a cup, keeping an eye on the kitchen clock. Ten minutes went by. Then another ten. After thirty minutes had passed, I knew something had to be wrong, unless Spider had called Church and Rocket just hadn't let me know. I reached for the phone, then paused. I hated to bother my sister in case my niece was sleeping. I knew the phone could wake Marianna. If the men were in Church, then someone at the clubhouse would know something. There were always Prospects hanging around in case the members needed anything.

It only took me a minute to slip on a pair of shoes and start walking to the clubhouse. The compound was eerily silent as I made my way down the road. There weren't city blocks set up inside, but it felt like the clubhouse was roughly a mile from Rocket's home. I didn't see a single member or Prospect, nor did I hear any bikes. Where was everyone? As I neared the front gates, I saw far more bikes than were typically parked in the area and only one Prospect who appeared to be on guard duty. The bikes didn't just line the clubhouse, but they wrapped around the sides and some were double-parked.

Unease settled in the pit of my stomach making it bubble and flip. Something was wrong. Really wrong. Rocket hadn't said anything about expecting another club, and after everything we'd discussed all night, I knew he'd have said something if he knew. What the hell was going on? Was there a party? I was starting to wish I'd called Luciana before I made the hasty decision to come here.

Making my way up the steps, I pushed the doors open and stepped inside. I saw cuts from two clubs I hadn't met before, and more than one pissed-off look was thrown my way. I rubbed my hands on the ass of my denim shorts, and wished I'd put on something else. When I'd gotten dressed, I hadn't intended to leave the house. I tried to wear more out in public than I currently had on, and the way a few of the men looked at me made my skin crawl.

Teller came from behind the bar and hurried toward me, gripping my arm and tugging me into the shadows.

"What are you doing here?" he asked.

"I was looking for Rocket. He left this morning to get breakfast and he's not back yet. I thought maybe Spider had called Church, and I was going to wait here for him." I looked around again. "What's going on, Teller?"

"Wait. Rocket isn't with you?"

"No. I thought maybe he was here. Are you saying no one knows where he is?" I asked, feeling panic start to well inside me. If they thought he was with me, and I didn't know where he was, what had happened to him?

Spider came through the crowd and frowned when he saw me and Teller in the corner of the room. He stopped to talk to a few men as he made his way over to us. Then he folded his arms and stared at me.

"Rocket's missing," I said, and damn near broke down just saying the words. I felt the tears well up and couldn't hold them back. "He went for breakfast and didn't come back. I thought he was here."

Spider's back went ramrod straight and he held Teller's gaze a moment before turning to face the room. He cupped his hands around his mouth to project his voice, then yelled out, "Anyone seen Rocket today?"

The Hades Abyss members shook their heads and looked at me uneasily. If they hadn't seen him, who had let him out of the compound? How did he leave with no one knowing he was even gone?

"Spider, what's going on?" I asked. "Where's Rocket?"

He looked at Teller again. "Philip is on the gate. Go find out when Rocket left and which way he went."

"He was just getting breakfast," I said again, hoping if I repeated it enough that maybe Rocket would magically return with bags of food, and without a scratch on him.

Spider put his arm around my shoulders and pulled me against his side. I grabbed onto him, fearing that if I didn't, my legs would buckle. Had the club who'd taken me seen Rocket and decided to get revenge? Was he hurt somewhere? Maybe even dead? I didn't want to think about living without him. He was my everything.

Two of the men wearing different cuts made their way over to us, distrust in their eyes as they looked at me. I didn't know who they were, or why they were here, but they made me nervous. They appeared hard, cold, and didn't seem like the type of men to care for the tears currently slipping down my cheeks.

"What's going on?" one of them asked. I read the stitching on his cut. *Crow. Reckless Kings MC.*

The other man was even more intimidating as he gazed at me. His cut said he was the President of Devil's Fury MC. I hadn't heard of either club before and didn't know why they were here. Had they done something to Rocket? Were they allies of the Hades Abyss or did they intend to harm my newfound family?

"Crow. Grizzly. This is Rocket's old lady, Violeta. She said he went to get breakfast for them and never returned."

The younger one, Crow, studied me. "Is she part of the trouble we were told about?"

I tried not to wince. They made it sound like I'd caused the problem with the Chaos Killers, even though I hadn't. Yes, because they'd kidnapped me, Rocket had hurt them, but that was their own damn fault. Rocket hadn't gone looking for danger, not until I'd been taken. Now I didn't know what he was thinking, other than he wanted them all wiped from the face of the earth.

"The Chaos Killers abducted Violeta when she and Rocket were celebrating at a nearby hotel. The men who took her were killed once we located Violeta. It's the same crew who shot me earlier this year. I'm not quite sure what put us in their crosshairs, but I'm ready to end it," Spider said. "At first, I'd thought they were just after our business or the cargo we were carrying that day. Now it seems like something else is going on. That's why I called the Devil's Boneyard and Dixie Reapers, and in turn they called you."

"Could Surge find him with his computer?" I asked. "Maybe there's a way to track Rocket?"

Crow rubbed a hand along his jaw. "If he has a cell phone with him and the GPS is turned on, it's possible he could be tracked that way. Then again, if he found trouble when he left here, he may not have a phone with him anymore. Wouldn't hurt to try and see what Surge can find."

"I brought Outlaw with me," Grizzly said. "He can help Surge. Between the two of them, they should be able to figure out something, or at least give us a direction."

Spider's arm tightened around me. "Sweetheart, I don't think you should stay at the clubhouse. This crew might get rowdy in a few more hours. If anything happened to you, Rocket would be ready to take some heads and kick everyone's ass. Not to mention Luciana wouldn't be too happy either."

"Your wife?" Grizzly asked.

Spider nodded. "Violeta is my wife's younger sister. The baby of the family. Their other sister, Sofia, is with Saint at the Dixie Reapers' compound."

Understanding lit Grizzly's eyes. "The girls who Casper saved from Mateo Gomez in Colombia. We heard about them, but until now I didn't realize they'd been claimed by any of the clubs. I only knew you were watching over them."

"What is with all of you taking in strays?" Crow asked. "The Devil's Boneyard and Devil's Fury both have rescues from human trafficking at their compounds, or did until the women were settled elsewhere. Except the ones you decided to keep for whatever reason, like Cinder's wife."

My back stiffened and I glared at the man. Beautiful or not, scary or not, he was an asshole. "I don't like you much."

He arched an eyebrow and stared at me.

"You're an asshole. I'm not a stray, and neither are my sisters," I said.

Grizzly chuckled, but Crow didn't look too amused.

"Stop being a dickhead," Grizzly told him. "You know damn well that you'd have taken them in too if someone had asked. Your club helped Meg, and you'd take in any other woman who was in distress."

"Women are too much fucking trouble," Crow muttered.

I leaned a little heavier against Spider and studied the men in front of me. Grizzly seemed like a good enough sort, now that I'd gotten over my fear as he'd approached, but there was a sadness in his eyes. Crow, though, was brimming with anger, and I had to wonder if a woman had recently hurt him in some way.

"I'll get Outlaw and send him to Surge's place," Grizzly said. "And, sweetheart, Spider is right. This clubhouse isn't going to be the right place for you once these guys start letting loose. Your man would want you somewhere safe. I'd trust my brothers with my life, but once they start drinking or women show up, then they tend to act a bit stupid."

"If you're Rocket's old lady, where's your property cut?" Crow asked.

"I didn't get it out of the closet. I was just worried about Rocket and didn't really think past the fact I had on clothes and needed my shoes. He's been gone probably an hour or more. I know a half hour passed while I sat in the kitchen waiting for him, but I don't know how long he was gone before that."

"I'll get Teller to walk you home and stay with you," Spider said. "He'll keep you safe until we figure out what's going on with Rocket. Don't leave the house, Violeta. Not even to come here or go anywhere else in the compound. Those bastards got someone inside our gates once and they could do it again. Surge has done his best to make sure the other Prospects are legit and haven't been turned, but I can't say for certain that I trust them."

"But you'll send one home with her?" Grizzly asked.

"Teller is my friend," I said softly. "He'd never hurt me."

Crow snorted. "Honey, there are a lot of reasons a man would turn on those who trust him. And if you aren't his woman, then I don't see him being loyal to you if a better opportunity presents itself."

"Teller's a good kid," Spider said. "I thought the same of Marcus, but he got in over his head. I haven't decided yet what I'll do with him whenever he's found. But I'd trust Teller with Violeta or my wife. He'll defend them with his life if need be."

Crow glanced out over the crowded room. "You going to tell anyone else what's going on?"

"Not until I know more," Spider said. "Depending on what Rocket's gotten himself into, I may need the help of both your clubs. No sense riling everyone up until we have more details, though."

"Forge is here somewhere," Crow said. "He'd be your best bet from my club as far as getting your brother back. Maybe he could coordinate with Bear. I didn't bring Shield, but they could always call him if they need more help with the computer shit."

"I brought Demon with me," Grizzly said. "With three Sergeants-at-Arms and two Presidents, we'll find your man and bring him home."

Teller came back inside, a frown tipping his lips down at the corners. When his gaze met mine, I knew it wasn't good news. I waited, hoping I was wrong, but the first words out of his mouth weren't exactly reassuring.

"Philip said that Rocket left nearly two hours ago. He didn't say where he was going or when he'd be back." He hesitated. "He didn't head toward town. Philip said Rocket pulled out and went the opposite direction. Toward the highway."

What? Why would he do that? If he was just getting food, he wouldn't have gone to another town, would he? I looked up at Spider and saw resignation there. My stomach knotted and my skin turned clammy. I broke free and hurried toward the front doors, barely reaching the edge of the porch before I threw up until all I could do was dry heave.

He'd left me. Rocket had left and lied when he'd walked out this morning. He'd promised to love me, to protect me, and now he'd abandoned me? I didn't understand. Had everything been a lie? Or had he gotten a message that made him leave the way he had?

I felt a hand run up and down my back and looked over at Teller. I broke down and cried again, curling against him as he held me. I wanted Rocket. I couldn't remember even being this scared and worried when the Chaos Killers had taken me. If Philip was right, and Rocket hadn't gone into town, then it was doubtful someone had taken him. He'd gone voluntarily. I just didn't understand his motivation for leaving.

"We'll find him, Vi," Teller said. "I don't know where he went or why, but I'm sure he had his reasons. Anyone with eyes can see how much he loves you."

"He left," I said, my voice cracking. "He left me."

"Take her home," Spider said from behind Teller. "I'll send Dread over to check her out, maybe give her something to calm her stomach."

"Come on, Vi," Teller said, leading me toward the steps. "We'll binge-watch all those eighties movies you like, and I bet Rocket is back soon."

I let him walk with me to the house, then sat on the couch while he turned on a movie. I got up and went to the bathroom to rinse out my mouth and brush my teeth, splashed some water on my face, and tried to pull myself together. Rocket was always saying how strong I was, but I wasn't acting like it right now. For him, I needed to believe that everything would be fine.

When I got back to the living room, Dread was waiting for me. He folded his arms and looked me over from head to toe, then dropped a bomb on me.

"When was your last period?"

I blinked, glanced at Teller who had just turned three shades of red, then focused on Dread again. I tried to remember when I'd last needed tampons, and I knew it was at least a week or two before Rocket had asked me to marry him. Possibly longer. I never really kept track. The cramps usually hit about two days before I started to bleed so I had enough warning to get supplies.

"At least three or four weeks? Possibly five. I don't really remember for sure," I said.

"Has Rocket been using condoms?" Dread asked.

"No. He said he wants to have kids with me," I said. "Do you think I'm pregnant? Because I think I threw up from the stress of Rocket being missing. I doubt I'm already carrying a baby. We've only had two nights together with everything else going on."

Dread smiled faintly. "It only takes once. You could very well have conceived the night you stayed at the hotel with him."

He reached behind him and pulled out a small white box, then handed it to me. A pregnancy test. Then the humor of him carrying that around in his back pocket hit me and I smiled.

"Do you keep these on hand for a reason? Make all your dates pee on a stick?"

He scowled at me. "No. Once Rocket claimed you, I bought a few of those to have on hand just in case. Spider can't have kids, so I didn't have to worry about it with Luciana. Although, maybe I should start testing the club whores randomly. The last thing we need is that kind of surprise. I think it's time to dump the bowl of condoms in the clubhouse too and get a fresh batch. Who knows how old those are."

"I'll take care of it once Rocket's back," Teller said. "Spider wants me to stay with Violeta for now."

Dread nodded.

"Fine. I'll take the test, but I don't think I'm pregnant."

I stood and snatched the box from him, then went to the bathroom, trying not to think about the fact there were two men in the living room who knew I was peeing on a stick. Men who weren't my fiancé. If anyone should be here for this, it was Rocket.

I read the instructions before taking the test. When I finished, I set the test on the counter, then flushed the toilet and washed my hands. While I waited the three minutes, I changed the sheets on the bed and picked up Rocket's dirty clothes, tossing them into the hamper. By the time I'd picked up the laundry from the floor, I realized my hands were trembling. Looking into the bathroom at the little white stick, I had to admit I was scared. Having Rocket's baby would be amazing, if I was sure he'd return to me. Slowly, I approached the counter, holding my breath as I stared at the little test.

Positive.

Holy shit.

I pressed a hand to my belly and closed my eyes a moment. It seemed Rocket had gotten his wish. We were going to have a baby, which meant it was even more imperative that we find him. I wasn't raising this kid on my own, having to explain their daddy vanished one morning. I had no doubt that Spider would watch over us, let us stay in this house, but I wanted the man I loved to be by my side through the pregnancy, and help raise our child. I wanted Rocket.

Walking back to the living room, I faced Dread and Teller. "You were right. I'm pregnant. I still don't think that's why I threw up, though."

"Maybe not, but at least we now know. I'll pick up some prenatal vitamins for you and make sure a healthy breakfast and lunch are delivered," Dread said. "And as much as I know this is an impossible thing to ask you right now, you need to be as stress-free as possible, and even if you don't have an appetite you need to eat. Your sister lost her baby because she'd thought Spider was dead, and it's possible your previous miscarriage was also due to stress. For the sake of your baby, I need you to calm down."

I nodded, knowing he was right. It wouldn't be easy, but I'd try. The thought of losing Rocket's child made my heart ache.

"I'll do whatever I need to, just please bring him back to me," I said.

"We'll find out where he is, then we'll go after him," Dread said. "If you need anything, let Teller know. Even though he needs to stay here with you, he can contact one of the other Prospects."

"Spider doesn't trust them," I said.

"Then call me or Spider. If you can't reach us, just work your way down the list of every patched member in the club. Someone will get whatever you need," Dread said.

"I'll take care of her," Teller said. "But if Rocket was going out for food, that means she hasn't eaten and will definitely need the meals you mentioned."

"I'll grab breakfast when I pick up the vitamins," Dread said. "I'll be back in a half hour. Lock the door and keep the other Prospects out. If Spider doesn't know that he can trust them, then I don't want them near Violeta, and I know Rocket wouldn't either."

"No one is getting to her while I'm here," Teller said.

I didn't want to point out that we'd been hit with some sort of dart previously when we'd been together in the living room. I just wanted all of it to be over. If Rocket had gone after the Chaos Killers, then I hoped his brothers found him before he got himself killed. Either way, the other club needed to be stopped. I only prayed that I didn't lose Rocket in the process.

Chapter Ten

Rocket

I'd lied to her. Lied to the woman I loved, the one I wanted to marry. She was probably scared out of her damn mind, or pissed as fuck that I'd vanished, but I needed to handle this. Spider meant well, but this wasn't the type of thing you handed off to someone else, even if it was Specter who promised to remove the threat. The Chaos Killers had come after my woman, and I wanted to make damn sure every last one of them was dead. My computer skills weren't anywhere near as good as Surge's, but I'd managed to track down the nearest Chaos Killers, and I was going to take the fuckers out. I might not have Spider's military background, but I had street smarts that had served me well, not to mention every trick I'd learned while handling club business over the years. But I needed to handle this shit before my club figured out what I was doing. I had no doubt Spider would rip into me when he found out.

I'd already wiped out one nest of the assholes, and a nest was the only term I could think that suited them. They were like fucking poisonous snakes or rabid sewer rats, and I was going to exterminate them. The second hideout was a few yards from where I was hiding in the trees and shrubs, watching for any patterns so I could make my move. When I realized they left the back door vulnerable every fifteen minutes, I waited until the coast was clear, then ran to the building.

There were two nine millimeter handguns at my waist, extra clips in my pockets, a large knife at the small of my back, another knife in my boot, and two sets of throwing knives attached to my belt. I'd come prepared, and had plenty of ammo stashed in my saddlebags on the bike. I might not be able to take out every Chapter, but I could at least get rid of the problems closest to my woman. From what I could see, the bastards I'd hit this morning and this group were Nomads and didn't have allegiance to a particular Chapter of the Chaos Killers, which meant it was possible they wouldn't be missed for a bit. Vi should feel safe in her own home. The fact she didn't pissed me off and I was going to make these fuckers pay.

I slipped up behind one of them, placed my hand over his mouth and held tight as he struggled. With one smooth swipe, I used one of my knives to slice his throat. He gurgled, and once he stopped fighting to break free, I let his body slump to the floor. His sightless eyes were staring at the ceiling and I sneered down at him. I hauled my foot back and kicked the asshole in the ribs, not that he could feel it. One down, five more to go. Unless there were a few I hadn't seen during my surveillance.

As much as I wanted to make them suffer, to draw things out, I knew that wouldn't be wise. I didn't have backup, and if they figured out someone was taking them down, then it would be harder to kill them all. I'd taken down two more, slitting their throats and stabbing them through the heart, before someone realized what was happening. Unfortunately, there weren't three left. There were six, and they were actively searching for me.

The building didn't offer much in the way of places to hide, so I blended with the shadows as best I could and bided my time. I picked them off one at a time, using my knives so I could move silently and not give away my location, until I was down to two who had partnered up, apparently smarter than the rest.

Not that the safety in numbers shit was going to help them. I pulled one of my guns, and when the perfect opportunity presented itself, I put a bullet between their eyes. After I made sure the building was clear, I checked the next location and got back on my bike. Knowing that Surge would try to track me once it was discovered I'd gone missing, I'd shut off my GPS. Didn't mean someone hadn't planted a tracker on my bike, but since no one had tried to stop me yet, I didn't think that was likely.

I got to the third location within twenty minutes, and had to wonder why there were so many of them so close together. From what I could tell, they looked like temporary setups, something that had happened over past few months. Until they'd shot Spider, none of us had given them much thought, but I was wishing that we had. It was one thing to gather the Chapters, but none of these were part of a particular Chapter, and they were all spread out. Each location had been fifteen to twenty minutes from the previous one. There was a bad feeling in my gut that said I was missing something huge. It wasn't until I'd observed the third spot that I realized what was going on. The Nomads were gathering women and young girls. Three were dragged into the building, bound and gagged. My heart hammered in my chest, and I knew there was no fucking way I could get in there and take out the fuckers without risking them killing every innocent they'd snatched.

"Your Pres isn't going to be very happy with you," said a voice from behind me.

I spun, my gun in my hand before I'd even thought about drawing it. The man who came out of the shadows was dressed all in black, but it was the ink that drew my attention. When I lifted my gaze to his, I knew that I was well and truly fucked. If there was one thing I knew, it was don't piss off certain men. You don't piss off your Pres, you don't piss off another club's Pres without expecting retaliations, and you sure the fuck don't piss off Casper VanHorne or Specter.

"Thought you were busy with personal shit," I said.

Casper shrugged. "I was going to deal with my wife, something I've needed to handle for a while. Then I got a call from Specter saying someone was looking into the Chaos Killers in this area. Decided to check it out, and what do I find? You, fucking shit up."

"Am I supposed to sit on my ass while my woman is in danger? Or while they're in danger?" I asked, pointing to the women and girls now disappearing into the building. "I'm sorry, but I'm not wired that way."

"You can't take out that building on your own," Casper said. "It's not some falling-down shack like the last two places you hit, which I'm having cleaned up. Thanks for the extra work. You made a fucking mess."

"They deserved worse."

Casper shrugged. "These men are bad, but there are worse monsters out there. At least the Chaos Killers don't hide their true faces, they aren't like the men and women who place the bids that torture the victims, or those who purchase them after. They aren't hiding behind computers and false accounts. I'd rather face a monster that doesn't try to pass itself as a human."

I could understand that. Didn't mean that I wasn't going to find a way into that building and remove the threat. I watched, trying to figure out if they had security other than the armed men. I didn't notice cameras on the outside of the building, but that didn't mean they weren't discreet.

"If you're determined to do this, you're going to need help," Casper said.

I eyed him. "Aren't you getting a little old for this?"

He arched an eyebrow and just stared. It was the most unnerving look I'd ever received and I was wishing I'd kept my fucking mouth shut. I'd heard about VanHorne and what he was capable of, but I also knew he was getting older. Not that age seemed to be slowing Spider. Once a badass always a badass.

"You want help or not, boy?" he asked.

"I want my woman to feel safe," I said.

He nodded. "Then sit and wait. I have backup coming and they'll be here in about fifteen minutes. No way to get those women and girls out with just two of us. The second we make a move, they'll be in danger."

I could wait fifteen minutes. I'd wait longer if it meant these fuckers wouldn't be walking out of here or hurting anyone ever again. As the minutes ticked by, I studied the structure from every angle, quietly walking through the wooded area so I could see how many armed men were outside and if they had any patterns they followed. When I made my way back to Casper, I froze and stared at the men standing with him. Their cuts didn't have any words, other than their names. But the colors stitched to both the front and back told me enough.

"They're here to help," Casper said. "If you still intend to do this, you aren't going it alone. Or…"

"Or what?" I asked.

"You can go home to Violeta and let us take out the trash. Specter already has his pawns in place to hit the Chaos Killers full force, and the Devil's Boneyard are going to extract the girl your club promised to save."

"I owe it to her to take them out, to end their reign of terror. The women and children they've taken deserved justice," I said.

"And Violeta deserves to have the man she loves return to her in one piece," he said softly. "Go home to your fiancée. We can handle these men while Specter takes care of the rest. You've done your share, Rocket. Let someone else step in now."

I glanced at the men standing with him, then looked at the building again. He was right. If I went in there and didn't come back out, then Violeta would be alone, and she'd never forgive me. I couldn't do that to her, couldn't leave her forever. Rubbing the back of my neck, I knew that VanHorne was right. I needed to step back and let someone else finish what I'd started today.

"You have my word that none will survive," Casper said.

"You've done your part," said one of the men, his voice scratchy like he'd smoked a pack a day for years. "Now let us do ours."

I nodded and stared at them a moment, then walked to where I'd stashed my bike. I turned my GPS back on before sending Surge a message that I was on my way home, then set my phone to do-not-disturb mode. They could track me if they needed to, but I wasn't ready to talk just yet. I knew I was in for the ass-chewing of a lifetime, but I wouldn't change a damn thing. Well, except scaring Vi. I had no doubt that she'd been terrified, and I felt like a complete dick for doing that to her, but if I'd told her what I planned she'd have tried to talk me out of it.

I was about fifteen minutes from town when I picked up an escort. Knox and Yankee flanked me, but I heard others behind me. When I pulled through the compound gates, I stopped my bike but didn't turn it off. Yankee glared and even Knox looked pissed the fuck off.

"The Pres would like a word with you," Yankee said. "Several in fact."

"I need to see Vi and let her know I'm all right."

"She's taken care of," Knox said. "Teller is with her, and Dread has been trying to force-feed her. She was so fucking worried about you that she came to the clubhouse, then ended up puking when she realized you were missing and no one knew where the fuck you were."

I winced and an ache started in my chest. I'd fucked up, I could admit that, but I'd done what I thought was right.

"Where's Spider?" I asked.

"In his office at the clubhouse," Knox said.

I pulled over to the clubhouse and parked my bike, then went inside. I saw that we'd gained a few guests since I'd been gone. Despite the fact I wanted to go straight home to see Vi, I made myself walk back to Spider's office, wondering if I'd be tossed from the club or if he'd let me stay for Vi's sake if nothing else. I knew I shouldn't have taken off the way I had, but I'd do it again in a heartbeat if it meant that Vi would be safe, along with all the other women those bastards had stolen and abused.

Knocking on Spider's door, I didn't wait before pushing it open and stepping inside, then pulled it shut behind me.

"Congratulations, you're a fuck-up," Spider said.

"I know I shouldn't have left like that, but it felt wrong asking someone else to take care of the problem. They hurt Violeta, could have killed her."

He nodded. "Yes, they could have, and you made those men pay. It wasn't necessary for you to take off after the others. Casper wanted you to know the third location was handled and the women and kids were safe."

Spider went quiet after that, just watching me. His silence was scarier than if he'd started yelling and cussing at me. I tried to wait him out, but I needed to know where I stood.

"Do I need to turn in my cut and leave?" I asked.

"No. But I do need to make an example of you so someone else doesn't try this shit. Tossing you from the club would only hurt Violeta, and Luciana. Besides, you have responsibilities at home. Can't have you drifting out there with no purpose or way to earn money."

"Responsibilities? If you mean Vi, then I already know I fucked up. I didn't want to scare her, but I felt like I needed to handle this."

Spider leaned back in his chair, making the leather creak. "I'm not going to demand your patch, but I'm going to cut your share of the profits for the next three months while you prove you can follow orders. However, that being said, your woman needs medical attention you can't afford it, send her to me. I'm not going to have her suffer for your stupidity."

"How much of a cut?" I asked.

"I'm going to cut your share by thirty percent. I'd slash more than that, but I don't want Violeta to suffer as well. While I don't mind covering medical expenses, anything else she needs will still be your responsibility. After three months, if you haven't fucked up and I think I can trust you to do as you're told, then I'll give your full share to you moving forward." Spider put his hands behind his head. "I understand why you did it, Rocket, but it doesn't make it right. You scared the shit out of your woman, and had all of us scrambling to find you when we could have focused our efforts elsewhere. It was a selfish, shitty thing to do. I expect better from you."

"Sorry, Pres. I know I fucked up, but it was something I felt needed to be done. I'll take the punishment without complaint, but I'd really like to go see Vi now."

He nodded. "You do that. Be careful with her, Rocket. I know you think she's strong, and in some ways, she is, but I watched that girl break today when she thought something had happened to you."

I swallowed hard and left, not stopping to say hi to anyone. I needed to get home, see my woman, and assure her that I was fine, and that I wouldn't pull this shit ever again. No matter how much I wanted vengeance or to wipe out any threat to her, I'd handle it in a way that wouldn't worry her. Or at least, in a way that allowed her to know where I was.

My house was quiet when I pulled into the driveway and I saw Dread's bike, as well as Fox's. The fact the club doctor and the VP were here made my gut clench. Had something happened to Vi and Spider just hadn't told me? He'd said that I'd scared her. Was there more to it than that? I hurried inside and stopped in the doorway to the living room.

Vi was stretched out on her side, her head in Teller's lap while he smoothed his hand over her hair. Even though her eyes were closed, I could tell she'd been crying. Dread and Fox both sent a glare my way, and even Teller didn't look that impressed with me at the moment. I quietly approached and knelt next to the couch, then ran my fingers down Violeta's cheek. Her lashes fluttered, then her eyes opened.

She stared a moment, then tears started slipping down her cheeks as she launched herself into my arms.

I caught her, holding her against my chest, as she cried. Teller got up and joined Fox and Dread on the other side of the room.

"I'm so sorry, baby. I never meant to scare you."

"I thought you were hurt, or dead. I didn't know where you'd gone or why. You just... left. You left me," she said, her voice breaking.

"Never, Vi. I'd never leave you," I promised. "I love you, so fucking much. I'm sorry I was a dumbass and didn't tell you where I was going, or at least that I'd be gone a while."

I glanced over my shoulder at Dread and Fox. "Can I have a minute alone with her?"

"Don't upset her," Dread said. "The stress isn't good for her."

My heart slammed against my ribs as I contemplated what that meant exactly. Was there something wrong with my Vi? I knew stress wasn't good for anyone, but he made it sound like there was something else going on. After they left, and Violeta managed to stop crying, I sat on the couch and held her.

"Something you need to tell me?" I asked.

"You didn't just leave me," she said, then grabbed my hand and placed it on her belly. "You left *us*."

Us? I looked at my hand, then lifted my gaze to hers. Pregnant? Vi was pregnant? "You mean we're having a baby?" I asked.

She nodded. "Dread made me take a test when I threw up earlier, but I still say it was just the stress and fear over you being gone. I'd been fine until then, so I doubt it was morning sickness."

"I'm in a bit of trouble with Spider," I said. "He's cutting the percentage I get from the club by thirty percent for the next three months. At least now I understand why it wasn't worse. He'd said he didn't want you to suffer for my stupidity, but he knows about the baby, doesn't he?"

"Dread told him."

"Casper VanHorne, Specter, and an MC that shall go unnamed right now are taking care of the Chaos Killers. Casper said that the Devil's Boneyard are going after Addie. Not sure if anyone knows where to find Marcus, or if he's even still alive," I said. "But you're safe. At least, from the Chaos Killers. I can't promise my way of life won't bring more trouble to the door later."

"Then we'll face it together. Right?" she asked, staring at me expectantly.

"Right. No more lies about where I'm going. I won't keep you in the dark about anything, unless Spider says otherwise. If the Pres says not to tell you, then I won't. I've fucked up enough already." I ran my hand up and down her thigh. "Any special instructions for this pregnancy? Things you aren't supposed to eat, drink? Things you can't do?"

She stared at me. "Is that your way of asking if we can still have sex?"

I shrugged a shoulder. "Maybe."

"You're such a guy. Is sex all you think about?" she asked, her eyes flashing with amusement.

I rubbed my hand against my beard. "Well, when it comes to you? Pretty much. Even when I shouldn't have been thinking of you that way, my dick still got hard. Then I hated myself for it, but now you're my fiancée. I figure I'm allowed to think about you naked every few minutes."

"Dread didn't say anything about not having sex. He's concerned that if I get overly anxious that I could miscarry, since I couldn't carry a pregnancy to term before, and with Luciana miscarrying not that long ago... Well, he just wants to make sure everything turns out all right."

"She can have sex," Dread said from the doorway. "Just take it easy. If there's any spotting or all out bleeding, then take her to the ER. I loaded your fridge and cabinets with healthy food and drinks for her. It would be a good idea for her to cut out caffeine completely. I also set an appointment for her with an OB-GYN in town, someone I trust to treat her right and not fuck up anything. I put the card on your fridge. Spider arranged for the club to be billed for any visits for the next few months."

"We're heading out and taking Teller with us," Fox said. "Until we get word that Addie is safe, Marcus has been located, and the Chaos Killers have been eliminated, we're going to do routine patrols by your house. Not taking any chances."

"Thanks." I hesitated. "And thank you for taking care of her today while I was gone."

"She's family," Fox said. "Simple as that. You do something stupid that keeps you from coming home one day, we'll watch over her and your kid. But you should probably curb that desire to run off and do shit you know will piss off Spider. Just sayin'."

The *dumbass* was implied and I deserved it. After the front door shut and we had the house to ourselves, I lifted Vi into my arms and carried her back to our bedroom. The sheets on the bed were different from the ones this morning, and I noticed none of my dirty clothes were lying around the room. I was admittedly a bit of a slob, and Vi seemed to only handle the mess for so many days before she picked it up. I'd have to do better while she was pregnant. The last thing she needed was to clean up my messes.

I shut the bedroom door and let her slide down my body until her feet touched the floor. As much as I wanted to make this last, to worship every inch of her body, I didn't think I could manage slow and easy right now. I'd be careful with her, but I was also aware that the second I felt her pussy around my cock, I'd lose what little sense I had left. I couldn't seem to resist her.

"Clothes. Off." She smiled softly as she started removing them, and I shed my own in record time.

When we were both naked, I kissed her hard, gripping her hair with one hand and her hip with the other. Her nipples were already hard and brushed against my chest, just upping my desire a few more notches. There wasn't a single thing about Violeta that I didn't love. She wasn't just beautiful on the outside, but she was sweet and loving. She had a beauty that shone from within.

"Love you, Jesse."

"I love you too, baby."

She pulled free of me and backed toward the bed, then stretched out and parted her thighs. Her pussy was already wet and my cock jerked at the sight of her open and ready for me. I stepped closer and ran my hand up her leg, loving the feel of her soft skin against my rough fingers.

I spread the lips of her pussy open wide, then brushed my thumb against her clit. Vi gasped and her body tensed, but her gaze was locked on me. Slowly, I lowered myself to the floor beside the bed and leaned forward. The second my tongue touched her, she moaned and her thighs clamped down on my shoulders.

"Jesse... more. Please."

Holding her open, I tasted and teased, flicking my tongue against her clit before plunging it inside her tight channel. Within minutes, she was coming on my face, and I lapped up every drop. Vi shuddered from the force of her release, and yet she still reached for me, wanting more. I wiped my beard before standing and pulling her ass to the edge of the mattress. As I entered her, I leaned down and claimed her lips. She didn't shy away from tasting herself on my lips and it just made me even harder.

The first few strokes were nice and easy, then the little temptress squeezed her inner muscles and my dick felt like it might explode. I growled softly as I started slamming into her, taking her hard and fast, just the way we both liked it. She came again and the rush of her release coating my cock was enough to trigger my own release. I came so fucking hard I saw stars and felt it leaking out around my dick.

"Fuck me, Vi."

She laughed softly. "No, I believe you did the fucking."

I lightly swatted her hip. "Smart-ass."

Withdrawing from her body, I collapsed on the bed next to her. Then what Dread had said about being careful hit me and I leapt off the bed, spreading her thighs again.

"What are you doing?" she asked, her body shaking with silent laughter.

"Making sure I didn't hurt you. You're not cramping or hurting?"

Her gaze softened and she reached for me. "Jesse, I'm fine, and so is the baby. Lie back down with me."

I crawled back onto the bed and pulled her against me. "One of these days, I'm going to make it last longer. I swear I see you naked and it's like the caveman side of me comes out and I can't seem to hold back."

"I don't recall complaining."

I kissed her forehead. "Maybe you should. You deserve better."

"I deserve better than the man I love? The one who loves me? The father of my unborn baby?" She looked at me. "Is that what you're saying?"

Well, when she put it like that... didn't mean I felt worthy of her. I wouldn't let her go, though. Not now, not ever. Fatigue was pulling at me after the morning I'd had, but I fought to stay awake. I didn't want to miss a moment with Vi. It was still sinking in that we were going to have a kid. I was going to be a daddy, something I'd thought would never happen. Forty was getting a little too close for comfort and I hadn't had a serious woman in my life since high school. I'd figured the family thing just wasn't in the cards for me. It seemed Fate thought otherwise.

I heard my phone chime in the pocket of my discarded jeans and I extracted myself from my fiancée long enough to get it. After pissing off Spider, the last thing I needed to do was ignore a text or call. The message made me smile and a weight lifted from my shoulders.

"The Chaos Killers are gone. If there are any left, they're off the radar. Specter and Casper blew every last one of their clubhouses, if you could even call some of those buildings a clubhouse. Addie was extracted before the chapter in the Florida panhandle was taken down," I told her.

"And Marcus?" she asked.

I pressed my lips together and shook my head. "They found his body. It seems he went after his sister, expecting them to uphold their end of the bargain, and they repaid him with a bullet."

"That's so sad."

"He made his choice and paid the price. It is what it is, darlin'."

We cuddled in the bed a while longer, until her stomach rumbled, then I had the fun experience of attempting to cook something out of the crap Dread had put in the kitchen. What the hell was I supposed to do with asparagus and cauliflower? Looked like Google was about to become my best friend.

Epilogue

Violeta
Four Weeks Later

I smoothed my hands down my dress, then lovingly caressed the property cut I'd put on over it. Once the dust had settled and things had returned somewhat to normal, Rocket had insisted we get married right away. To him, that meant go to Vegas and do it that night. I'd talked him into giving me a few weeks to put together a decent wedding, and he'd conceded.

"You ready?" Luciana asked.

"To marry Rocket?"

She nodded.

"I've been ready since I got over my initial fear and started to realize I liked him more than any other man I'd ever met. And that was before I'd even seen him shirtless."

Luciana snickered.

"Oh, like you're one to talk! You weren't even in Spider's house one day before you offered to be his woman, and don't even tell me that by the time you went to bed that night it was only about being safe. He rocked your world and you wanted more."

She stuck out her tongue.

"I thought you were the eldest sister?"

I turned to the voice behind me and smiled at Charlotte. The Reckless Kings were passing through and heard about my wedding, so of course they'd crashed it, and brought Charlotte with them. She was the baby sister to Brick, one of their patched members, and I already knew we'd be good friends.

"Only by age," I said. "The longer she's around the Hades Abyss members, the more childish she acts."

There was a knock at the door and Dread poked his head into the room. "If you don't hurry up, Rocket is going to come in here and get you."

"I'm ready," I told him.

I stepped into the hall and Spider was waiting for me. I'd asked him to walk me down the aisle, and he'd accepted. Even if my father had been alive, I would have never wanted him here. As we neared the main part of the clubhouse, I heard a violin start playing. The moment I'd searched for a band or pianist, I'd been informed that Knox played the violin, and he'd offered to play at the wedding.

Rocket was waiting, along with Bear, who had gotten an online certification to officiate weddings. He looked amazing. Even though he wore his cut, he'd purchased a button-down shirt that was charcoal with lighter gray striping. He'd paired it with his dark-wash jeans and his Harley Davidson boots, but just looking at him made my knees weak and my heart race.

Spider handed me off to Rocket, and the moment our hands touched, I felt a flutter of excitement. Even though he'd claimed me, I would officially be his wife after today. I couldn't wait to share his name. Violeta Jones. Bear had promised to only use Rocket's club name during the ceremony, but the marriage certificate would have his real name on it.

Bear cleared his throat and I felt my cheeks warm.

"What?" I asked, and everyone in the room chuckled.

"It's the part where you say I do," whispered Rocket with a smile.

"Oh. Oh! I do. I definitely do!"

That drew another laugh from our friends and family, but I didn't care. When our vows were over and we both wore matching wedding bands, my heart felt so full that I thought it might burst. Rocket kissed me softly, our first kiss as man and wife.

"Love you, Vi."

"Love you more."

He grinned, then scooped me into his arms and started toward the front door of the clubhouse. Spider's hand clamped down on his shoulder. "Where the hell do you think you're going?" Spider asked.

"Uh…" He looked uncertain. "Home?"

"Nope," Spider said. "You're staying for the reception, and when you leave, you'll be going on your honeymoon."

"Honeymoon?" I asked. "We didn't book one."

"No, but I did," Luciana said. "You have three nights at the best hotel in St. Louis, and dinner reservations for tomorrow night. Anything else will be up to you. If you want to sightsee, then you can."

"And when do we check-in?" Rocket asked, not sounding the least bit excited.

"Tonight," Spider said.

I looked up at my husband. "We don't have to go."

He opened his mouth to respond, but Luciana interrupted him.

"Yes, you do. Violeta, you haven't seen any of this country except for the one trip down to Alabama when we were in trouble. It's not right that you're caged here and don't go out and have fun."

Rocket's jaw snapped shut and he gazed down at me. "She's right. We'll go after we've visited with everyone."

"And opened presents," Charlotte said, grinning as she wormed her way between Spider and Rocket. "We brought gifts!"

Rocket sighed, then kissed me softly. "Well, wife, it looks like we're entertaining this crew for a while longer. Then we're going on a short honeymoon. And when we get back, you can pick a room for the nursery and we'll go shopping."

I smiled and reached up to tug on his beard. He'd let it grow out again, and he'd also been asking me for weeks where I wanted to put the nursery. I hadn't given him an answer yet, mostly because I was scared that I'd set up the room, then lose our baby. Keeping that thought to myself hadn't been easy, but I didn't want him to worry.

Rocket carried me over to a table decorated with ribbons and flowers. He sat, then placed me in his lap even though there was a perfectly good chair next to him. As we opened the first present together, I realized that I had everything I could ever want. The love of a man who adored me, a baby we'd created together, and a family who meant everything to me, whether we were related by blood or not.

When I'd come to the Hades Abyss, I'd thought I would be tortured, maybe even killed eventually. Instead, I'd healed emotionally and physically, grown stronger and more confident. And I'd found love. Recent events had proven something to me, though. While I was safe, protected, and cared for, there were other women out there who weren't so lucky. Women who had the misfortune of attracting the attention of the wrong sort, or trusting someone they shouldn't.

"Jesse," I said softly, hoping no one heard me use his name.

"Yeah, Vi?"

"When we come back, do you think I could talk to Surge about the other women the Chaos Killers took?"

His brow furrowed. "Why?"

"I want to help them. I don't know how, or if there's anything I can do, but maybe if they see how happy I am with you, then it will give them hope. Casper VanHorne might have brought me here, but it was you who saved me. Now I want to save them."

He nodded. "We'll figure something out. Right now, we need to open presents and cut that ridiculously tall pink-and-white cake. What the hell, Vi? It looks like a flamingo threw up on that thing."

I threw back my head and laughed, knowing that he wasn't wrong. It hadn't turned out quite the way I'd imagined, but then nothing in our lives ever seemed to go according to plan. And I was learning to love it.

I'd found my happily-ever-after, and now I wanted everyone else to have one. My gaze slid over to Charlotte, who was talking to Teller, her hands waving as she explained something to him. Then I noticed the way both her brother, Brick, and the Reckless Kings' President, Beast, were watching her. Brick looked ready to rip off poor Teller's head, but Beast... that wasn't brotherly concern on his face. If I didn't miss my guess, he was jealous.

I smiled, wondering just how much of a nudge she would need in his direction, and whether or not he'd act on his feelings. Only time would tell.

From Harley

Thank you for reading *Saint/Rocket Duet*! Whether you're a new Harley Wylde reader or you've been with me from the beginning, I appreciate your support. If you have a moment to leave a review at BookBub, Goodreads, or one of the retailers, that would be awesome.

Dedication: Some women are lucky enough to marry their soul mate. I got that and so much more. My husband is supportive of my writing, encourages me when I get frustrated, and believes in me even when I don't believe in myself. So thank you, to the man who keeps me going even when I'd rather curl up with a book and read.

I'd also like to thank my readers. You guys are so amazing! I can't tell you how much I appreciate you. There are millions of books out there, but you chose to read mine. Sending you lots of hugs!

And last, but not least, thank you to the owners, editors, and proofreaders at Changeling Press! You guys keep me from getting too crazy with the storylines, then polish the mess I send you so that it shines. I'd also like to say a huge thank-you to Bryan Keller, the cover artist for the Bad Boy Romance Multiverse. You always give me the perfect cover for each story.

Thank you again for taking a chance on my books!

Harley

Harley Wylde

Harley Wylde is the International Bestselling Author of the Dixie Reapers MC, Devil's Boneyard MC, and Hades Abyss MC series.

When Harley's writing, her motto is the hotter the better -- off the charts sex, commanding men, and the women who can't deny them. If you want men who talk dirty, are sexy as hell, and take what they want, then you've come to the right place. She doesn't shy away from the dangers and nastiness in the world, bringing those realities to the pages of her books, but always gives her characters a happily-ever-after and makes sure the bad guys get what they deserve.

The times Harley isn't writing, she's thinking up naughty things to do to her husband, drinking copious amounts of Starbucks, and reading. She loves to read and devours a book a day, sometimes more. She's also fond of TV shows and movies from the 1980s, as well as paranormal shows from the 1990s to today, even though she'd much rather be reading or writing.

Harley at Changeling: changelingpress.com/harley-wylde-a-196

Changeling Press E-Books

More Sci-Fi, Fantasy, Paranormal, and BDSM adventures available in e-book format for immediate download at ChangelingPress.com -- Werewolves, Vampires, Dragons, Shapeshifters and more -- Erotic Tales from the edge of your imagination.

What are E-Books?

E-books, or electronic books, are books designed to be read in digital format -- on your desktop or laptop computer, notebook, tablet, Smart Phone, or any electronic e-book reader.

Where can I get Changeling Press E-Books?

Changeling Press e-books are available at ChangelingPress.com, Amazon, Apple Books, Barnes & Noble, and Kobo/Walmart.

ChangelingPress.com

Printed in Great Britain
by Amazon